Sidney Kerr

WAIT FOR YESTERDAY

A Novel

SIDNEY KERR

WAIT FOR YESTERDAY

This book is a work of fiction. Names, characters, places and incidents either are products of the author's imagination or are used fictitiously. Any resemblance to actual events or locales or persons, living or dead, is entirely coincidental.

Library of Congress Control Number: 2006906988
ISBN 0-615-13228-6

First Edition

Mimosa Publishing
103 Mimosa Street
Hereford, Texas 79045

(806) 364-2734

FOR CLIFF—Your patience and perseverance have not gone unnoticed. I hope you find it worth the wait.

ACKNOWLEDGMENT—To my editor and my friend, and her most important and appreciated role, My Sister, ROXY GASKILL, for all the long hours of editing and encouragement.

ALSO BY SIDNEY KERR

THE BAR4 SPREAD

A family saga set in NeeDee, NM, spanning 1935-1956, The BAR4 Spread is the story of Buck and Alta Ramsey, and their friend and partner, Ariola. Together, they build a ranching and financial empire, only to have it crumble because of an early mistake. What they never lose is their love for each other.

ORDER

MIMOSA PUBLISHING
P.O. BOX 265
HEREFORD, TX 79045

(806) 364-2734

WAIT FOR YESTERDAY

Mimosa Publishing

Chapter 1

Just two spindly weeds, that's all they were. Parched, thirsty, nearly dead from the hot New Mexico sun, they were still more than Buck could bear. Clutching both in one hand, he twisted and turned. He had choked the life out of them before they finally broke loose from the hard ground. Flinging the weeds toward the graveled road, he knelt before a tiny tombstone and stroked the alabaster lamb that topped it, then traced the words below it, Our Baby.

His eyes moved down and rested on the words that told the whole story—Megan Ramsey, October 12, 1938. She would have been eighteen. How would she feel about all this mess? Perhaps if she'd lived, things would have been different.

Shame flooded him, thinking a baby, his baby, could have kept him from being the piece of worthless trash gripping her headstone. He lay his head on the lamb, caressing it before moving on to the next stone.

Lt. Joseph Luther Pitts, February 2, 1921—May 1, 1943. Joe had been so proud of their family—the Ramsey family. Despite their mere ten-year difference in age, Joe and Buck had bonded as father and son from practically their first meeting. After all, twenty-four and fourteen was a wide span separating man and boy, especially while scrambling to dig out a living on that farm. The timing was right. They needed each other.

Buck had tried to be a good dad and he believed he had been. Even Jimmy, with all their clashes, knew Buck loved him. It had gnawed at him for a long time, but after they lost him, Buck had convinced himself that Jimmy knew he loved him—loved them all.

Nick was the only one of the four boys who called him daddy, but he had been a father to all of them. The older three had always called him Buck, and it just seemed natural. He had never considered asking them to call him anything else. They were comfortable with calling him Buck and it satisfied him. He always believed they looked upon him as their dad. Nick had never called him much of anything until he had started calling him daddy.

A few minutes ago, he'd realized the past twenty years didn't mean squat.

He moved over to Jimmy's grave. The fine gray marble headstone was identical to Joe's. Two words, Jimmy Pitts, were chiseled in tall block letters across the stone, with July 2, 1925—August 10, 1948 in finer, smaller lettering under it. No dignified double name, like Joe's *Joseph Luther*—just Jimmy—but his birthday celebrations made up the difference. On each July 2nd, the firecrackers came out and popping began. It went on for a week—sometimes longer. He was king of the hill for that week, and he needed it.

Buck moved to stand in front of the fourth one. This one, small and ground level, was inscribed Alta Ramsey, June 15, 1905—June 10, 1956. She'd nearly made it to her birthday. That had become her goal during those last weeks. A birthday party would have gotten her whole family together in one room for a change and that's what she wanted most.

They were all attentive, coming often, but only for short visits, and noticeably, painfully—at least to Alta—absent when Buck was present.

That party never took place. Five days—five lousy days, but oh, she had tried. The family did finally get together—for her funeral, but after that morning they had scattered again. They still were and would be for a long time. He was about to give up. Alta had asked him not to give up, but she was not here to help him anymore.

The understated funeral was completely private, exactly

as Alta had requested. The service had been the morning of her death. No one other than the family had been notified—she was a very private person.

After a call from the funeral home that the interment was complete, the family, along with Ariola, Ramona, John Kraft and Father Michael, went to the cemetery. They joined hands and sang Amazing Grace just as the rising sun was glowing pink and orange across the wild grass of the little cemetery. After Father Michael spoke, the small group recited the Lord's Prayer.

They returned home and Ramona served a big breakfast. Gathered around the kitchen table, they talked about Alta Ramsey, sharing memories that came to mind as they ate.

She died convinced she had left her sons only a tarnished memory of a mother nothing like she had portrayed herself. If she could have been there, she would have known each one present remembered her exactly as the woman—the wife, mother, grandmother and friend—that she had always tried to be.

They continued short, but frequent, drop-in visits to the house, yet Buck often felt each of them was only carrying out Alta's wishes, caring little about actually seeing him. She had repeatedly reminded them a family should remain close, but each time he read a quickly scrawled note left on the kitchen table, or Ramona mentioned one or the other of them had stopped by, he felt sure that wasn't the closeness Alta had hoped for.

Buck was still at Alta's stone, his face contorted with grief and disbelief.

He was determined to carry out Alta's request, yet had just stormed out of a meeting with Billy Jack and Nick, along with Ariola and the attorneys, for the reading of their mother's will.

She had, as her half of their joint estate, bequeathed the house and several sections of grassland to Billy Jack, and a comparable amount of cash and bonds to Nick.

Billy Jack, stunned by the enormity of it, perhaps a little reluctant at the prospect of managing it, spoke up quickly, but stumbled, searching for the right words. Buck and Alta had been more than generous through the years, he said, and with their help, plus a lot of luck, he was comfortable financially.

He had assumed that Alta's estate had gone to charities worked out by Father Michael. He'd not been expecting anything.

Buck was quiet as one of the attorneys explained that it was a joint-bequest, from both Alta and Buck.

Nick had remained silent as the talk went back and forth, but when he finally spoke, the dozen words he spit out brought the meeting to a crashing end. Everyone else was silent, all looking to Buck and Nick. Neither of them said anything else.

Searing pain, worse than Buck felt the morning they had buried Alta, burned through his chest as he heard Nick's tight-lipped growl—and Nick the only one of them who had called him daddy—"You just don't get it, Buck. We don't want anything from you."

Buck was on his feet and out the door. No one had called after him. No one had spoken at all.

Later, when he'd managed to pull himself together, he had wondered more than once what had been said after he'd left, but he never asked anyone. Perhaps he really didn't want to know.

He was in the cemetery on impulse, but now realized what had brought him here. He needed a little help from Alta to get on down the road.

He turned back toward his car, looking again at the other stones as he passed. He needed another look. It might be a long time before he was back this way.

Chapter 2

Buck drove around for the better part of an hour, trying hard not to think about the meeting. An occasional caustic thought of it would cross his mind, but he mostly tried not to think at all.

He crossed a cattle guard and pulled into the shade of a tall cottonwood that thrived on the banks of a small pond. He sat there awhile, then killed the engine and looked out over glassy green, rather stale looking, water, but at least he was in the shade and the pond offered a diversion.

Getting out of the car, he walked across the stretch of grass bordering the lake, and sat down on a long log that rested partially on the bank, then disappeared into the water. A similar log had saved Jerry the day Jimmy had drowned. It was just a remnant of an old elm tree in the tail water pit, yet something to hang onto, and Jimmy had managed to put Jerry there.

Buck dipped his hand into the water. It was cool, but his hand came back covered with bits of green slime. After rubbing it hard against the log, much of it remained, but he didn't bother with it anymore.

The New Mexico sun finished the job for him. As he sat looking across the tiny expanse of water, his hand dried. That dried muck made it stiff and itchy, so he used the log again. Small spots of blood appeared on his knuckles.

Ignoring his stinging hand, which was now swelling a bit, he stood up and walked close to the bank, occasionally picking up a pebble to skim across the water, but never slowed enough to watch the rings form. About halfway around, he stopped in the shade of another cottonwood. He swiped his shirtsleeve across his forehead, then spit on his bloody knuckles and rubbed them down his jeans. It hurt, but he paid little attention to the pain—even smiled, for at the same time he had done that unsanitary deed, looking down at the raw knuckles, he heard Alta as plain as if she had been standing beside him. *Buck, I told you. Your knuckles are going to rot off if you don't quit that.*

He doubted it. They never had. Still, he knew she would be saying those very words. That gentle nagging—the only way she ever did it—was one of the things he missed most about her. She was always looking after him. He still needed it.

Buck continued resting in the shade and looked again toward the water. It was glassy smooth, with not even a breeze to ruffle it. The only sound was an occasional plunk, no doubt a frog seeking relief from the heat in the cool water. It looked peaceful. Standing there, taking it all in, he longed for some of that peace. What would Alta be thinking, what would she be saying, if only she was with him under this old tree?

He realized now, that in the early years, Alta had held back a lot. Only near the end had she begun speaking her mind, knowing he needed to be straightened out a little. Closing his eyes, he could again hear her, her voice softer now, Buck, I told you not to run off and do something wild like you did after Joe and Jimmy died. You have to keep this family together.

"I will, Alta, I will," he said aloud.

He'd never been one to talk to himself, but at the moment he was torn between what he knew Alta expected of him and what his hurting heart demanded. Yes, he would do that for her, but for now, he had to heal himself.

"I will, Alta, but not right now. Baby, I just have to go—but I'll be back, I promise."

Chapter 3

Buck headed back toward home—but he drove quickly, not at all like the meandering drive he had taken after leaving the cemetery. No point in idling along as he had done for the past hour. At times, hitting ruts at that speed along the dirt roads nearly cost him control of his car. He fought it. He had no intention of ending up in a ditch with some farmer finding his body, calling the sheriff or the undertaker, then have the folks click their teeth with glee or sympathy for Nick and Billy Jack. He was simply in a hurry.

In a hurry for what? Back to what? Why had he left in the first place? How would things have worked out if he'd stayed? All unanswerable questions, but it didn't matter anyway. He'd done it. He'd run out of that office, jumped in his car and sped off like an upset child.

More than an hour had passed since he'd left. They didn't just sit there doing nothing, saying nothing. Something had happened, something was said.

He should have stayed, tried to reason with Nick. He could have taken a little of Nick's bile—could have taken a lot of it—he deserved it.

If he hadn't been so gutless, he would have stayed and worked things out with both boys. With Ariola's help, it might have all been settled by now, at least smoothed over a little, so they could have had something to work on.

For now, though, there was just pain. And it wasn't only pain for himself—he was hurting plenty, for sure, but it was Alta's gift they had turned down. It was her sons telling their mother they didn't want what she had worked her heart out to give them. He didn't feel up to walking back in as if nothing had happened.

He was driving along just fine when his vision began to blur. He could hardly see before finally realizing it was only tears.

He had not cried at Alta's funeral—none of them had. There had been plenty of tears beforehand, but none on that morning. It was as if she—and all of them—had been set free.

Reliving all this was too much for him. Pulling off the highway, Buck laid his head on the steering wheel and sobbed, but felt little relief. In fact, he felt foolish, but at that moment all he wanted was to stay there and cry.

When a car approached, he immediately pulled back onto the road. He could not chance anyone seeing him. No one he knew—not even a stranger—must see him slumped over the wheel and stop to offer help. He needed help from no one but Alta and it was too late for that. Now it was his turn to help her, and he'd do it.

He couldn't waste anymore time. He'd go home, get his ideas down on paper and be on his way again. Writing it down might take away some of his pain, but he doubted it.

Chapter 4

Buck strode into his office without glancing toward Mary Lou or Pauline, who were at their desks. Pauline rose to follow him as she usually did when he came in.

"Let him be," Mary Lou said.

It was she who had talked to Ariola. After repeating his message word for word to Pauline, she had yet to convey to Pauline the implications she had gathered from the emotion in Ariola's voice. His tone had given more meaning to his message than the words could.

"He needs me. Oh, I know he needs me," Pauline said over and over in a quavering voice, but reluctantly sat down.

As the senior BAR4 employee of the two, as well as Buck's secretary, she had the unofficial title of office manager, but on this point Pauline gave in to Mary Lou.

"What can we do?" The words turned into a soft moan as she spoke. Mary Lou didn't answer because she didn't know.

Inside his office, Buck was faring no better. He fumbled with a piece of paper. His plans had been to dash off a quick outline of his intentions, but he couldn't get started.

He finally wrote down one word: Hospital. Tapping his pen on the desk, he studied that one word, then turned back to work. Next came a number—3,000,000. Thinking for a moment longer, he added a dollar sign in front of it.

Three million was probably fair enough. That was close to Nick's inheritance. If Nick couldn't, or wouldn't, accept the money, it would still be put to good use.

John had taken care of the medical needs of NeeDee in an inadequate hospital for years. In the past, Buck, Alta and Ariola had often talked of launching a matching-funds drive. It had been Alta's illness that had brought Nick back to NeeDee, but they, especially Alta, had been hoping he would stay. Without mentioning it to Alta, Buck and Ariola had taken an option on some suitable property.

There would be no matching-funds drive, but a new hospital would be built. Buck studied the figure once again. Three million should take care of everything. If it didn't, he would add more later.

Next came the first complete sentence. Call Kirk Andrews.

Kirk, a NeeDee boy, was now an architect in Denver. Kirk had gone to school on a BAR4 scholarship. He would appreciate the work and take a personal interest in the project.

After that, Buck wrote quickly, outlining a rough plan for getting the project underway. He picked up the paper and looked at it intently. Satisfied, he laid it down and dashed off a note at the bottom of the page.

Ariola—please take care of this for me. Pick up our option in the Givens Addition. Call Kirk and get started on the plans. Get all the input you need from John—Nick, too, if you can. Surely, he'll do it for you—and Alta. I'll call you, but don't wait. Start now. I know I can count on you—always have. Thanks.

He didn't sign the note, just folded it, put it in an envelope with only a large A scrawled across the front and handed it to Pauline.

Buck drove hard, not consciously heading for Denver, but he ended up there, actually about fifteen miles north, before pulling off the highway, then a short distance up a graveled lane.

The little road looked as if it might lead to a house, but he didn't see one. If there was, surely its occupants wouldn't mind his parking. Even if they did, he was too tired to drive another mile. There was some hope, too, that he was tired enough to be able sleep.

He did sleep, waking only when the sun streaming through the window, paired with a pesky fly, brought him out of a deep slumber. He had slept hard several hours, but didn't feel rested. Stiff, dry-mouthed, and needing to relieve himself, he got out of the car and walked up toward a grove of small aspen, looking for a more-secluded spot. He found it behind a large sign, then walked slowly back to his car. As he opened the door, he looked again at the sign.

For sale by owner. 160 acres. Good timber, good water, good pasture.

Good luck, he added to the list, hoping the owner would have more luck selling this property than he was having at giving his away.

He turned around, not considering why he was heading back to Denver instead of further away. In fact, he would have just as soon sat out there beside the road from now on, but he figured someone would show up and let him know he wasn't welcome there either.

He checked into the first motel inside the city limits, then walked across the street to a greasy-looking café. He wasn't hungry, even dreaded the prospect of eating, but he thought it might do something for his blinding headache. The food didn't help.

He went to his room and flopped down, angled across the bed, on top of the spread. Alta had always admonished him about that. She was doubtful of the cleanliness of motel bedspreads. When he had pointed out on more than one occasion that she didn't mind pitching in around the ranch and getting plenty dirty, she always came back with a perfectly logical retort, at least to her way of thinking—well, that's our dirt. It's different. Oh, how he wished for some of that logic now.

Lying down was as much of a failure as the food. Never having been one to lie around in the daytime, much less to nurse a headache, Buck got up and began aimlessly driving over the city, turning up any street that looked unfamiliar, avoiding Broadway or Colfax or any part of the business district.

His desk calendar had a red star scribbled in by Pauline on a date less than two weeks away. He would have been here in a matter of days anyway, down on Colfax juggling some of the investments Alta had wanted Nick to have.

He couldn't tolerate the idea of attending that meeting, or any meeting. The thought of checking ledger sheets, returning calls, making calls—making any kind of decision—was unbearable to him.

He zigzagged across the city the rest of the afternoon, stopping only a couple of times, once to watch some swans gliding across a pond bordering a park, again to get a coke and a package of peanuts, but for the most part he just drove. He didn't do much thinking or planning. His only intent was distance—the distance of time and of miles—between himself and his family.

Late in the day he turned onto the highway and headed north again. He noticed the lane where he had slept the night before, but didn't stop this time. As he drove, pine and aspen groves became thicker and he noted fewer and fewer side lanes. The beauty of it was wasted on him.

Making his mind as blank as possible was still his major need and if he could have accomplished that by squeezing his temples with both hands instead of driving, he would have been parked by the side of the road doing just that.

That need could have been the reason he had paid no attention to the gas gauge on his Buick. It would have done little good anyway. Gas stations had been left far behind. The car began handling differently, and he instinctively glanced down at the gauge.

He didn't find a lane this time, but he did manage to coast onto a narrow clearing by the side of the road before the car coughed and died.

Oh, hell, he thought. Alta had admonished him many

times to clean up his mouth. Maybe he would. For now, though, it was nearly dark, so he pushed off his boots and slid from behind the wheel to the far side of the seat. Tossing his hat into the back, he leaned against the smooth leather. He looked out the window, but no stars were visible.

In fact, nothing was visible. The hazy outline of the trees soon turned into a solid black wall. Nighttime fell quickly in the wilderness, and that was fine with him. He closed his eyes, but noticed the darkness had not blocked out his headache.

Chapter 5

Buck slept through the night without dreaming, yet awoke so cramped and stiff he thought he might have had nightmares the whole time. If he had, he could recall none of it.

A faint noise against his window woke him. It didn't startle him awake, he just gradually became aware of a sound so soft it could have been a squirrel scampering across the car. In fact, he only opened his eyes out of curiosity.

When he did, a face appeared at the window, about eye level with him. At that height, it could have been a child peering in, but when his sleepy haze turned loose enough for him to take a closer look, the face seemed to be about a hundred years old.

The face was filled with steel blue eyes, their coldness offset by an amicable glint, and a near-toothless grin that was only partially visible beneath scraggly silver and black whiskers, matted in spots with brown tobacco juice. It wasn't a pretty face, but it was friendly.

Buck sat up and rolled down the window. The man continued grinning, but said nothing.

"Morning," Buck said.

"You come pretty close to the edge, feller," the old man said. "You'd have been in a pretty pickle if you'd hit this rut."

Buck leaned toward the door and looked out. The man was standing in a foot-deep crevice. The front wheel of the Buick was resting only a few inches away from it.

"You'd have hit high center for sure." He still seemed amazed at Buck's good fortune.

"It's about time I had some good luck," Buck replied.

"Been on a losing streak, huh?"

"So to speak. I ran out of gas."

"That is pretty rotten luck," the old man replied. "Especially considering that the nearest gas station is about twenty miles up the road, or about the same back to Denver, depending on which way you're going."

Buck didn't reply, but slid over to the driver's side to get out since the little man was still standing next to the car. He also noticed that if he had gotten out on that side, it would have been quite a drop to the ground.

He came around the car and the man stepped up out of the rut. He wasn't as small as he'd appeared to be, but he still only struck Buck about shoulder height. He was thin and sinewy with little meat on his bones. Muscle mass had left him as he'd aged, but he didn't appear to be uncertain about standing, talking and holding his own with a stranger, much larger, much younger than he, and with an ominous look about him that came from a two-day growth of beard and rumpled, lived-in clothes.

"Which way you headed?" he then asked.

"Makes me no difference," Buck replied dully.

That could have ruffled the little man, but it didn't in the least. He simply asked with a casual air, "You ain't runnin' from the law, are you?"

Buck grinned. "No," he said emphatically.

"Then it must be a woman. Woman trouble, huh?"

Buck smiled again but said nothing. The smile seemed to satisfy the man.

"Woman trouble. I've had my share of that, too." He gave Buck another toothy grin, then added with a knowing nod, "In my day, I have."

"How would a feller go about getting some gas?" Buck asked.

"I have a barrel up at my place, but we'd better push you out of here first."

Buck looked at him quizzically.

"Ain't you noticed where you're parked?"

Buck looked around, but still failed to see the need for moving the car. The man jerked his head in the direction of a small sign at the entryway to the narrow road onto which Buck had steered his sputtering car the night before.

"If a runaway truck has to have this, that little Buick won't mean a thing. It would be just like a bunch of shoats heading for the slop trough. The big ones win every time."

Buck could now see his mistake, but the little man continued. He didn't often have the pleasure of visitors and he wasn't about to miss this chance to talk.

"I seen it once myself. A long time ago, but I still remember it like it was yesterday. This feller had parked here, and about the time he did, this big blue tanker comes barreling in here and blows that little Ford to smithereens. Fortunately for him, the man had just gone up behind a pine to take a pee. Funny thing about it, he wouldn't claim the Ford. It was worthless after that anyway, and I guess he was afraid he'd get in trouble with the law. It's against the law to park here, you know."

"Well, I guess I've pressed my luck. Do you think we could push this one down to the shoulder a ways?"

"You bet. Just take her out of gear, and she'll practically roll back out. Just be careful not to run her into that rut. Then you'd be in a pickle. I've got a little tractor back up at the house, but she ain't runnin' right now, so you'd just have to stand here by the side of the road and wait until somebody with a chain came along."

"Guess I could call into town and get somebody out here."

"I don't have a telephone, either," the man said.

He paused, then added, "Don't see any need for too many of them fancy do dads people are so crazy about nowadays."

He nodded his head and waited.

Buck nodded along with him, affirming the old man's

belief.

"Well, then, how about that gas?"

Buck didn't care which way he was going, just as he'd said, but he was ready to get started.

"Sure thing. My place is just over the ridge there. Could have built her a little closer to the highway, but I didn't want to see anybody, and didn't care about anybody seeing me, either."

"Well, I'm sure glad to see you this morning. Buck Ramsey's my name." He stuck out his hand.

The old man still had a firm grip. "Paul," he said.

That was all he offered. He took off, angling up the hillside, Buck beside him. For the first time, Buck noticed he was barefoot. The rocks and pinecones and occasional dead branches appeared to be harder on Buck's alligator boots than they were on the old man's bare feet. They passed the remains of a foundation. The old man jerked his head in its direction.

"There's where my granddaddy built his first cabin. Of course that was before the highway had even been thought about."

"So you've been in these parts awhile."

"Reckon so. I was born here."

He cackled and added, "And that's a while for sure."

They were soon on his front porch. He stopped at the door and slipped on blue canvas tennis shoes, minus strings for easy access. He motioned Buck through the open front door.

"Splinters in there. My maw scrubbed it so much a man can't walk to the kitchen without getting a splinter. Reckon she probably scrubbed herself to death, but it made her happy."

Buck again nodded in understanding. He had yet to hear anything from the old man with which he could disagree.

"Privy's out back, if you need it," the old man said.

"Thanks. I believe I will."

"Through there," the man motioned toward the kitchen.

"There's a water bucket and pan out on the back porch. I aim to cook us some breakfast before we get to that gas barrel."

"That sounds real good," Buck said.

He hadn't bothered to stop for lunch or dinner the day before, and had given little thought to breakfast, but now that it had been mentioned, it sounded good.

As he returned to the back porch, he stopped, dipped water from the bucket and poured it into the wash pan sitting beside it. Picking up a bar of soap covered with dried grime from its last user, he wet it and rubbed his hands together briskly. It lathered well, better than he had expected. He reached for a towel hanging on a nail above the pan. The towel was in a little worse condition than the soap had been, but it did the job.

As he stepped back inside the kitchen, he glanced through the door back to the living room, and noticed three pairs of boots lined up in a neat row against the far wall. All three, apparently hand tooled, had an expensive look about them, but some were in better condition than others.

The first, a brown pair, short topped with red roses adorning each side just below heavy cloth pull straps, high heeled and pointed toes, had obviously been polished and shined many times, but their burnished glaze failed to cover scars that told a story of hard use.

In the center, glowing like the star of the show, stood a pair that looked to Buck to be tall enough to nearly reach the old man's knees. They were deep turquoise splashed with numerous bright yellow stars along with a few suns and moons. They appeared to have been worn gently.

The third pair, nice looking, but plain black boots, likely served the old man if he was required to look presentable enough to make a trip into town. They were worn, but still looked as though they hadn't been used much.

"Good looking boots in there," Buck said.

"Stage props," the old man answered. "I use them on the rare occasion I'm forced to appear to be something I am not."

He'd had his back to Buck, busy laying thick bacon into a black cast iron skillet, but turned to continue his story.

"I had a pan of biscuits ready before I headed out down to the road to post a letter a while ago. They're in the oven, but still need a few minutes."

Buck decided he was going to hear a story whether he wanted to hear one or not, so he pushed his chair back from the table and waited.

"Them tall ones there. They're my movie star boots. I was out in L.A. one time and got a part as an extra on this picture. Actually, it was a pretty good little part for a beginner. I was supposed to play a sissified city dude stumbling around some ranch chasing after the gal the big guy was sweet on. Well, I guess some assistant writer or someone took a liking to them boots, because he wrote me in as taking the gal away from the big guy. First thing you know I was fired and the writer was fired, too. I don't think they finished that picture—at least I don't recall seeing it."

"Did you get any more parts?" Buck asked.

"A few." The old man hesitated, then continued. "Does the name Paul Sloan mean anything to you?"

It didn't, but Buck pursed his lips and shrugged as if it might.

"That's me," Paul said.

That appeared to be all the explanation he was giving, but then went on with his story.

"I got in one Gene Autry picture," he added.

"Oh, yeah. I used to see some of those myself, and my boys really liked them."

Buck grinned, and added, "Here I am having breakfast with a guy I might have watched in a movie."

"Not likely. I played a member of the posse in that one."

"But you might have. They always put me close to the front for those fast rides because I could sit a horse real good. Some of those poor suckers were having to hold onto the saddle horn with both hands."

He stopped, enjoying the remembering.

"Them boots, though, they were a drawing card all right. Used to wear them in a lot of parades. And rodeos. They always wanted me to ride the colors in the Grand Entry. Wanted to see them boots. And like I said, I could sit a horse real good."

"So you did some rodeoing, too?"

"Some," Paul said. He was back at the bacon, but talked as he worked. He turned each slice more than once, giving it no chance to burn. It would be crisp, evenly done, perfect when he laid it on the waiting ironstone platter.

Paul quickly put the bacon, scrambled eggs and biscuits on the table. He then reached into a bowl on the window ledge and pulled out a bridge, popping it into his mouth before sitting down.

Buck noticed the old man now had a fair set of teeth in his mouth.

"The shorties in there, they're my real rodeo boots. You can tell it, too. Had the hell beat out of them."

Paul opened a biscuit and filled it with butter before closing it and taking a generous bite. Melted butter settled in beside the tobacco juice on his whiskers.

"Some of the boys thought I was real vain, changing out of the tall ones before I rode. Of course, they wondered why I beat them most of the time, too."

He continued in a solemn tone, "What they didn't know was, I just rode a little harder. I was smaller than most of them and I wanted them tall ones to be nice and fresh for the dance after the rodeo. The girls appreciated it. Nothing worse than getting those pretty high heels stepped on by caked-on muck."

To his credit, Paul didn't say the precise word.

He talked while eating, giving little thought to either, just enjoying the past and present.

They finished the meal and Buck rose, starting to clear the table.

"Leave all that be," Paul said. "Let's get that gas down there. I'll do this later."

"Even got last night's mess over there in the sink. Likely have to draw a bucket of water before I start."

Buck insisted mildly, but was overruled.

"Now, Maw would be a different case altogether. She'd have them dishes done before she stepped out the door. Me? I don't have to please nobody but myself, and I'm easy to please."

They went out the kitchen door to a shed where a barrel of gasoline was kept. A small red can, large enough to hold the few gallons it would take to get back to Denver, stood beside it. Obviously, Buck wasn't the first person who'd had to depend on Paul's kindness.

Chapter 6

Paul filled the can, and they walked down a narrow road toward the highway, Paul carrying it. Buck had protested about that, but he insisted.

"Only way I know of to keep up my strength. You know that old story. Start lifting a calf the day it's born and by the time it's grown—"

"Oh, hell. Why didn't you just hoist that barrel up on your shoulder and bring it on down?"

"Couldn't spare that much gas," Paul said dryly, then chuckled, knowing he had bested Buck.

As they walked, Paul offered a simple explanation as to why they were returning to the car by way of the road instead of across the hillside as they had arrived at the house earlier.

"I'm aiming to mail my letter. The mailbox is down this road at the highway. I only cut across there this morning when I spotted you parked in that runaway lane. Sure didn't want to see another thing like that little Ford. Don't think I could take it at my age."

"I appreciate it for my part, too," Buck said. "I do have a little unfinished business."

He was thinking about the hospital. Paul stopped at his mailbox, put in his letter and lifted the metal flag. He had set the can down for that chore, and Buck picked it up before the old man had a chance at it.

"I have a few calves of my own," Buck said.

"Figured you to be a cattleman. You don't look exactly like any of the cowboys I've known—most of them have a look about them, you know. Riding through too much foul weather, most limping a little from placing their trust in one too many spooked horses, then drinking too much to kill the pain of it all—but I did figure you for a cattleman. One of the big boys, that is."

"Well, I admit I do most of my ranching from behind a desk."

"There's no shame in that. Has to be done. Couldn't work any other way. If you tried to put one of them real cowboys behind a desk, it would be—well, it just wouldn't work."

"I guess that's exactly what I've been trying to do." He liked the old man's logic.

He'd tried to do just that to Billy Jack—and to Nick, too, in a different way. Putting Billy Jack behind the BAR4 desk and expecting him to just step in and take over when all he wanted was his own little spread would be sentencing him to a life of misery.

Nick—with three million dollars worth of stocks and bonds and real estate to look after, would have to scramble to find time to do a decent job of practicing medicine when doctoring was all he really wanted to do.

He and Alta had figured it wrong—yes, he was going to place a fair share of the blame with Alta. If she were here now, she could see it, and would be helping him to make it right again. They had both wanted—Alta more than he—to see that the boys were financially secure, hoping to spare them the struggles the two of them had faced in the beginning. He then reconsidered that. He had a feeling he and Alta had been closest when there had been adversaries to be faced together. Not only financial, there had been so many other times—the heartbreak of losing Joe and Jimmy—and Megan, especially Megan, when he knew neither could have made it without the other. They had shared so much, until the cancer. She had kept that from him. His chest hurt when he though about it—the cancer and the shutting out.

When they'd left the cabin and started down to the highway, Buck had been dreading the prospect of getting enough gasoline to take him back to Denver, or to the next town up the way, for that matter. The empty tank gave him license to while away the morning, or even a week, talking to Paul. The three gallons of gas would force him to make a move of some kind.

Paul's comment had set him to thinking. By the time they'd made that short walk from the mailbox to the car, and Paul had sloshed the gasoline into it, Buck knew what he had to do. It wasn't the easy way out, might not amount to much, but he would soon be heading back to NeeDee.

Chapter 7

Once Buck had gotten back to Denver, he wasted no time. He filled the gas tank, checked out of the motel, and headed for NeeDee. A big part of the bravado he'd felt at Paul's place had left him. He thought for a moment about staying another day or two, to do some thinking, but soon discarded that idea. There was no reasoning-power left in him, and doubting there would be any time soon, he decided to just plunge right to it. Back home, looking at Alta's picture, being around things that still held her ambiance, perhaps he could get a glint as how to approach this situation.

There was no question in his mind about the hospital. It would go forward, with or without the money that Alta had intended for Nick. If he had reconsidered, that would be fine. Whether he accepted his inheritance or not, the new hospital would go on. Buck worried that Nick had not softened any, but couldn't let go of hope so soon, all the while conceding that he deserved those scornful words.

The house was another story. Remembering Paul's philosophy, Buck could accept Billy Jack's reluctance to step in as manager and majority-owner of the BAR4 outfit, but the house was entirely different. Alta wanted Billy Jack and Donna and those three little boys in that house, to make it their home. Buck intended to fight for that, for Alta. She had wanted that home for them from the beginning. His face softened, remembering how Alta had everyone scurrying around, moving the two of them to Willowbranch before Billy Jack and his family had returned from Hawaii. She had been disappointed when they moved into Stone Creek instead, but had assumed it would be only a matter of time before they would accept the house.

Alta had insisted on spending her last few weeks in the hospital so there would be no memories of hospital beds and nurses. She wanted only joy to fill that house, and he was going to make sure she got that.

He was hopeful. Bill had sounded mild that day, his usual demeanor. He had simply said that since he was comfortable financially, such a large inheritance could be put to better use. *Inheritance.* That was the key word here. That inheritance had been from Alta. In one moment, Buck was angry. Why should Bill refuse his mother's gift? In the next, he could see Bill's reasoning. He didn't care for management. He was a cowboy, pure and simple. It took some of both to keep the BAR4 running smoothly, but the cowboy in him outweighed the other. But the house? Why should he refuse the house? Maybe he wouldn't. Buck had rushed out soon after Nick had spoken, not giving Bill time to finish. He couldn't. W*e don't want anything from you, Buck.* After those words, he'd left.

Those thoughts sobered him even more. Could he have expected the boys to react any differently than they had? Would he have, if he'd been in their place? It had been a month. The sharp pain of their mother's death had begun to subside, but it was still there. Now reality was seeping in. It seemed they wanted as little as possible to do with him and he could hardly blame them.

He was home, but just pulling through the BAR4 gates gave him an uneasy feeling. How could that be? Home was home, supposedly a shelter, a place to heal. He hated the sudden ache in his gut.

The house was empty. Surely Ramona hadn't taken off, too. Why not? Was he the only one with that privilege? Could he expect everyone to simply sit and wait for his return? He had taken off before and come back to find everything moving along as normally as possible, considering the circumstances, but that had been Alta's doings. He began to feel panic creeping into his chest.

Maybe Ramona had already gone home for the day. Not this early, not Ramona. Well, why not? She had been the only one here for the past two days. He picked up the phone and called her. No answer.

He wheeled and went out the back door to the Bull Barn. No cars in front. Pauline and Mary Lou had left a little early. He couldn't fault them for that. They set their own time, putting in long hours most days. His desk was as he'd left it, except for the two days mail that had been sorted and stacked neatly in piles. The routine business had been taken care of, answered by Pauline and signed in her neat script. As always, a copy had been left for Buck's inspection, but he seldom looked closely at it. He could depend on Pauline. He flipped through the stack that needed his attention, dreading it. All the enthusiasm had been taken out of him.

A copy of the Givens option, signed by Ariola, and notarized by Mary Lou, was lying to the side of it all. So Ariola had gotten things rolling. But where was he?

He was beginning to think he had made a mistake after all. Why should he have come home when there was no one to come home to?

No, when he left Paul's place, the old man's words had made him realize there surely must to be a way to work things out with the boys. It might never be the same, but it would be something.

He went outside, walked across the pasture a few minutes, then followed the white pipe fence back to the house. He got into his car, not sure which way he would go until he reached the gates. As if the car had a life of its own, it turned toward Stone Creek.

He almost drove on after seeing the several cars parked in front of the house, but he didn't. Donna was at the front door before he had knocked.

She hugged him, whispering against his cheek, "We're so glad you're home, Buck."

He looked beyond her and saw Ariola, John Kraft, Nick and Ramona sitting with Billy Jack and the little boys. He stiffened and turned away. Donna thought for a moment he was about to leave. He did turn, but only his face—so none of them would see the tears in his eyes.

By the time he had regained his composure, Billy Jack had joined Donna.

"Buck, you're just in time. We're about ready to eat."

"No, I—"

"We really need you, Buck. John and Ariola are here to throw around some ideas about the hospital."

"Oh, no. I just came by to let you know I'm back. We'll talk tomorrow."

"Please stay, Buck," Donna added.

"No, really. I need to get back to the house." He rubbed the stubble on his face as if his pitiful looks were reason enough for refusing to stay.

When he'd stepped onto the porch, he had intended to come in, but as he was about to go inside, he had looked beyond Donna and saw Nick disappearing through the kitchen door.

Chapter 8

During Alta's last weeks, Nick had taken an apartment across the street from the hospital. After her death, he kept the apartment, but had continued going out to the ranch on weekends, or at least one or two nights a week for a meal with Buck and Ariola. Things had changed. Buck hadn't seen him since the night at Stone Creek.

Nick took little interest in the progress of the hospital plans. John Kraft understood. Nick was trying to do his share toward getting it underway by covering for John while he was at the building site, and by being on call most nights.

At the same time, John had the growing fear that Nick would be leaving as soon as the hospital was complete and additional doctors had been recruited. Nick went about much of his daily routine in uncharacteristic lethargy. The only time Dr. Kraft witnessed the old Nick was during medical emergencies, or as he dealt with the critically ill, especially the very old or very young. It was then that the physician's heart in John swelled with such pride he thought it would burst. Recognizing that much skill, or compassion, as the need arose, he thought he must somehow find a way to convince Nick that NeeDee was the place he should be.

Each time things settled back to normal, however, and John had time to reflect on the situation, he was still at a loss as how to bring Buck and Nick together. He would mull and puzzle and sort until he had to take something, sometimes for heartburn, other times for headache.

When all else failed, he would finally revert back to the philosophy of a long gone old friend. Let them skin their own skunks.

Nick sat at a corner table in the commissary, drinking the last dredges from the coffeepot. He did unplug it, but didn't bother to refill it, doubting that anyone else would be foolish enough to drink coffee at two thirty in the morning. He didn't expect anyone else would be coming in until the morning shift of nurses arrived. He wasn't winding up his shift. He didn't have one. He just came in when they called him and stayed until he finished, which was ordinarily a little earlier than tonight, but often not until John Kraft arrived at eight o'clock sharp every morning.

Nick was about to get up and rinse his cup when Freda Bailey came in. She went straight to the sink and started the water running for making another pot, too intent to even notice Nick.

"What on earth are you up to, Freda?" he asked.

"I thought you went off at twelve o'clock."

She jumped her funny little sidestep, startled at hearing the soft drawl from the corner.

He ordinarily had little interest in the comings and goings of the staff, but seeing Freda making a pot of coffee at two thirty in the morning piqued his curiosity. He distinctly remembered his last view of her had been her rear end bent over searching under the counter in the nurse's station. The view had been more memorable because her skirt had hiked up enough to prompt him to give her a sharp slap on the rump as he passed by.

"You'll have to do better than that to get any attention from me," she had said dryly.

After retrieving her purse, she had raised up to her full height, which was several inches taller than Nick. Turning toward him, she had continued in a tired voice that still managed its pithy sarcasm, "In fact, I'm so beat, I don't believe it would have done any good if that had been John Wayne patting around on me, much less a skinny little runt like you."

He had ducked his head, properly chastised, then looked

at her like a scolded puppy before they had turned and gone their separate ways. He did get in a sideways grin before she disappeared around a corner, and so did she. Now she was back.

She came over and sat down across the table from him.

"Nah, I never made it out the door," she said.

"I made the mistake of looking in on Mr. Everett on my way out. Poor old fellow, I don't believe he's going to make it 'til morning."

Her voice lowered as she continued, "Nobody should have to die alone."

"Well, you're going to be the one who does if you don't start getting a little more rest," he said.

"Nah, I've been dozing some in the recliner. It's not that I've been doing anything for him, it's just that he needs someone in there. The girls are doing his vitals right now, so I thought I'd get some coffee while they were working on him."

She then added matter-of-factly, "I think I'll need to be awake now until morning."

"Freda, you're too soft hearted for your own good."

Uncomfortable with praise, or any word directed toward her, kind or unkind, she was quickly on the defensive.

"Cut it out, Nick," she said. "It's just that I called his niece to tell her he was sinking, and the poor thing couldn't come. Her mother, Mr. Everett's sister, is in the hospital in Tucumcari nearly as bad off as he is. She'll be here in the morning, but I think it will probably be too late."

She got up to fill her cup. He shook his head in refusal at her offer to bring him more. She brought her own cup back, intent on a little visiting before returning to Mr. Everett's room.

"Besides," she continued, "you're really a good one to be talking."

Nick perked up, knowing he was in for another tirade. Always protesting—that had become his role—he expected those affection-coated lectures and actually enjoyed them.

"Explain yourself," he said.

He slid down in the straight chair to stretch his legs, and listen to Freda, although he knew he'd probably heard it all before.

"Well, for starters," she said, "you could be in a city hospital where you could at least have some kind of schedule. You're a surgeon, for crying out loud. You could have all your surgery done before noon and play golf all afternoon."

"Even surgeons have to do an occasional emergency appendectomy," he said with mock indignation.

"Well, not as many as the emergency broken collar bones these cowboys around here bring in from rodeos and bar fights," she countered.

She was right about that, he must admit. There had been a rash of those lately. Seven of them all in the last month, to be exact, and that was a bunch—at least for a small town like NeeDee. And he did stay pretty busy with broken arms and sudden fevers in the middle of the night, as well as the occasional emergency appendectomy.

He didn't mind. There was nothing else he would rather be doing than working, but he couldn't tell her that. He had to shoot back, else it would have ruined their repartee for her—for him, too.

"Freda, I couldn't do straight surgery. You know what a lousy athlete I am. Getting beat every day on the golf course might cause me to lose my self-esteem, and that would affect my skills as a surgeon. At the least, it might start me to drinking to drown my morose. Straight surgery would be a bad deal all around, for me and for my patients."

He was trying his best to sound solemn—and she, working hard at sounding brusque.

"Well, at least you could have a wife and kids to go home to instead of sitting here talking to me," she said.

That was an easy one. Despite being ten years older, and several inches taller than he, she loved to hear his answer to that one. It always took on a similar form, but sounded great every time.

He sat up in his chair, propped his arms on the table and looked at her earnestly.

"Now Freda, we've been through this before. You're the only woman in NeeDee who would have me, and you're definitely the only one I would have. So where are we?"

"Tonight, I finally got up the nerve to make a pass at you and what did you do? You flat out told me you prefer John Wayne."

Freda grinned and stood up. "I guess I had better get back to Mr. Everett's room."

After rinsing her cup in the sink, she turned at the door and grinned again at Nick.

"Well, now don't give up, boy. I think John Wayne is taken."

He sat a while longer, then stood up. Laying his hand on the knob for a moment, he turned back to the cabinet and poured himself another cup of coffee. He had no place else to be. He would go check on Mr. Everett. Freda might need the company.

Chapter 9

Buck stewed around the office for a couple of days, working as a rote process. His enthusiasm had vanished, but a feeling of obligation hung on. To whom, he wasn't sure—certainly not to himself. The boys? They apparently weren't interested. There were dozens of BAR4 employees and their families—he most surely felt a responsibility to them. Yet the driving force behind his actions was Alta—his promise to Alta.

When he had put everything back into Pauline's basket, instead of pushing the buzzer, he called loudly through the door for her.

She came immediately, picked up the basket and turned back toward the door without having spoken a word. In the past, if there was no time for visiting, she still usually had some comment, either pleasant or tart. Today she said nothing.

When he realized she was about to leave without saying a word, panic gripped him. A feeling of nothingness swept over him. He wasn't sure she could hear him, and she barely did.

"Can't you stay for a second?"

Placing the basket back on the desk, she sat down in a nearby chair, still silent, near tears.

"Of course," she finally spoke. "I wasn't sure you'd want to talk."

"I need to talk to someone, and a friend is the best choice. You fit the bill for that," he said, hesitated and continued, "I hope you still do. You always have."

The tears came, although she fought them. "Of course," she managed between sobs.

Seeing her need, some of his composure came back. He

walked over, sat in a chair opposite her, and extended his handkerchief. She took it, but only dabbed her eyes. She was much too dignified, and too much in awe of her boss to blow her nose in front of him. There was no way he would ever be able to change her, so he didn't try. She managed things her way.

"I just don't know how it got this far," she said, and swiped at her nose.

"I do," he said, "It was my sorry ass." Apologizing immediately, his opinion of himself hadn't changed, he only regretted having used such language in the presence of a lady.

She shook her head, refuting his words. Still busy with the handkerchief, she couldn't say anything, but wanted him to understand that she didn't agree with his self-contempt. In fact, she felt a little foul language might be justified under the circumstances. She loved Nick and Billy Jack as she would have loved the sons she never had, but she loved Buck, too.

He wanted to talk, but both of them were at a loss for words. In the past, there had been so much to discuss, with never enough time to get it all in. She was his confidante as well as his executive secretary. Many times he used her as a sounding board before he had approached Ariola or Alta. He depended on her. She had an analytical mind and was good at helping him sort details. It had always been in the back of his mind that her expertise made him appear to be a better businessman than he really was. She made him shine. After spending a few days on a project, and adding her own spin to it, the Houghton touch, Buck called it, she was ready to get back to her desk, but it was usually only a matter of time until he called on her again for more input.

Today, she didn't have reams of information to offer, only questions, yet she couldn't put them into words. When she tried, more sobs came out instead. Even if she had been able to, she somehow knew Buck was in the same quandary. He couldn't manage the answers any better than she could ask the questions.

It was Pauline who finally broke their impasse. The two couldn't yet talk about Buck's personal hurting, but they could, however, work out the business end of his plight. There was the hospital construction. The architects were already working. Optioned land would soon have a clear title and be ready for purchase. Suppliers would be submitting bids. All of this called for money. Stacked on the corner of Buck's desk, the thick files of documents that had been intended for Buck's and his stepsons' signatures represented several million dollars, but right now, they were only paper.

As they talked, it became clear what had to be done. The stacks of documents would be dealt with later. She would go through his portfolio and research the stocks that could most easily, and most profitably, be sold.

That would solve the immediate cash flow problem. As for Buck's personal hurting, she didn't know how to deal with that.

She rose, red-eyed, but happy to have a project that would help Buck—and at the same time, stall the need for the talking she dreaded—and returned to her office.

"I'll get this back to you," she said, indicating his sodden handkerchief. He wanted to tell her to throw it away, but he only nodded, knowing it would be on his desk the next morning, laundered and ironed—not that he'd had any other occasion to loan her a handkerchief, but he did know Pauline.

Early the next morning, Pauline began working on the cash flow.

Buck hung around the office, thinking about calling Billy Jack. He nearly picked up the phone, but finally just walked down to the barn and saddled up. Alta always said a person could see the most important things on horseback.

Out at the Stone Creek place, Billy Jack puttered in his

barns, thinking about calling Buck, but instead, he saddled up and rode fences the rest of the day. About sundown, he told Donna he believed he would drive over to see Buck.

Near that time, Buck was unsaddling, wiping down his horse, then going in the house to shower away his own dust and sweat. He pulled out of the BAR4 gates just in time to catch the best of the setting sun.

They missed each other by two miles.

Chapter 10

As Buck approached the gates, he didn't have a destination in mind. He pulled under the arch, and by the time he had covered the fifty yards to the pavement, it was decided.

He could have turned back toward NeeDee, where he might have caught up with Nick at the hospital and tried to do some talking, or driven out to the building site, or to the airport where Ariola was due to land. He could have just stopped at the café for a cup of coffee, but he headed West again. He had to be on the road, still didn't know where he was going, and really didn't care. Perhaps he just wanted to be out of the house before dark.

Soon after sundown, it was time for another decision. He turned North—toward Denver, or maybe one of the little towns on up the road, or perhaps some place far beyond. He drove into the night, parked by the side of the road to sleep, and pulled in to Denver about daylight.

Why back to Denver he could not phantom. His board meeting was only three days away, but he had brought nothing he would need. The meeting hadn't entered his mind when he headed for Denver. He'd walked out the door with nothing; no briefcase, not even a change of clothes. In fact, he hadn't decided whether or not he would even show up for the meeting—might be just as well that he didn't. What could he offer?

Why not just take off and drive for a few days? The more he studied it, the better he liked that idea. Nick and Billy Jack would have a chance to think things over and he could do the same.

He drove all over town, but somehow never left the city. The streets had yet to come alive with the morning bustle.

He looked at closed shops as he drove. Some of them, in fact, a good number of them, didn't look too prosperous, yet people would soon be opening their businesses, whether they really felt like it or not. Perhaps very few of them were actually enthusiastic about going to work, but most would.

So why couldn't he be man enough to take care of what had been dumped on him, whether he liked it or not? He'd just been running up and down the road like a fool.

He didn't care much for this town, hardly knew anyone here. Of all his Denver business associates, he could think of none that he would invite himself to breakfast with, or call, for that matter. His only reason for being here was to get away from a chance encounter with anyone he knew.

Buck pulled into the parking lot of a rundown diner, not the kind of place he would likely run into any of his investment banking associates—just what he had in mind.

He got out of the car and was nearly to the door before a familiar voice calling from across the lot stopped him.

"You still in town?" Paul Sloan came hobbling up, using a crutch to manage a slightly soiled cast on his right foot.

"Looks like you could use a pair of those," Buck said as casually as if he had been expecting to meet the old man right at this exact spot for breakfast.

"Well, I do have another one in my room, but I slid it across the floor trying to kill a cockroach and the danged thing landed under the bed too far for me to reach. I hate roaches more than anything."

Buck held the door open while Paul gingerly made his way through it. He wondered for a moment, but it was only a fleeting thought, how the old fellow would have managed if he hadn't been there. Paul Sloan would have done just fine without him.

He was curious enough, however, to ask what the old man was doing in Denver at daylight, wearing a cast, and hobbling over from a rundown hotel.

"Well, it's a long story, but first, what about you? I thought you were headed out of town the last time I saw you."

"I was and I did. I went back to NeeDee then came back here, but I still haven't figured out why."

"Sounds like you're still suffering from that wild hair."

"I guess you could say that," Buck said.

They found a booth. Buck was standing behind Paul, feeling edgy again, hands outstretched in readiness. He now doubted the old man's ability to slide into the seat. After Paul had managed to do it, Buck was again glad he'd left him alone. Paul might have thrown his crutch at him.

"Let me get this straight. You've moved into town? Into that fleabag over there?"

"Yep," Paul said, "I've moved into town, but I take offense at your derogatory remark about my new abode. It's downright luxurious—compared to my cabin, anyway."

A waitress had been standing by with pad and pen, waiting silently until they had finished the exchange and noticed her.

"Let's get us a couple of plates of eggs started and then I want to hear more."

"I need about a slab of bacon to go with mine," Paul said.

"It seemed more trouble than it was worth getting over here to eat, but now that I've made it, I sure am glad I've run into somebody to buy my breakfast."

"Well, I believe I owe you one. You cooked mine the last time I saw you."

"I guess you want the trucker's special then," offered the waitress, still patient.

"Sounds good," Paul agreed.

"Make that two," Buck said, "And we sure need some coffee."

"And lots of orange juice," Paul added.

With that taken care of, Buck was anxious to hear the rest of the old man's story.

"So how did you end up here, and with a cast on your foot?"

"Well, it started not too long after you left the other day."

The waitress returned with coffee and Paul stopped talking and devoted his full attention to sweetening his coffee heavily. He then took a few sips.

Buck hadn't known the old man long, in fact, had only spent a few hours with him, but that had been long enough to learn something about him—and to accept it. Paul Sloan wouldn't be hurried, whether it be gassing up a car or telling a story. The only thing for Buck to do was join him. He picked up his cup and matched Paul sip for sip.

It tasted good to both of them, and soon revived Paul enough to continue.

"I, uh," he got that much out before stopping to add more sugar to his cup, then stirred it silently.

Buck watched him, then said, "Paul, all that sugar, no wonder you only have a few teeth here and there."

"Gives me my energy."

"Well, go ahead and tell me. What about that cast?"

"Like I said, it was pretty soon after you left. I'd headed back to the house. Then I looked up about twenty yards in front of me and there was a damned skunk. He was in a fast trot, and you know that road leads right to my front porch."

"So you kicked him down the hill," Buck said, smiling.

Paul didn't smile back.

"I wish it had been that simple," he said. "What I did was circle out around him, aiming for the back door. I wanted to get my twenty two and pop him before he had a chance to run under the house."

"So you fell off the porch?"

"I wish you'd quit trying to outguess me, but I'll be

damned if you aren't nearly right."

"What happened was, I popped him all right, but he just stumbled a little and kept on making straight ahead. Well, it took me a couple of seconds to get another shell in, and by that time he was so close, I had to go down the steps to get a good bead on him. I jumped the last step and broke my damned ankle, although I was so full of it I didn't even know it was broken at the time."

The old man was so excited about recounting the story, it entered Buck's mind that he might be spicing it up as he went along. So what? He was enjoying listening as much as the old man was enjoying telling about it.

"I guess it was like when I was riding bulls. I just didn't feel the pain. Well, I got him good with that second shot, but he still made it under the house before he fell."

"I figured I'd better try to get him out before he stunk up things more than he already had, so I cut me a long piece of barbed wire and doubled it to stiffen it up some, then bent the end to make me a hook, and—"

"Paul, how about your foot, for crying out loud?"

"It was broke. I already told you that. Anyway, it was my ankle, not my foot. Pay attention."

Properly chastised, Buck promised himself not to ask any more questions unless it was positively unavoidable.

The waitress brought their breakfast just then, and Buck thought he was probably in for another wait. He was right.

Paul picked up his flatware and cut, then crosscut his eggs. He had ordered them sunny side up and that's what he got. They needed little more than salt and pepper to be ready to eat, but he worked meticulously until the three eggs were one rounded yellow heap.

With that done, he laid his knife on the edge of his plate and took a bite. After that one bite, he also laid his fork down and continued his story.

Buck hadn't waited. He was well into his breakfast before Paul had begun talking again.

"Well, I hooked him pretty quick, and it was a good thing. He had really sprayed things up. I got me a shovel and scooped him up and dragged him off down the hill a right smart ways from the house. I dug me a hole and got him covered and had nearly made it back to the house. Then I stepped on a rock, a little bitty old thing, but that's all it took for me to know my ankle was broke. I went to the ground and stayed there for the next three or four hours."

"How'd you manage to get to town?" Buck asked, then added, "Your eggs are getting cold."

Paul looked down at his plate of food and picked up his fork. He took a few bites, then laid it down again. It appeared that he didn't have too much of an appetite after all, but he did drink his orange juice. He then raised the empty glass toward the waitress and she was there immediately with more juice.

With that taken care of, Paul continued talking.

"A neighbor from down the road a few miles stopped at my mailbox. They always do that, and bring it up to the house if I haven't picked it up. Doyle likes to stop and talk a few minutes, but that Lois, she's just snoopy. As soon as she finds out I'm not dead or dying, she's ready to go. Well, she was really ready to go when they got there and she smelled that skunk. Wouldn't let Doyle put me in the car. Doyle stayed there with me and she went home and sent their hired man back in Doyle's old pickup. She sent some ragged quilts and they made me a pallet in the bed and brought me to town."

"The hospital was nearly as contrary as Lois. I thought they weren't ever going to let me in to get my ankle worked on. They put me in this little room and these two big ole' orderlies scrubbed me with something that smelled so much like castor oil I thought I was going to have a movement before they could get my ankle set."

Buck grinned and shook his head. He finished his food

and pushed his plate aside to work on his coffee and orange juice. Paul noticed, and began picking at his food as he talked.

"Well, after they got it set, they put me to bed and made me stay a couple of days. When Doyle came yesterday, they let me out, but Doyle said the cabin was still in terrible shape. He tried talking me into staying at their house, but I wasn't about to be in the same room with Lois all day long. I doubt that she would have let him bring me out there anyway. He was probably counting on me to turn him down, but I thought it was right neighborly of him to invite me."

"Now don't be too hard on this Lois. It might be that you just painted too good a picture about that skunk and all, but I believe I can still detect a slight skunk odor about you," Buck said. "Maybe she had good reason not to have you staying in her house."

Paul looked aghast. He'd had Doyle buy him a new set of clothes from inside out to wear when he checked out of the hospital. The orderlies had thrown his others away without asking. He'd been barefoot when Doyle had brought him to the hospital, but now he wore one bright new tennis shoe.

Doyle must have also brought his razor and his partial because he had a bright smile and was clean-shaven.

"Might be a hint of it still in your hair. Don't worry. Ramona can get that out with some tomato juice. She'll sop some tomato juice on your head and cover it with a hot towel. Let it set thirty or forty minutes and rinse, then presto. No more skunk."

"Ramona? Who is this? A beauty operator you know?"

"No."

"Who, then?"

"My housekeeper. You're going home with me."

He looked at Buck, confounded.

"The hell, you say."

It was not as hard as Buck had figured it would be to talk Paul into going home with him. After his initial objection, he agreed to at least let Buck take him to his cabin. He hobbled over to a pay phone and called Doyle. Doyle wouldn't need to come into town to get him after all.

"A friend of mine from New Mexico is here and will bring me out to the cabin," he told Doyle.

His casual tone didn't quite cover the pride in his voice.

Buck was pleased. He guessed that meant he had a friend in Denver after all.

They went up to Paul's room and gathered his few possessions, a shaving kit, two or three paperback books and a nice Stetson hat. As an afterthought, he asked Buck to get his other crutch from under the bed.

Buck dragged it out and handed it to Paul.

"Well, there's a little good news for you under there," he said. "You got him."

Paul had been propped against the door, holding it open. His eyebrows raised, at first puzzled by the words, then settled back to their permanent scowl as he grinned.

"Oh, yeah. That damned roach," he said.

He checked out of the hotel, and they headed for his cabin. He was anxious to get home to check on his place. Doyle had reported each day that things were fine, but he was not apt to check as closely as Paul.

The deciding factor in whether or not Paul would be going home with Buck was the offensive odor that hit them as they were going up the porch steps. Inside, there was only a faint skunky smell in the front room, and even less in the kitchen, but enough that Paul was agreeable to spend the next few days with Buck at the ranch.

There wasn't much to Paul's getting ready. He asked Buck to reach in his closet and retrieve a canvas duffel bag. He rolled up three pairs of Levis and stuffed them in the bottom, but was more careful with four bright western-cut shirts, smoothing them carefully before folding and laying them on the jeans. He added a double handful of socks and underwear plus a few handkerchiefs. His shaving kit was still full from his stay in town. He started to place it in the duffel bag, but hobbled over to his dresser for a bottle of Old Spice, adding it to the grip.

"Just in case Ramona's tomato juice doesn't work," he said.

On the way back through the kitchen, he stopped and opened his refrigerator, pulling out a coffee can. He dug deep into the coffee and removed a jar full of fives and twenties. After stuffing the roll into his shirt pocket, he wriggled the jar back out of sight.

"Don't worry, that's not what I used the other morning. This is just where I hide my stash."

"Whatever, it was the best coffee I've had in a long time."

It looked as though Paul was ready to go, so Buck headed for the front door, carrying the duffel bag. He stopped and turned back again when he realized Paul was not following. He had hobbled to the cabinet.

"Just where are your crutches, Paul?"

The hospital had put a walking cast on his foot, but Buck was sure they had not intended for him to discard his crutches so soon.

Paul pulled a faded lavender flour sack out of the drawer and popped it open, then hobbled over to the three pairs of boots in the front room. When he bent over to pick up a boot, he tottered enough that Buck was by his side immediately. He swore a little under his breath and handed Buck the flour sack.

"Here. Throw those in there."

He glanced down at his cast, and growled, "Don't worry. I'm not planning on being at your place long enough to wear any of these. It's just that if any rowdies break in here, these boots are about the only thing there is to steal."

"No problem," Buck said as he filled the sack. He then went back to the bedroom and brought Paul's crutches to him.

Paul was leaning against the wall by his sack of boots. He took the crutches reluctantly but Buck had a feeling he was more grateful than he would let on.

"If I use these, you're going to have to tote that stuff," Paul said.

"No problem," Buck said again. He picked up the sack and duffel bag, this time walking behind Paul. He couldn't be trusted to follow.

Buck closed the door and waited for Paul to lock it, but he had headed on down the steps.

"Aren't you going to lock up?" he asked. "I thought you mentioned getting broken into."

"Don't have a key," Paul said. "Never have. Breaking in just covers anyone who might come in uninvited. Nobody ever has, but in case they do, at least they won't ruin the door busting in."

By the time they got there, Paul was beginning to get a good feeling about being on a working ranch again. He hardly wanted to admit it to anyone, but his last few working years had been on various dude ranches. He made them a good hand, for what they wanted from him; smiling and talking and spinning yarns around the campfire—and wearing his showy boots—was all that was required of him.

From the way Buck talked, he might even be able to hobble out to the corals and, at least, lean on the fence once in a while.

Chapter 11

The sun was barely up, but it was already getting hot. Billy Jack reached for the canteen hanging over his saddle horn and swigged a little of the cool water, washed it around in his mouth to loosen the dust, then spitting it out, he wiped his mouth on his shirtsleeve. After that, he really drew down. It took several swallows to satisfy him. He had the cap nearly tight, but twisted it back off, took a small sip, and squirted it between his front teeth. He replaced the cap, grinning from this juvenile action. Buck had taught Jimmy, Joe and him to spit.

Nick had been too young to get the hang of it. By the time he was old enough, he already had an aversion to watching such crude behavior, much less taking part in it. Nick invariably stomped back to the house as the rest of them, plus one or two neighbor boys, whiled away many a Sunday afternoon with spitting contests. Over a period of time, Jimmy established himself as the champion, often managing a good twenty feet.

He wished Nick had been more of a spitter. He would have been good at it. He was good at everything he set out to do. Of course, that would have knocked Jimmy out of one of his few claims to top spot. Still, taking part in such antics might have loosened Nick up a bit. Jimmy wouldn't have minded anyway. He would have been happy to have Nick out with the rest of them. And who could know? Maybe Nick would have never out-spit Jimmy, no matter how hard he tried.

Bill's mind was on the good times—those spitting contests, Buck's teaching them to ride horses when he could barely handle a horse himself. They all got better than Buck at riding —all of them except Nick.

He had nearly as much of an aversion to horses as he did for spitting, but when comparing the two pastimes, his reasoning was that spitting left a person less smelly than riding.

"Old Nick," Billy Jack said aloud as he watched the last of the tiny spot of moisture drying up where it had landed a good ten feet out. Then he smiled. *Well, I've still got it.*

He jiggled his spurs lightly and Old Chigger moved forward across the pasture. Chigger had been on this trail so many times, he knew exactly where they were headed. If the horse could only manage to check the windmill, Bill knew he could have stayed at the barn and sent Chigger out alone. He reached forward and patted the horse's neck, feeling a ripple of response under his hand.

Bill's thoughts returned to Buck. He had driven over to the house last night, but Buck wasn't home. He had called this morning, but Ramona reported he was not there, and she hadn't heard from him. Neither had Pauline. Bill didn't know exactly what he intended to say to Buck anyway. He just knew he had to get something started. He hadn't intended his comments to come out the way they had although he was pretty much overwhelmed by the size of Buck's and his mother's intended gift.

When Nick spoke up, his words as sharp as his surgeon's scalpel, the meeting had ended. Everything ground to a halt and Buck was gone before Billy Jack had a chance to say anything else.

As soon as he got home from the lawyer's office, he and Donna had their first fight. Before he could even tell her what had happened, she hit him with the news that she had let both the hired hands off for a week.

The two cowboys were first-time ranch hands and good workers, but too young to resist when adventure called. A more seasoned cowboy would not have asked, but they did, and a more seasoned ranch wife would have given it a lot more thought before sending them on their way so quickly, but she had. They were headed to a rodeo in Wyoming.

Ken Jones, a buddy of Tommy's—Tommy being the older of the two, so—mostly by self-declaration—their head wrangler, had stopped by on his way North.

Ken was driving a pickup with a topper on it—handy for sleeping, or changing clothes. He was pulling a two-horse trailer, but just hauling one horse. He had only intended to have a beer with them and buy a couple of bales of hay for the road. Thirty minutes later, Tommy and Buster were at the back door asking for time off and an advance on their wages.

Their friend had a horse go lame, thus the lone animal in the trailer. A man couldn't depend on enough luck to get through a week of rodeo with only one horse. Tommy didn't mind loaning him old Blue, but hated to send his favorite horse off by himself. Ken needed another horse in there. Hauling on one side left the trailer unbalanced. Buster had never been to such a big time rodeo. Tommy might just jump in and try his hand at Cheyenne—Buster, too, for that matter.

Tommy's earnest logic, if his plea could have been considered logical, had won Donna over before Tommy, himself, was convinced. In the end, it was she who had to persuade the boys to take off. She could help Billy Jack if need be, or they could get Buck to send someone over from the BAR4. She had written their checks and made sandwiches for the road while they were loading old Blue and their gear. They were off in less than fifteen minutes.

She would now finally get her chance to help Billy Jack. He had been teaching her to ride, but that was for their enjoyment. Now she could really work. She would at last be a real ranch wife.

Billy Jack, mad when he came through the door, was furious when Donna told him what she had done. It was he who was supposedly the rancher, and he would decide whether or not the help could take off for a rodeo.

When Donna explained her plans to help him, he was quick to assure her she didn't know how. It had escalated from there, with a lot of shouting on his part, and a lot of crying on hers. When Bill finally realized it didn't matter that she had sent the hands off, telling her what he was actually upset about, she was hard-pressed to offer sympathy.

It was now she who was on a rampage. Having watched in-fighting among her own father and his brothers, all now completely estranged from each other, she could not face the possibility of years of the same with Bill and his family.

Bill had not intended for it to be this way, he had pleaded to Donna. He was just overwhelmed. She knew they had both expected to be receiving only a deed to the Stone Creek place. That was great with both of them. The house and such a huge acreage and the management of it, had been a bombshell to Billy Jack. The two of them needed to talk.

Their reasoning finally took hold, or perhaps they were too drained emotionally to continue. In any case, they agreed they must find a way to explain this to Buck.

Ranch hands come and go, but Buck was—well, Buck was Buck.

He and Donna weren't mad anymore and wouldn't be again for a long, long time.

Billy Jack thought about all this as he rode. She wasn't with him as she had planned. He had left early, long before Juanita, their housekeeper, would be there to look after the boys. He didn't want to wake Donna, but he did leave a note on his pillow that explained how he felt about her much more adequately and tenderly than words coming directly from him would have been.

He vowed he would get back to Buck. He needed Buck as much as he needed Donna and the boys. All these thoughts whirled in his head. It was good that he was riding alone. He had plenty of time to think.

He thought about his childhood, filled with year after year of what could have been considered rugged work, but looking back, it hadn't seemed arduous at all. Today, he realized that was because his mother had worked beside them, turning work from toil to challenge.

She'd never stopped. He smiled as he thought about the ceremonious evening when Buck, Ariola and Joe, with Joe the ringleader, had banned Alta from the fields. But that hadn't stopped her. She'd found work. She was still at it weeks before her death.

And Buck. He hadn't been in on much of the fieldwork —he'd been busy in a different way, but he'd worked every day.

Yet he'd found time to do the little things with his kids that might be taken for granted, for after all, that's what dads do.

He knew one thing for sure. As soon as he got home, he was going to teach his boys to spit.

Chapter 12

When they arrived at the ranch, Buck drove around showing Paul the layout before stopping at the house. Paul appreciated the sight of the sleek, fat registered Herefords clustered in a holding pen, but Buck, watching Paul as they drove, taking in the vast expanses of pasture—scattered herds, one or two cowboys checking on them—was convinced Paul still had the heart of a range cowboy. As a young man, he had been out in the big pastures, and still would be if age hadn't caught him.

Buck drove for an hour, then headed back to the house. He did need to check on a few things, but was also concerned that he might be pushing the old man. Paul's face looked more drawn than it had when they left Denver.

Buck stopped under the portico, but before turning off the engine, he pulled out again.

"You can see the house tonight at supper. Right now, I'll just take you to the bunkhouse where you'll be staying so you can rest a little if you want to."

Paul's brow furrowed in question.

"All the beds are upstairs," Buck said.

"Besides," he added, "I figure you might enjoy your stay a little more if you have some privacy. You wouldn't want Ramona hovering over you. And this way, you can scratch and belch when you want to, or—"

"Clear enough," Paul cut in.

Another question was on his face as Buck pulled up to a long, low building. It matched the house, in that it was of rough brick painted white and topped with the same red tile roof, but the resemblance ended there. The main house was two-storied, huge, on the verge of being a mansion. The workmanship on this one looked just as nice, but with none of the architectural detail of the big one. It was plain, except for the porch that extended its length. Paul counted six doors. It reminded him of a motel—only nicer than any he'd ever stayed in.

"This is the bunkhouse?" Paul questioned.

"Sure is. Only you'll have the suite that belonged to my boy, Jimmy. You don't have any objection to that, do you?"

"Of course not. I'm just taken by it. I've lived in my share of bunkhouses, but this is something else. The ones I lived in were just that. Bunkhouses. You bunked there, all right, but you wanted to get on down the road as soon as possible. Looks like I could tolerate this for a long time."

"Well, I hope you will."

Buck got out and hurried around the car to hand Paul his crutches from the back seat. He grabbed the duffel and flour sack before Paul could object, and carried them in. They walked slowly, Paul groaning a little, laying it onto the long ride. Inside, Paul whistled under his breath, then said, "If I don't stay long, it won't be because it's not nice enough to suit me."

"Well, if you don't mind, I'll just hang up your clothes. I'd like to see you lie down to rest for a while."

"You've just been needing someone to mother, haven't you, Buck."

Buck smiled, not even bothering to answer. He went about the business of putting away Paul's clothes and shaving kit, and when he came back to the front room, Paul was stretched out on the sofa.

"You have a mighty nice bed in there," Buck said.

"This is fine. You do sound more like my mother by the minute," Paul growled. He had put his Stetson on the coffee table, but reached over and got it to cover his face.

"I'll come back for you at suppertime," Buck said.

When Paul didn't reply, he wondered if the old fellow might already be asleep. If he wasn't asleep by the time

Buck left, he would be soon after.

Some time later, Paul was startled back to wakefulness, or at least a semblance of it, by the ringing of the phone. His eyes flew open to unfamiliar surroundings, confusing him about where he was for a moment. The phone was on the table by his head. He could reach it from where he lay, but let it ring several times. Finally answering it, he still wondered if he should have—that it might be for someone else. When he picked it up, he was relieved to find it was Buck calling him to eat.

"I'll be right there to get you. It's too far for you to hobble," Buck said.

"I think you're probably right."

For once he was agreeable to being pampered.

He sat up and reached for his hat. It had fallen off his face some time during his sleep, or perhaps when the phone had jerked him awake. He brushed it off a little, but only out of habit. It certainly hadn't gotten dirty from Jimmy's floor. The dark plaid rug under the table was spotless. He lay the hat back on the coffee table, then spied an empty hat rack by the front door. Hobbling over, he hung the Stetson on it. While standing there, he tried to rub away some of the wrinkles in his shirt, but didn't have much luck. Maybe he should change, but decided against that. The most he was going to do was comb his hair, then put in his partial and use a little mouthwash.

Paul was on the front porch looking for Buck's car when he drove up on a golf cart. He got off and leaned against it.

"See if you can handle this thing."

"I reckon it wouldn't be much different than a tractor," Paul said. He made his way down the steps with both crutches under his left arm so he could hold onto the rail with the other hand. Placing them in the empty rack behind the seats, he moved gingerly toward the running board.

When he winced with pain at having all his weight on his cast, Buck reached out to help him step up, but pulled back, knowing the old man wanted to make it on his own.

"I thought you might need this to zip around the place," Buck said.

Paul nodded, but said nothing. He was studying. Buck had left it running. Paul was not exactly sure about how to handle the cart, but he certainly didn't want advice. They got off to a jerky start, but were soon sailing along.

"Go through the courtyard and you can buzz right up to the kitchen," Buck said. "It'll be a whole lot easier for you than the front door."

He could have bitten his tongue. Implying that Paul couldn't handle his crutches was a habit that would have to change if he wanted to keep Paul around—and he did want the old man to stay as long as he would. Buck enjoyed Paul's tart wit, and besides, it was nice to have someone around he could talk to without any agenda. The silences were comfortable, too. On the way down from Denver, they had gone miles at a stretch with no word spoken.

Apparently, Paul took the remark only as it had been intended because he simply mumbled sure thing as he passed under an arched gateway and into the courtyard. Buck had left its swinging doors propped open just for this purpose.

"We'll leave that open for you," Buck said.

"I've opened my share of gates through the years," Paul replied, "but that will make it a mite easier for me on this thing." By this time, he was approaching the kitchen door, and having as much trouble stopping as he'd had when first starting out. They passed perilously close to a huge terra cotta pot of flowering vine, but jerked to a halt without incident.

"I think I could use a little practice out in the wide open spaces," Paul admitted. Buck silently agreed, but only said, "No problem. We'll do that tomorrow."

They were to eat in the kitchen, but Ramona was bustling around with last minute preparation. Her glance at

Buck told him he'd better take Paul into the library until she called them. Ariola was already there, reading, but when Buck and Paul came in, he closed his book and spent the rest of the time talking and listening, mostly listening—Ariola had a knack for drawing people out.

Buck sat back, learning a lot about Paul Sloan and a few things he had never known about Ariola. He noticed Paul had his own brand of finesse.

After eating, Ariola helped Ramona with the dishes, his usual habit, while Buck and Paul remained at the table with one last cup of coffee. There was a light knock at the kitchen door, but it opened before anyone had a chance to get it. Three small boys rushed in. Buck was up and across the room. There was some scuffling as each one tried to be the first to get to Buck, so by the time they had untangled, he was already scooping them up. He was quick, but not so quick that Paul had missed Buck's paling face at the sight of them and their parents, who waited in the doorway. It was obvious that it was Buck whom they had come to see, so after introductions and a little chatting, Ariola suggested that he accompany Paul back to the bunkhouse.

"I'm your neighbor out there, you know," he said.

"I know," Paul said as he gathered his crutches.

As they headed toward the door, he added, "I'll even offer you a ride on my cart, but I'd appreciate it if you'd do the driving."

Chapter 13

Billy Jack didn't try to explain anything. Neither did Buck. A lot of hugging had gotten everything off to a good start.

Buck had been in countless situations where he had been rebuffed coldly, only to come back with a stronger position that had won him the battle, if not the war.

Of course, there was no comparison between what took place in the law office, and what Buck had dealt with in those business meetings.This was family. Everyone present had been grieving. They had been discussing Alta's wishes for her sons, but the sons happened to disagree with her wishes.

Donna had sent Buck and Billy Jack out of the kitchen and put the three boys at the table to eat the last of Ramona's peach cobbler. Afterward, she got them started on puzzles that would keep them occupied for as long as the men needed to talk.

That didn't take long after all. They didn't come to any decisions, but each man expressed his feelings enough that both were satisfied knowing things could be worked out. Billy Jack was able, in his slow deliberate way, to explain that he didn't want to step into a management position, being handed everything Buck and Alta had worked so hard to build.

They did continue talking for a long time, but not about the settling of the estate. They talked as neighboring ranchers would talk—about the cattle market, the bottomed out wheat prices, the progress of current fence building, even about the best fishing streams for the boys.

Buck was as anxious as Alta had been to see that Nick and Billy Jack were well set financially. He wanted to do everything possible to ease Alta's fretting. In those last weeks of her life, there had been too little time, and not enough energy on her part, to rationalize that their good upbringing was gift enough.

Buck didn't say so, but in his heart, he knew that as well as carrying out Alta's last wishes, he was trying to ease his guilt about the pain he had caused. He had to get his family back. He felt like a stranger among them, that nobody really cared what he did.

While the men talked, David and Jeff had worked and reworked the puzzles. What they really wanted was to go outside and watch the sky for shooting stars. Donna finally sent them on their way with a nod. That wasn't at all like her, but when they found their mother in such an agreeable frame of mind they quickly upped the deal to walking down to the pasture to look at the horses.

They failed in that attempt to expand their territory, but happily scrambled atop the thick wall in the far corner—the darkest corner—of the courtyard. Never mind they could see a light from the bunkhouse only a short distance away, plus the lighted kitchen window, they felt brave and adventurous. David swore he saw two shooting stars. Jeff missed them, but he had no doubt that his older brother had spotted them. That was all that counted. They were a team. Donna stood by the window awhile, watching the boys. She could barely make out their small forms through the darkness, but an occasional soft giggle reassured her. She finally turned away and went about cleaning up the few dishes from the cobbler, wanting to keep herself busy.

She wondered how Billy Jack and Buck could find so much to discuss. Billy Jack had always been on the quiet side. However, she noted this evening might be the longest the two men had ever talked. She had a good feeling about how things were going.

Matt was stretched out on the wicker settee in the breakfast area. Donna, seated beside him, cradled his feet in her lap. He had fallen asleep before Billy Jack finally gathered up his family to take them home.

Buck carried Matt out to the car and placed him in Donna's lap while Billy Jack brought the two proud sentinels back from the courtyard wall. They skipped happily along behind him, not quite ready to give up their posts, but content anyway. It was the latest they had ever been allowed to stay outside alone.

Buck stood at the gate until they turned onto the highway. He kept watching until the taillights were swallowed up by the darkness, then walked back to the house. He was keyed up and drained of energy at the same time.

It was time to go to bed, but he felt no dread of the empty house. It was returning to what it had always been—home.

Chapter 14

Buck was ready to drive out to the building site at sunrise. When he got there, he didn't find much building going on—none as a matter of fact. It was impatience on his part, but he had expected some noticeable progress. A number of pieces of heavy equipment were scattered across the area, but the only activity was a surveying team on the east edge of the property, and a crew clearing a few scrawny mesquite trees from the other side. Although the future complex was inside the city limits, it was overgrown, littered with trash, several empty cans and a couple of old tires. It looked more like the beginnings of a dump ground than of a hospital.

Buck parked on the far side of the land. The street was unpaved. That would have to be changed, he thought, as dust settled across the hood.

The land beyond was a pasture but no cattle were in sight, though a four-strand barbed wire fence stood ready. For a moment, Buck eyed the pasture as a future park, but quickly changed his mind. He was predisposed to buying up everything around him, but there was always something else. Beyond this pasture lay another, and yet another. It could be endless. He had to break away from that. He'd promised Alta.

With that thought, he was suddenly nervous about seeing Nick, of being in this spot. Sitting there, making furtive glances, he was disgusted with himself, but at the moment he couldn't fight it.

They had taken the option, but he had not driven past the property since. The old Buck would have driven onto it, to walk it, checking the lay of the land and envisioning how the hospital might look.

This new Buck seemed intent on slinking in unnoticed. It took him a while to get his fill of self-pity—self-loathing, too, he guessed—but with his allotted time for pity and hate gone, he circled the acreage. Making sure to stay out of range of the surveyors, he started walking but hadn't gone far when he heard a horn honk. He turned and waited as Ariola came walking up. Buck notice Paul sitting in his car.

"The old codger had such a hard day yesterday, I thought he might sleep in this morning, or I would have brought him myself," Buck said by way of a greeting.

"I think he's pretty much of an early riser," Ariola replied. "No problem, though. I enjoy his company. We had quite a visit last night after we left the house."

"He's had a somewhat checkered past, and doesn't mind talking about it," Ariola added, chuckling.

"I believe you're right," Buck said.

With that settled, they continued their walk.

As they walked, they talked and Buck gradually loosened up. It was almost like it had been in the old days, throwing ideas back and forth, good ones discarded as soon as better ones came up. Circumstances had been different then. There had been a few lawyers, but no architects or construction consultants. They'd had, instead, ideas and courage—and just plain guts. Every detail of a project had been worked out before they'd taken it to the bank, whether it had been to Mr. Hayward, as it had been in the beginning, or later, to the huge financial institutions from which they operated today.

They discussed the feasibility of a single story structure with long halls to be walked, versus the higher construction cost of a multi-level building. Should nurses living quarters be included in the complex? A myriad of other decisions would have to be made before the actual planning could even begin. By the time they got back to their cars, the one thing that had been decided was they would turn such decisions over to the architect and John Kraft—and hopefully, Nick. It was Ariola who was more optimistic about Nick. Buck was uncertain whether Nick would have anything to do with the project, much less stay in NeeDee to practice.

Two more cars pulled up. At least it was beginning to look as though something was happening. John Kraft and Kirk Andrews were in Kirk's car, and Nick, with Tom Fraser, a big man who barely fit into Nick's little blue bug, pulled in beside them.

Tom managed John's tiny hospital, but was not the administrator—at least he'd never officially had that title—yet that was his job. He oversaw the staff, including any hiring and firing—although there was very little of that.

A head nurse was in charge of the medical staff, but she answered to Tom. One woman, serving as dietitian and chief cook, planned the food, assisted with the cooking along with supervising the serving of it and the cleanup following, then answered to Tom. Likewise, did the office staff—and the maintenance crew. So Tom was definitely an administrator.

He would move into this new facility, doing the same job, but on a much larger scale. Now Tom would also have a board to deal with. There would be lots of changes, to be sure, but everyone was confident Tom could handle it.

When the four got over to Buck and Ariola, there were handshakes all around with much reaching across one another until everyone had greeted everyone else. The shuffling ended with Nick standing beside Buck. Buck stuck out his hand. Nick shook it firmly as Buck had taught all his boys to do. He had always told them a firm grip was the mark of a man. After releasing his hand, Nick punched him lightly on the shoulder. Yet when Nick said *good morning, Buck,* his voice seemed cool—at least in Buck's mind.

Buck's jaw knotted, but he pulled something from deep

within his gut and responded crisply, "Good morning, son."

The group talked, the two doctors and the future administrator discussing their needs in the working facility, the architect commenting, but mostly listening, then scribbling rapidly in a small notebook, and Ariola offering suggestions about the financial arrangements. Only Buck was silent. He had written the check. It lay on his desk. Ariola could pick it up whenever necessary. That was as far as his involvement would go, as far as he wanted it to go.

Buck didn't intend to walk off like a pouting child, but he did feel like getting away. He broke in, telling them he would take Paul back to the house.

"Paul?" Nick questioned.

"An old man who came home with me. From Denver yesterday," Buck said.

"You'll love him, Nick," Ariola added. "Come over to the car and meet him."

He glanced around and added, "You guys just keep at it. We won't be long."

As they approached the car, the only thing visible was Paul's cast propped on the dash. Peering in the open window, Nick gave it a professional once over. Paul squirmed up a little, but was still lying halfway down.

Ariola, standing closest to Nick, said, "Paul, I'd like you to meet Buck's son, Nick Pitts."

Paul stuck out his hand. "So this is the doc. I might have known—he seems to be more interested in my cast than in me."

"Just habit," Nick said and grinned.

Nick stretched his arm inside to reach it. As they shook, he added, "I'm pleased to meet you."

"Same here."

Paul hadn't seen the three men approaching, else he would have been sitting up—at least in a more dignified position. Now he was faced with the problem of getting the heavy cast off the dash without as much moaning and groaning as he had put in while placing it there. Having it elevated seemed to relieve some of the pain that shot through his toes.

"Looks like you have a little swelling there," Nick said. He hadn't gotten beyond inspecting the old man's cast.

"Probably. Them toes has always been on the blue side though. Got me a case of frostbite up North one time, and they haven't hardly been any good since."

"We'll keep an eye on them."

"You can check on him out at the house sometime," Buck spoke up. "I'm going to be taking off and be gone for a few days."

The words had just spilled out of his mouth. He hadn't planned on going anywhere—not even to that Denver board meeting—but now he had a sudden urge to be gone again. He didn't know where it might be. He just wanted to be on the move.

Paul looked at him in alarm. He hadn't planned on coming to NeeDee then left stranded, without a way to get back to Denver.

Buck caught the look. "Just for a short while, Paul."

Nick's reaction had been as troubled as Paul's. Could Buck be thinking that his being gone was a prerequisite to Nick's going out to the house?

"Sure," Nick said, hesitated, then added, "Or maybe Ramona or someone could bring him to the hospital."

Paul could not ignore the polite tension between the two, and he suddenly felt himself the center of a family squabble. He didn't like it. It gave him just enough of a spurt of adrenaline that he was able to get his leg off the dashboard with a minimum of noise from his pain.

"Hell. No problem. If I can just get someone to haul me to the bus station, I need to get back to check on my cabin anyway."

Buck stepped up to the window and stood beside Nick.

He, too, peered in at Paul.

"You're not going anywhere right now and neither am I. I don't know what the hell got into me. I'll haul you back to Denver in a few days when I have a real reason for going—that board meeting."

"That's right, Paul," Nick cut in.

"You hang around here with us. I'll be happy to come out to the house to check on you."

"Damn right, he will. I'm inviting him out there. No, I'm telling him to come out there. I'm still his old man."

"Yeah," Nick again took up the campaign.

"I don't know which one of us is the biggest horse's rear end."

He was talking to Paul, looking him in the eye, but he glanced at Buck.

They both straightened up and faced each other.

"I do. It's me," Buck said with a grin that he hoped Nick would return. "I'm six inches taller than you."

Nick responded with a lopsided grin that broadened into a smile. Then he grabbed Buck in a bear hug.

Chapter 15

That scene brought Buck and Nick back to friendlier terms, but it didn't keep Paul out of the hospital. He'd been in pain before leaving Denver, at times worse than others, but now the torment was constant, becoming intolerable. He'd been too agitated to take proper care when he'd removed his leg from the dashboard.

As soon as they got back to the ranch, Paul excused himself. He had Ariola drop him off at his door. Needed to rest, he told him, thought he'd better just lie around and keep off his feet.

Paul lay on the sofa all morning, his leg propped on a pillow. He couldn't touch the lunch Ramona sent out. Not even the last few nips from his pint of Jack Daniels helped.

His foot throbbed, the pain shooting to the top of his cast, up his leg, and into the groin at times. It was so swollen the circulation was cut off. Needing some relief, he nearly had someone call Nick, but changed his mind. What could Nick do about it? He had no doubt about how to take care of it himself.

He'd had an old uncle in this same situation. He remembered watching him one hot afternoon, had even been posted as a lookout. Being only six or seven years old at the time, Paul was not quite sure what he would have done if he had spied Aunt Marge or Granny coming down to the orchard to check on him. He decided later that he would have run to meet them with a good story—he'd been bitten by an ant, maybe a snake or spider, anything to get them headed back to the house with him. He was extremely loyal to Uncle, and when Uncle explained that it was the only way to get rid of the pain, Paul wanted to help. If it took a little lie, Uncle was worth the risk.

As it happened, they didn't come looking, so Uncle had the whole afternoon to work on his cast. By the time they did come, Uncle was in a poor state. He had applied vinegar-soaked rags to his cast to soften it up enough that he was able to whittle away the offending section, but in the process, he had scratched and cut at his foot until it was a bloody sight when Aunt Marge finally found him.

After getting him to the doctor's office, and the rest of the cast sawed off, several infected sores and red streaks were exposed. It turned out that Uncle had already scratched quite a lot with a straightened-out metal clothes hanger to relieve the itch and burning going on inside the cast. Paul remembered Uncle was laid up for the whole summer, resting in the porch swing, watched closely by Aunt Marge. Paul spent much of that time cooling Uncle with a funeral home fan, knowing it was the least he could do since he had taken part in the whole sorry mess by serving as Uncle's lookout. Aunt Marge made that clear. It had cost him the summer, but Uncle had needed his help.

That was many years ago; times had changed. Maybe vinegar was more potent now. Uncle had been careless in scratching his leg; he'd be more careful.

He was more or less stranded in a strange place, surrounded by people he didn't know, and besides, he could take care of himself—always had.

Pushing Uncle's troubles to the back of his mind, Paul called Ramona and inquired about her pickling supplies. Surely she put up pickles. Yes, she did, several varieties, in fact. Would she have a gallon of vinegar she could spare? Yes, and she would send it right down since it would be hard for him to handle on the golf cart. Ramona didn't question the nature of his need, but she did think it was an unusual request, in fact, strange enough that she told Ariola about it as soon as he came home.

It was late afternoon before Ariola walked in to check on Paul. It seemed to be a replay of that afternoon Paul had served as Uncle's lookout. He wasn't in as big a mess as Uncle had been—after all, he worked the whole afternoon, whereas Paul had only a couple of hours—but he was aching and burning considerably more than before starting work on his cast. He was, in fact, in enough misery that he didn't complain when Ariola and a cowboy loaded him up and took him to the hospital. Paul stayed there long enough to miss his ride back to Denver with Buck. On the positive side, he met Freda Baily, his nurse, and was there long enough to become very well acquainted with her.

Chapter 16

Paul was aware of being tightly bound from shoulder to toe. The binding was cool and smooth and slightly stiff. He felt constricted but not extremely uncomfortable—simply confined to one spot, as if someone didn't want him to move. That was all right with him. He really didn't care what went on. He felt some pain, but not much. In fact, there was so little of it, he had the puzzling idea that the pain might be in someone else's body, not his own.

The second thing he noticed was a white cloud above him. It floated lazily back and forth, the white tinged with gold and bits of blue. It then began to swirl. The faster it moved, the smaller it became, finally turning into a beautiful face hovering in place of the cloud. Ah, no, he thought. What'll happen to old Jake now? Here I've died and left my poor old dog to Lois's mercy.

Doyle would come by for a few days to feed him, as he'd promised when Paul had left with Buck, but Lois would soon put a stop to that. Then Jake would be on his own, having to make his living by snapping up indolent squirrels—and those were hard to come by. Most squirrels were quicker than Jake—not only because of Jake's age—squirrels were just generally quick.

He started to fret. The beautiful face, thinking Paul must be in more pain than he should, tried to soothe him.

"You just take it easy, young man," the beautiful face said.

He hadn't ever considered that angels talked. He didn't know what they did, but he'd never associated them with a voice, even such a sweet sounding voice as he now heard. He should look around and try to clear up this puzzle. The answer came when he looked beyond the beautiful face and saw Buck standing there.

"You son-of-a-gun," Buck said. "You've really fixed yourself up, haven't you? You don't have a cast anymore, but you're hooked up to more chains and pulleys than a trapeze artist."

"Don't rub it in. A man's got to do what a man's got to do."

Even as his woozy state hung on, he was still more interested in the beautiful face than in anything Buck Ramsey might have to say.

That ephemeral beauty had turned into an ordinary looking nurse by now, but while realizing she wasn't an angel, she was a sight much more appealing to him than Buck.

"Don't agitate our patient," she said. Paul knew he had someone on his side and turned a docile face toward her to express his appreciation.

Buck wasn't through, however.

"You'll spoil him, Freda. Just like you do every old goat that lands in here."

"This one's special," she said. "He deserves a little spoiling."

Paul looked up at her smiling face and fell in love.

When Buck had to leave for Denver a few days later, he left Paul happily basking in Freda's, and the rest of the staff's, care. He was still hooked up to his chains, and could not have gone with him anyway, but that was fine with both of them. An orderly came in to shave him one morning, and, in a hurry to get to the next patient, gave Paul a little nick on the chin. It drew some blood. Freda sent him on his way. He was on a tight schedule, she said, so she would finish Paul. From then on, she shaved him and combed his hair—after the orderly had bathed him and changed his hospital gown, of course. Paul noticed right away that she had a knack for shaving, even better than the old barber who had given him a weekly shave and haircut long ago. She didn't give him a steaming towel treatment as Cleotus Roberts had, but otherwise, she did a much better job than that old barber. Much better, Paul thought, and much prettier, too.

On Saturday morning, he stared out the window with a woebegone look on his face. It was Freda's day off. She planned on sleeping late, then going to the beauty shop. He turned his head—the rest of his body still being well immobilized by the chains—at a slight rustle in the doorway. She stood there with a shaving tray in her hand. That sight gave him such a start he tried to sit up, nearly upsetting his pulleys in the process.

Her nurse's intuition took over. She rushed to him, set the tray on his bedside table and busily righted the contraption. Then she adjusted his pillow and smoothed his bedding, making him comfortable with professional efficiency. He hadn't spoken until she finished and stepped back.

"What are you doing here, honey?" he asked, unable to mask his pleasure.

He must have called a lot of women honey through the years. She assumed as much by the flip tone he'd used in the beginning, but now it had a special sound to it—to her, anyway.

"I couldn't let your whiskers go the whole weekend, but I was afraid if Willie got hold of you, he might scar you for life."

She didn't tell him she couldn't face the day without seeing him. He didn't tell her how lonesome he had already begun feeling without the prospects of seeing her. They just smiled at each other.

After his shave, she sat in a straight chair beside his bed. They chatted, jumping from subject to subject, each silently amazed at how easily the conversation flowed. He finally insisted that she at least sit in the recliner if she intended to stay longer.

He regretted saying that because she took it as her cue to leave. At the same time, he was concerned that she was spending her day off with him when she should get away from the hospital. She insisted that she had nothing special to do. She could come back that evening, maybe read to him for a while—if he wanted her to.

"Why don't you come earlier and eat supper with me?" he asked.

"Why, yes, I don't suppose that would hurt a thing."

"Then we have a date?"

She stepped back from his bedside a little. She could feel her cheeks flush and she hated that. She hoped he hadn't noticed, but he had.

"Well, we'll not call it a date, if that bothers you. Anyway, if I took a beautiful woman like you on a date, it would be to the nicest club in Denver."

"And I'd be happy to go—if we were in Denver. But we're here, and this is as nice as it's going to be for a while. So yeah, I'll come back and eat with you, Paul. And yeah, we have a date."

She stepped closer again, and they smile at each other. Then, without any conscious thought of it, she abruptly reached over and kissed him on the lips. But in the next moment, reason again gripped her. Surely this must be against some hospital policy or the other.

Freda then darted for the door, and looking back, she saw Paul still smiling.

Chapter 17

The supper went well, and did for the next evening and the next—then became a daily ritual until Paul was finally released and driven back out to the bunkhouse by Ariola.

The kitchen allowed some limited special ordering, and after Paul noticed that Freda enjoyed the baked chicken, he began requesting it. When Freda walked in with her tray—she usually picked up whatever was the standard meal for the evening—Paul insisted they trade. It galled him to have to play such silly games in order to make things special for a beautiful woman. It hadn't been too many years ago—at least it didn't seem to be so many—since all it had taken was his silver money clip thick with rodeo winnings to get the lady of the moment and himself the best table, the best service and the best wine.

When Freda hadn't been able to stop by for a while, his thinking took another turn. Yes, it had been a long time ago—so long that he wanted to do this right, or at least the best he could do among all his chains and pulleys.

She was beginning to tire of baked chicken but soon caught on—he was trying to make the most of their hospital meals, as if he had planned their evening. She always accepted that chicken graciously—delighted that he wanted their time together to be festive.

"You're spoiling me," she'd say, nibbling at her dinner.

"I wish," he'd answer, his standard reply.

Another grin would follow. She hardly noticed how much she was beginning to look forward to those grins.

The morning shave also became part of Freda's routine unless she was tied up with an emergency. When that happened, Paul told the orderly he didn't mind waiting for Freda.

It was all right with Willie. He could hardly keep the crotchety old rascal still enough to do a decent job, he told the rest of the crew during his coffee break, whereas the old coot just smiled at the sight of Freda and was meek as a lamb waiting its turn at the teat.

Freda was an extraordinary nurse, and gave her full attention to every patient in her charge, but in Paul's case, her capabilities seemed to reach far beyond. He simply blossomed under her care. Her company each evening might have been a factor, but whatever the case, he gained weight and got some color back. The kitchen staff took their share of the credit, and Freda encouraged that, going out of her way to give them *all* the credit. She had never played favorites, but more than that, she was determined that the staff have no room to speculate about her feelings for Paul.

She didn't want Paul getting any ideas either, but he was getting plenty of those on his own. He was old enough to be her father. He dreaded the thought that her feelings might not match his—his were far from fatherly.

He pouted when Freda was too busy to make rounds with Nick. The various nurses who accompanied Nick noted that he was the same cantankerous old man, no different from the day he had checked in, but Nick only smiled.

Buck was glad he had brought Paul to NeeDee. He didn't know why he had taken such a liking to the old man—never questioned it—but he was happy Paul was here instead of back in his cabin. He never doubted that Paul would have taken the vinegar to his cast, if he could have coaxed Doyle into bringing him some and he was sure that Doyle would have given in to him just as Ramona had. Paul would have been in such misery—Buck didn't like to think about it—by the time Doyle had come back the next morning.

Buck was accustomed to delegating. From the looks of

Paul when he dropped in, he knew whoever was taking care of him was doing their job well, so he went about his routine. He was in and out of town. So was Ariola, but both managed to spend time at the hospital whenever possible.

"I figured he would be raising hell and rearing to get out of there," Buck remarked following an hour with Paul.

"I imagine they'll have to keep him quite a while longer unless he wants another cast, and I doubt that he would tolerate one any better than he did before," Ariola replied.

"Even so, he's turning into a lot better patient than I figured he would," Buck said.

Ariola had noticed the way Paul gazed after Freda as she finished whatever it is a nurse pops in and does. He was confident he knew the answer for Paul's newfound contentment, but he only shrugged and acted as amazed as Buck.

A few weeks later, Buck came back after several days in Chicago and found things had changed. Two cars were parked in front of the bunkhouse. One was Nick's. He felt a jolt of alarm at the sight of it—it had been some time since he had seen that dusty little VW parked there. The other was one he didn't recognize. He knew it only meant Paul must be out of the hospital, and Nick had come out to check on him, but he also wondered about the unfamiliar car. Perhaps some of his family had come to take him home. He didn't recall Paul mentioning any family. In fact, he made it clear that he had no relatives. Maybe Doyle had overruled Lois for once and had come for Paul. He doubted that. In Paul's own words, Lois had Doyle on a pretty tight leash. Why should Doyle come? Paul knew that Buck was planning to drive him back home as soon as he was ready to go—or as soon as he was able to go.

None of that mattered. Now his main concern was whether he should see for himself or wait until Nick had left. Nick would have things well in hand, so perhaps he should just stay away. If he did go out, would Nick be uncomfortable? That friendly exchange at the construction site was one step, but he was still unsure of how much closeness Nick was ready for. Should he ask Nick to come up to the house afterwards for some coffee? Would he come, even if he were asked? He disliked indecision from anyone—he detested it in himself. He headed for the bunkhouse.

Nick was not around, but Paul, still in pajamas, was settled on the couch. His leg, free at last of its chains and pulleys, rested on a thick pillow. Two more behind his shoulders propped him into a half upright, but comfortable recline.

"Good to see you home," Buck said as he came through the door. "But I wish you were up at the house. We could set up a bed for you in the library."

"I'll be fine here. Got me a nurse and everything." He winked and glanced across the room.

Freda was busy in Jimmy's kitchenette. The teakettle was whistling, and she was placing thin slices of cake on saucers. The saucers were pale pink, translucent enough that they glistened in the late evening sun. Buck didn't remember ever seeing such delicate dishes in Jimmy's place. When he spotted a wicker basket on the counter, it dawned on him. Freda had brought them—and the cake.

"Hi, Buck. Care for some of this?" she asked, setting a cup of tea and some cake on the coffee table for Paul.

"No, but it sure looks good. You make it?"

"She sure did," Paul answered for her while she beamed at him.

"So Freda's going to nurse you?" Buck asked.

"I had a lot of vacation coming. I'm taking off for a month to look after him," Freda said.

"Well, then, how about you staying at the house, Freda? So you won't have to be driving out if he needs something during the night."

"I won't be needing anything at night. Besides, I don't want her running in and out all hours. Wouldn't look right."

"She ain't exactly my nurse anymore," he continued.

"She's asked me to marry her."

"Paul," Freda squeaked and stepped menacingly toward him.

"Well," he growled, "I'll admit I did ask her, but she said yes quicker than a cat could lick his whiskers."

"And I will admit to that much," she said. Her cheeks colored as she squeezed into the end of the couch and stroked his bare foot.

"Paul, you old devil. I didn't bring you down here to steal away our best nurse."

"You're telling me," Nick said as he came out of the bedroom. "She would never give me the time of day."

He grinned, his eyes scanning the three of them, but lingering last on Buck.

"How about us going up to the house. These lovebirds need some privacy. Besides, it's been too long since I've had any of Ramona's tamales."

Chapter 18

During that walk from the bunkhouse to the kitchen door, Buck and Nick chatted, mostly about the weather. What a subject, when there was so much they could be talking about. By the time they'd gotten there, a dozen scenarios had flashed through Buck's mind.

He wasn't expecting any kind of showdown with Nick, nor did he envision a clear-cut reconciliation. What he did want was the impossible—for that terrible scene in the law office to have never happened.

Nick had been friendly that day at the construction site when he had tapped Buck on the shoulder—friendly, at the same time, distant. Buck knew that Nick would have made that casual gesture to anyone who happened to be around. He'd hardly seen Nick since.

What was he thinking? He'd seen him several times—in Paul's room, at the site, other places. But that was not the kind of seeing that he wanted, that he craved.

Nick had given Paul the best possible care. Of course he had. He was a doctor. He would have given anyone the same care. If it had been he, himself, there was no doubt about what Nick would have done.

Buck walked along with a lump in his throat and he hated the feeling.

As it happened, there was no chance for any kind of one on one conversation. Ariola and Ramona were at the kitchen table, having coffee. As they entered, Ramona stood up, ready to attend to their needs.

"Keep your seat, Ramona," Nick said. "I think I know my way around here well enough to get us some coffee."

He kissed the old woman on the cheek, and gently pushed her back into her chair.

She looked up at him, smiling broadly. "Well, I wouldn't know about that. It's been so long since I've had you messing around my kitchen."

He didn't bother to answer, just set two mugs of coffee on the table. Buck took his place in front of one and pushed the other over to an empty space, but Nick didn't sit down. He was bent over, prowling in the refrigerator, whistling softly as he looked, finally raising up, empty-handed.

"No tamales? I could eat half a dozen right now. Even cold."

"I've somehow gotten away from making tamales," she said, "but I'll get back to it since you miss them."

"You're the only one who has noticed I don't make them anymore," she continued, giving Ariola and Buck a pointed glance. She meant it, too. She was serious about cooking to please her Nicky.

"Thank you, Ramona." He planted another kiss on her cheek as he passed her, on his way to his waiting coffee.

"I do have some banana bread," she offered. All three accepted so she got busy. She served them quickly, then left the three men alone to talk.

The conversation soon centered on the construction. Ariola and Nick discussed it. Buck mostly listened, and drew some painful insights as he did. He concluded his interest in the hospital might not be as selfless as it could appear to outsiders. He had written the check for it, but only as a means of disposing of the money Alta had intended for Nick. He didn't regret that—the hospital was badly needed—but was heartsick about the circumstances surrounding it. Why couldn't Nick have said that day, *Daddy, I appreciate yours and Mother's intentions, but let's just use the money for a new hospital.*

There could have been any number of reasons for him to refuse it, but he had chosen the most cutting words he had ever spoken to Buck. *Buck, don't you understand? We don't want anything from you.*

With those words again ringing in Buck's head, gloom consumed him. Perhaps it was in his eyes, or the slump of his shoulders, but whatever it was, Ariola noticed, and glanced at him with concern. Nick didn't notice it at all.

Ariola watched the two, who had somehow begun discussing Ramona's tamales again. Something nagged at him. He listened until it finally dawned on him. They were like new acquaintances throwing about meaningless scraps of conversation just to fill the time.

Ariola wanted to be gone. The pretense was irritating, but he stayed. He would not leave his friend. When all that could possibly be said about tamales had been said, Ariola intended to be there to see that Buck didn't crumble in the face of an affable stranger.

"Well, how about Paul and Freda?" Ariola cut in. That was as neutral a subject as he could come up with, and one that interested all of them.

"I was never more surprised in my life to see Paul talk her into marrying him," he continued.

"Oh, no," Nick said. "I see them every day. She's as crazy about him as he is about her. Maybe more so."

"She's going to have her hands full," Ariola replied.

"He fought like—well, argued anyway—not much fighting he could do against those two guys who were building the ramp. We got out here before they had it finished. There wasn't going to be any carrying him up those steps, but they did it anyway."

"I got here right after Freda, and he seemed pretty calm," Nick commented.

"Well, that must have been because she came in," Ariola said.

"See what I mean?" Nick retorted. "She has a way with Paul like I've never seen."

"It was his lucky day when he met her," Buck agreed.

"You bet," Nick said. "How did *you* happen to meet him?"

"Oh, I just ran into him in Denver, and we got to talking."

He wasn't about to tell him he had driven until he'd run out of gas, ending up sleeping in the car at Paul's place.

"The next time I saw him, he'd broken his ankle trying to shoot that skunk."

They all chuckled, none of them unsympathetic, but each with his own vision of Paul's dealings with the skunk. He'd paid a price, but he'd won.

Paul told Buck over and over—that face-off was the turning point in his life, the luckiest day of his life. If it hadn't been for that skunk, he would have never come to NeeDee. If he'd never come to NeeDee, he would have missed out on Freda.

Chapter 19

Paul's bones were healing, but slowly—at least too slow as far as he was concerned. That, in turn, didn't help his temperament. He growled at everyone—everyone except Freda, of course, involved in taking care of him, most heatedly at the young cowboy who was spending his nights on a cot in a corner of the living room. Since Paul wouldn't hear of Freda checking on him after bedtime, Nick insisted that someone stay with Paul in case he needed help. He was notorious for refusing to use his crutches.

Carter Fields was a happenstance cowboy—if any kind of cowboy at all, just working on the ranch until he could save enough money to get out of town. His plans were to go up North and try being a lumberjack. He didn't know much about it. The little he did know came from reading—and more than that, from movies. Lumberjacks worked hard, with long hours and bad weather. But once they'd had their shower and got over to the bar, everything seemed all right—soft and mellow and relaxing, at least that was the way it appeared to be in the picture shows he'd seen about life in the big woods. Right now, Carter was ready for it. He had just finished helping Paul shower. The old man was as irritable as he had ever seen him.

"I've broke a thousand broncs in my day, but you and Nick and all these smart asses think I can't walk across the room without these sticks."

"Just doin' my job. If I wasn't getting paid real good, I'd take these sticks and stick them up your—"

Paul cut in, cracking the tenseness with a chuckle and a profound admission, "You could probably do it, too."

He took the crutches without further protest and shuffled over to the sofa.

"Oh, yes. You probably could. You're bigger than me, and a whole lot younger."

"Yeah, but you're still as hard as nails," Carter replied just to make the old man feel a little better—aggravation having taken a sudden turn to sympathy.

Paul reminded him of his grandfather. Carter had been a lot younger and more impressionable when his daddy had called him into the back room one night to help hold his grandfather in the bed while he was dying. Even as he was fading, Grandpa was putting up a feeble scrap and threatening to pee on them if they didn't stop holding him down.

In the end, his grandfather had relented and died in Daddy's arms. He hated to see Paul give up so easily.

"What really gets to me is them thinking I have to have somebody with me all the time. You should be out running around."

"I get some time off. And, like I said, I'm getting paid pretty good."

"Pretty good, huh? Just a while ago, you said real good."

"Well, it is real good, considering there's not too much you'll let me do for you."

"What I mean is, you shouldn't be here at all. You should be out running around, chasing some girls. Isn't there at least one young thing out there you could have a little fun with?"

The boy colored slightly. The old man was getting to him again. He was just about to offer some kind of hot retort when a soft tap on the door staved it off.

Paul scrambled for his robe with Carter helping him. They had both recognized Freda's knock.

The knocking was only perfunctory. She had opened the door and was moving toward Paul before Carter could get it.

"What are you doing here this time of night, honey?" Paul asked, tying the belt.

The robe was only a plaid hospital issue, but he had brought it with him when he'd left and had used it every day since, giving it up only long enough for Ramona to wash it. It was the first robe he'd worn in forty years.

He'd worn one then because it was hanging on a silver hook in the bathroom of an oceanfront home on the East Coast where he was spending a week. It was hanging there because Anita—he did remember her name—had placed it there and expected him to wear it. He did wear it down to breakfast every morning for that whole week, but it was left hanging on that silver hook and he hadn't worn one since. Neither had he seen Anita.

He now felt differently about a robe. It was comfortable. It also set a certain decorum that he intended to use as far as Freda was concerned. He knotted the belt again. There was no comparing Anita and Freda.

"Well, I was already in bed—because you told me I was tired and needed to go to bed early—but I just couldn't sleep. I wasn't tired and I knew it. So I just sat straight up and said to myself, well, if he is trying to run me off, he's going to have to do it face to face."

Paul was sputtering denials all the while.

"And, besides," she said softly, "I missed you."

"I think this might be a good time to leave," Carter said.

Freda walked him to the door. They spoke quietly.

"Don't forget what I told you, boy," Paul called after him.

Carter said nothing. Going down the steps, he heard the lock snap behind him.

"And what was that you told him?" Freda asked.

"Oh, nothing. Just horsing around."

She came to the sofa and sat beside him, giving him what she hoped he'd consider a provocative glance.

"Well, I know what I told him. I told him he needed the night off."

"Now, Freda," he protested.

"Now, Freda, my foot. We're adults. We're engaged. And besides, I'm a nurse. I should be taking care of you."

She paused only for a second and continued before he could say anything.

"Yes, I should be taking care of you, not because we're engaged, not because I'm a nurse, but because I want to."

"That's not the point," he protested again.

"Then what is the point?"

"It's just that I'm an old reprobate and you—you're so young and beautiful—"

"I'm not that young, and I'm far, far from beautiful."

She was thinking about how unattractive she really felt, and at that very moment she was admitting, that perhaps, she had deliberately set out to make herself unattractive.

"Oh, yes you are. I still can't believe you've agreed to marry me."

Freda listened while stroking his cheek at those lovely words, but at the same time, was thinking of Hayden. She didn't want to think of Hayden. It was Paul's soft voice that was soothing her.

She had trained herself not to think about Hayden, and hadn't in a long time. In fact, through the years, she had several times won herself months at a stretch free of any thought of Hayden, good or bad. Then, for no apparent reason, a little scrap of something he'd said, usually hurtful, would flash through her head. She preferred it that way; if she remembered him at all, it needed to be bitter. Freda could not tolerate dwelling on the sweet times or she might brood for days.

She had even pushed the spring of her senior year of college to a far corner of her mind because it had also been her spring with Hayden. Those first incredible weeks with him were filled with all-night study secessions that ended with hurried kisses before heading for class—everyone was always in such a hurry. With graduation in sight, tentative plans for their future began. There also began subtle hints of trouble— distant stares, no-shows for the studying then finally no-shows for the kissing. Yet, there had been hope. That hope ended when Hayden had left school without withdrawing. He'd left with Al, a guy who had sat in on a few of their study sessions. Someone said they heard Hayden and Al had gone to Canada.

Now here she was with Paul—her beloved Paul—and she was determined that Hayden would have no part in this moment. She felt Paul's fingers trailing along her arm, leaving warm, smooth tracks as they traveled upward from her wrist. Hayden had done that, over and over, night after night, then he'd stopped.

She flinched. Paul's eyes flew open.

"I'm sorry, honey. I was getting a little carried away. I don't intend for us to go too far."

She smiled at him, held his face between her hands and kissed him soundly.

"Don't you fret, darling. You keep right on. I'll tell you if you've gone too far."

Chapter 20

Freda Bailey, whose life a few months earlier had meant long hours at the hospital and an occasional dinner out with some girl friends, sat in a deep leather chair in the Ramsey library, watching five men play poker. She was the only woman present, but did not feel uncomfortable; Paul was at the table.

An open book lay across her lap, but she read little. She enjoyed watching people, especially these particular people—and most particularly, Paul.

They had a certain uniting element in common, a bond of sorts—something to do with their all being Westerners, she supposed.

Their personalities were far from similar and none of them looked alike, not even the two brothers.

Billy Jack was tall and lanky and sunburned, his blonde hair bleached white under the summer sun. Nick, shorter than Bill, with curly red hair and skin that would have kept him out of the sun even if he didn't already spend most of his time in the cool corridors of the hospital, looked scrubbed. Freda had grown to expect that appearance at the hospital, but she was surprised after she began meeting him every day in Paul's place to see that he still looked as if he were ready to step into the operating room.

Then there was Buck, his reading glasses perched on the end of his nose, hunched over his cards, concentrating on them as if this last hand of the evening was the most important matter he faced. She supposed that was why the majority of the chips stood in neat stacks in front of him.

Even Ariola, with his swarthy skin and coal-black hair seemed one of them. Paul, of course, was the epitome of the Western man.

She could not put her finger on it, yet she felt their kindred spirit.

She watched them, feeling at ease in this plush room although before meeting Paul, she had never set foot inside the Ramsey mansion. She had never wanted to. She was here now only because of Paul. She was included in every activity that Paul was, and she came to please him. She had never attended a barbecue at the ranch even though there was always an open invitation to the whole county. When the Ramsey Bull Sale came around, there were excited twitters among the hospital staff about who would attend and what they would be wearing.

If someone among them happened to receive one of those fabled engraved invitations to a special party inside the mansion, a united front was mounted to make sure the recipient had everything she needed, or thought she needed. Freda felt a certain distaste for this, at times disgust, but, as a loyal friend, she joined forces, and had more than once sent her diamond and pearl graduation earrings off to the party on happy ears.

Perhaps the reason Freda had never wanted to attend these parties had been Alta Ramsey, herself. There had been no parties since Alta's illness and death, but before that, with Alta frequently in Dr. Kraft's office, Freda had come to know her well enough to suspect Alta, least of all, wanted to attend her own parties.

Now Freda had become more comfortable with the Ramseys, in fact, perfectly at ease with them, but she knew she still would never attend one of those parties—if they ever started up again. She and Paul would be gone tomorrow and she doubted they would return to NeeDee. If they should come back, she still doubted she would attend a Ramsey party, or any other party.

After Hayden had left, when the crying had stopped, and after she had come close to flunking her analytical psychology class—her mentor finally convinced her that she was using all her energy trying to analyze herself—she did pull herself together and had graduated with honors. When she took her first job, new town, new people, she came prepared. A thick wall had gone up around her, protecting her from any more hurt. She wanted no parties. She was too busy—busy covering long weekends for the other nurses, or babysitting for them so they could go out for an evening with their husbands. She never failed to bake brownies for staff parties, but usually had a good excuse not too attend.

She felt safe behind her wall, but just to be sure, she became sloppy. Even so, through the years, a few would-be suitors had been able to recognize the real person hiding there. But no one had ever come close to getting past that wall—until Paul.

She had spent years grooming herself to be an outsider. Her short neckline haircut was perfect for jumping into the shower and popping on her white cap in record time. Doughnuts in the break room and lots of potato chips every evening while lounging on her patio kept her figure ample. That was behind her now. She was not about to let Paul eat all that junk food she'd lived on for years.

Being on leave from the hospital freed up more time to spend on her makeup, and she was letting her hair grow. It now curled softly over her ears. Paul noticed these changes, and declared he didn't know how she could get any prettier. Always responding that she had never been pretty in the first place, she now wanted to be pretty for Paul. She knew that if she was becoming more attractive, it was all because of Paul.

Her girlfriends insisted that she would need a completely different wardrobe for Colorado. They were right, of course. Paul had described his place as rather rustic, so, with the help of the girls, she was soon outfitted with several sets of matching pants and shirts. All the wool plaid skirts and jumpers went into a box for the charity clothes drive. A pale silky suit, her wedding suit, waited in her closet beside the other new clothes.

Tonight she was wearing Paul's favorites, lightweight denim pants and a yellow silk shirt. As she had dressed, she was pleasantly surprised. They fit a little less snugly than when she'd bought them—a good feeling. She thought of the way Alta Ramsey had looked in her clothes—sleek. She'd like to achieve that look someday—for Paul.

The game was winding down. She was glad. It had been a pleasant evening, but tomorrow would be a hard day. They would be driving to Denver, then be married the next day—Wednesday—the best day of all. She was glad it would be on a Wednesday—that silly little rhyme had been flitting through her head since they'd started talking about setting a date.

"Time to cash in, boys," Buck said, then swallowed the last of his drink and pushed back from the table.

Nick was ready—had been for quite a while—but he was not about to put any kind of damper on Freda's last evening with them.

"Here's the box," he said, retrieving a tooled-leather chest from the floor beside his chair and setting it in the center of the game table.

The others began raking their chips into convenient piles, ready to put them away.

"When I said cash in, I meant with greenbacks. Just throw in enough to cover whatever we started out with. We're giving the pot to Freda—a little wedding present."

Nick screeched and muttered a pitiful protest, just as he knew Freda would expect him to do. She laughed at that, and came over to join the men.

"Of course, Paul doesn't have to," Buck added, "since it's for him, too."

"Paul most certainly does," Freda spoke up. "I'll just use it to buy myself something frilly."

"Freda," Nick continued in his special—special to Freda, anyway—plaintive tone, "you know I've already chipped in at the hospital for that Samsonite. Besides, I had to throw in another five for something frilly. The late shift caught me in the break room the other night. When you open that suitcase, you'll find something frilly already in there."

"I'll gladly throw in my share," Paul cut in. He grinned at Freda and continued, "A girl can't ever have too many frillies."

Even as he pulled out his wallet, Nick continued. This might be his last chance to bicker with Freda. He was going to miss her—a lot.

"How many can you use, with an old coot like that? If I'd even dreamed that old broken down cowpoke was going to take you away from me, I'd have tried a little harder."

Freda came over and slipped her arm through Paul's.

"It wouldn't have mattered. You never had too much of a chance with me anyway, but after Paul came to town, you were done for."

"But getting beat out by an old coot like that—" Nick wouldn't give up the charade.

"Listen, boy, there's not all that much wrong with age. I've done things you haven't dreamed of, " Paul said.

He pulled Freda a little closer, then added, "And I intend to do a lot more."

They all laughed. Paul said it with impressive bravado, but wasn't sure he believed it.

He doubted that any of the rest of them believed him either. In fact, age was usually on his mind any time Freda wasn't around. If he were her age—oh, what a life they would have.

While Freda gathered her winnings, the men stood around, with hands-in-pockets stiffness, waiting their turn to say goodbye to Freda and Paul with warm handshakes and good wishes and sincere promises that might or might not be kept. They came to Nick last. He shook hands with Paul, then hugged Freda—or perhaps she hugged him. He mumbled into her shoulder, "The old coot is one lucky dog."

Paul was up early, waiting for Freda. He hadn't brought much with him when he had come home with Buck, but what little there was, was packed and ready to go. Freda had done that before she had left last night. He wanted to think she had only helped him, but it was not true. She had done it all, but that hadn't bothered him too much. Freda had a way about her. She could manage to make him feel that she was only doing what she wanted to do, and that she wouldn't be happy unless she was permitted to pamper him.

He knew Ariola and Buck would be around before they left—for another cup of coffee and one more goodbye. One of them could load his suitcase and his sack of boots. He surely wasn't going to let her do that. When they got home, things were going to change, too. He intended to be the one doing the pampering.

This was to be the happiest day of his life—in fact the beginning of his life, so why was he suddenly sad? Sadness had swept over him as he gave his boot one final swipe. It so filled him that he hardly noticed a catchy pain, sharp as an electric shock, racing through his chest. The pain was gone, lasting only a few seconds, now no more than a ringing in his head, but it seemed that the sadness had always been there—for as long as he could remember.

The feeling confused him, making him lose his balance. The brush was falling from his hand, but when he reached out to grab it, he stretched too far and fell off his chair.

The pain was back, now fighting the sadness for space, but without much success. He was accustomed to pain. The crash to the floor wasn't any worse than being slammed into the fence by a mean horse—perhaps not as bad.

Now he was really confused. He had thought he was on the floor, but he realized he was still on the horse. It wasn't an ordinary ride. He wasn't in the saddle—there was no saddle—he was lying on the horse's back, looking up into an endless haze, pale and shimmering. Thank goodness it was beginning to make sense, for there in the center of the haze was Freda's face, just as beautiful as it had been that first time he had seen her. No, something was different. She seemed upset, her smiling face now contorted and full of fear. That first time, he had been coming toward her, and she had been urging him on with a firm voice. Now he was moving away from her, and he could hear her crying, this time begging him not to go. He wanted to stay—oh, how he wanted to stay, but the horse would not stop. It kept moving. He floated just above its back, but he could not get free of it. He could hear her calling, stay with me, Paul, please don't go, don't leave me. He didn't want to leave her, but the horse would not stop.

He suddenly knew why the sadness had come upon him. He knew he was not going to get to take Freda to his mountain in Colorado. He knew he was never going to wake up beside her and show her the sunrise.

The battle between sadness and pain raged on. There was no clear winner, but the fierceness of it was making him tired. He was drifting further and further away from Freda, or perhaps it was she who was drifting. It was hard to tell. Her face was right above his, but she seemed far away.

He wanted to touch that beautiful face, but he was too tired to lift his hand. Then she picked it up for him and held it against her face—that beautiful face. She had stopped crying. She smiled at him just before she drifted out of sight. The sadness and the pain were gone, but he was so tired, he returned her smile and closed his eyes.

Chapter 21

They were half way to Denver and neither Buck nor Freda had spoken a dozen words. The only talk came from Ariola, and he did little more than comment on the countryside flashing beneath them. When it occurred to him that he was talking mainly to himself, he gave up.

When he was flying alone he sometimes sang, or at least whistled. He wasn't alone, it only seemed that way. Even if he had been, there would have been little singing. He had no heart for it, but managed a few soft, comforting refrains.

It was a smooth flight, so smooth the small mahogany box had yet to need the belt that held it firm in the seat beside him. He had belted it down to guard against its flying around the cockpit in case they did hit turbulence.

Freda couldn't bear to have Paul stowed in the back—just like some old piece of luggage. Buck didn't want Freda holding it in her lap during the flight. He was afraid she would cry all the way to the mountains—just as she had every time she looked at it before they left the NeeDee airport. He didn't want her to see it again until they got there. He suggested the two of them ride in the back seat so she could have a pillow to lean on—and the box would be out of sight. He didn't actually use those words—his wanting the box out of sight. He figured Freda would cry at any implication that she wanted it out of her sight yet he was certain she couldn't bear seeing it without breaking down. *The box* was how he referred to it, and how he thought of it. He hadn't reached the point of accepting the fact that Paul was now ashes inside that gleaming wooden box.

It had fallen on Ariola to break the news to Freda. Paul wanted to be cremated and have his ashes scattered over his mountainside. Freda had been more distraught at this news than she'd been at his death. As a nurse, she had seen death many times, but had never personally known of anyone being cremated. That was something one read about occasionally, some faceless person back east, but certainly not for her Paul.

She was dismayed at Paul's talking to Ariola about funeral arrangement in the first place. The two of them had never discussed such things. Certainly not, Ariola told her. She was his bride to be, so Paul only wanted to talk about their future, about all the good times ahead for them. Being a realist, however, Paul had turned to Ariola. Before mentioning funeral arrangements, Paul handed Ariola a list that needed to be taken care of, and Ariola had done so.

The deed to his mountainside had been transferred to Freda and she was now the beneficiary of his life insurance policies and joint owner of his bank accounts. She took this news no better than the cremation. She hadn't even known there was a bank account, much less life insurance. Did he look on her as some kind of brainless child? Why hadn't he mentioned any of this to her? Simple, Ariola thought, but he didn't comment. When Freda could think more objectively, she would realize that she would not have let Paul do any of this before they were married.

She would have thought making legal arrangements about his property ominous. She would have refused, but only in the most lighthearted way, probably laughing and saying she wasn't after his money, only his body—or some other amusing little phrase. With that carefree remark, Paul would have missed out on doing what mattered most to him—taking care of Freda.

Ariola only told her that Paul said he wanted all the business out of the way before the honeymoon—because he planned on the honeymoon lasting a long, long time. Hearing more—Paul's concern about their age difference, and his health—would have crushed her.

Ariola set down at the Auora airport. He didn't want to go into Denver because all he was interested in was fueling up, and eating a bite; he hoped he could persuade Buck and Freda to join him before they made the short flight out to Paul's place, spread his ashes, and returned home.

He had first suggested to Freda they rent a car in Denver afterward and drive out so she could look over the place. What a mistake. Nearly hysterical, she had screamed she would never set foot on that mountain. Wherever she stood, on any square inch of it, he would be there, part of him would be there, but she could never find him. She couldn't bear it.

Buck hadn't been much help to Ariola in convincing Freda to carry out Paul's wishes. Cremation was as foreign to Buck as it was to Freda. Buck was afraid that after the ashes were scattered, it would come to be people would forget he had existed.

He felt a kind of comfort any time he went out to the cemetery. Just looking at the stones, seeing the names, and the numbers under them—the dates put a time frame to their lives—brought him some peace. Of course, there was sadness and regret—lots of regret—with each visit, but the comfort outweighed the sadness.

In the end, Freda had realized Paul's choice was best. There would have been no reason to bury him in NeeDee. Paul had never been to NeeDee until he had come home with Buck, and they would have been leaving for Denver the morning he died.

Why bury him in Denver? Freda was the one with no ties to Denver. With Paul gone, she didn't plan on staying there. They had only intended to be in Denver until the new suite had been completed on the cabin.

That had been Paul's idea, also. She had insisted that, from his talk about the cabin, it would be just fine for the two of them, but she came out to the ranch one morning to find him on the phone talking to a well drilling company in

Denver. He then sketched off a rough plan for a bedroom, bath and screened porch. Within a few minutes, their lives had been settled. They would take an apartment in Denver, but before the first snow came, they would be in the cabin, their home.

Now she didn't want to look at it, not even from the air. When she heard Ariola's quiet words, "It's time," she squeezed her eyes shut and leaned hard against her corner.

Buck was also silent.

A small bag now lay on the seat beside Ariola. He had discreetly removed it from the box and handed the empty container to a flustered young airport attendant, his mouth agape when he realized what he had in his hands.

"Get rid of this for me, please. I don't want one of them," he motioned toward Freda and Buck, who were sitting at a table in the lounge area, "throwing box and all out the window. Might be dangerous for someone on the ground," Ariola said.

The young man was handling it like a hot coal, shuffling it from hand to hand.

"It's perfectly all right, beautifully made. You might want to give it to one of your girlfriends for a trinket box. Paul would like that."

Ariola had checked the aerial distance from the airport to Paul's place. Now they were here, but he was going to have to make another pass—Paul's place wasn't very large.

"Buck," Ariola said sternly. Buck came to life and reached over the seat. Sticking the tip of the bag out the window, he let it blow.

He was about half-finished when Freda sat up and opened her eyes.

"Here. Let me have that. He'd do the same for me."

"Good for you, Freda," Ariola said.

Freda slid across the seat closer to Buck. He kept his grip on the bag as she joined him. Both held onto the last of Paul until the bag was nearly empty.

"Okay?" he asked.

Freda nodded. He let go. Holding on for a few more seconds, she, too, relaxed her fingers as she said a last goodbye to Paul. Buck leaned back so Freda could get a closer look. She watched for a moment as it floated lazily toward the ground, then slid back into her corner. She didn't want to see where it landed.

"Done," she said before closing her eyes again.

She pretty well kept them closed until they were about half way back to NeeDee. They bolted open as she heard a slight sound, softer than the drone of the engines, yet distinctly separate from their noise. At the same time she felt a lurch. It was only a tiny jolt, as gentle as the sound, but enough to startle her.

"What the hell," Buck yelled.

Ariola was silent. He was busy at the controls. The plane had listed to the right and moments later the right engine sputtered and died.

In all of his twenty years of flying, he had never encountered so much as a reluctant prop on a plane, but he had read enough and talked to Jerry enough that he felt confident. The left engine was still good, but he didn't want to take a chance trying to get closer to home. He started looking for a place to land. He found it minutes later.

He had been trying to spot the most level pasture available, when a freshly graded road came into view. It was the typical, narrow ranch road, but, as luck would have it, flat and straight for at least a half mile, which was extraordinary.

He set the plane down in a rough landing before anyone said another word.

Freda broke the silence, murmuring, "What on earth?"

Her reaction was mild. She only felt a little woozy, and that from shattered nerves. None of them were more than slightly jarred.

Ariola was already on the radio but getting only static.

"I'll try again in a minute," he said. "Are you all okay?"

Freda looked at him, still a little dazed, and nodded.

She then said, "Thank you, Paul."

"He's already started taking care of me," she added.

"Yeah, thank you, Paul," Buck said, then to Ariola,

"What do you think? We hit a bird?"

"Maybe so," Ariola said. "I can't imagine it, but we must have."

They had gotten out of the plane and stood looking around. Sure enough, there wasn't a bird in sight as far as the eye could see.

Logic took hold of Freda. "Well, there must be a house close by, what with this nice road. Let's head for it."

Buck and Ariola looked at each other, knowing that a well-kept road could be headed toward a distant loading pen instead of a house. With no telephone or highline poles in sight, they thought this might be the case.

"Let's just sit here for a while. Then I'll try the radio again, or maybe someone will come along or spot the plane from the air," Ariola said.

Freda wasn't for that, but when she glanced down the road, first one way, then the other, and down at her high-heeled shoes, she gave in.

"Look at these." A throb of anger edged her voice and her eyes were now fixated on her feet. She couldn't look up.

Ariola caught the change in her demeanor. He disliked the thought of dealing with a hysterical woman in this desolate place. He patted her arm in concern. She seemed unaware of his touch, nor his presence.

"Look at these," she said again. "Of all the dumb things to do. They were to be my wedding slippers, so I wore them to look nice for Paul, I guess. Now what? I couldn't walk half a block in these things, much less down that road."

She used one shoe to push the other off her heel.

"Better keep them on. There are lots of goat heads and cactus out here," Buck reminded her.

She looked at him and threw one white pump as far as she could across the pasture.

Buck scrambled after it, keeping his eyes on where it landed. He didn't want to lose sight of that shoe and have to spend time searching for it in the grass.

"Damn you, woman," he was muttering under his breath as he went. He bent over to pick it up just as the other shoe zinged over his head and landed a few feet in front of him.

Buck's first inclination was to throw both of them further out into the pasture. In fact, he had them in his hand, arm raised, ready to throw, when he let it drop resolutely to his side. He realized—at least a little of it—how Freda was feeling.

Here she was, standing beside a downed plane in the middle of nowhere with two men she hardly knew. Of course, she *knew* them. Every person in NeeDee knew everyone else, if only by sight. Yet even in a town as small as NeeDee, people traveled in different circles. She was part of the medical community and they— Buck had never considered what circle he and Ariola might be a part of, if any. They seemed to be everywhere, yet nowhere. They weren't a part of her life any more than she was of theirs. They had all been drawn together because of Paul and now he was gone.

Had Freda really known Paul? He had lived his real life long before they met. Those hard-driving years he spent chasing the gold buckles of rodeo had left little time for women like Freda. Even if circumstance had allowed it, would he have looked twice at the mild girl in the bleachers? If he had walked into a drugstore looking for an aspirin after a rough ride while Freda and her girlfriends were having their vanilla cokes, would they have noticed a dusty cowboy?

The more aggressive women waited at the rodeo dances.

Paul would have headed there, back to his own world, and Freda would have remained in hers.

Yet, they had met. Freda said their time together was meant to be. That time had just been too short.

Buck continued thinking. What would it be like for her once they got back to town?

Was she to be treated like a widow? She wasn't a widow. Since he was so much older, could she have really loved him, other than as a dedicated nurse? Would they have stayed married once he got her up to that cabin? Those were questions people would be asking themselves and maybe each other. Perhaps Freda would begin questioning herself. At this moment, though, she knew the answers to them all, and he didn't blame her one bit for throwing the damned shoes.

He walked back toward the plane, regaining composure on the way. He guessed Ariola must have been soothing her while he retrieved the shoes—Ariola was good at that—for when he got there Freda gave him a sheepish grin and reached out for them. He moved his hand away quickly, out of her reach.

"Nooooo," he said. "I'm hanging on to these for safe keeping. If push comes to shove, I might have to give you my boots and wear these out of here myself."

He teased her for a while. He knew she could tolerate no more pity at this time. By the time she got her shoes back, she was feeling better, acting more like the woman Paul had loved.

As it turned out, Ariola got the radio to crackle to life about the same time a pickup pulled up behind the plane. A young man got out, and pushed his hat back to scratch his head before saying a word.

Ariola talked to Jerry and made arrangements for him to bring out a mechanic while the young cowboy visited with Freda and Buck. It was good they'd stayed put for a while since, sure enough, his house was fifteen miles back toward the highway and a loading pen fifteen miles in the other direction.

The young man stayed longer than he should have. A plane landing in the middle of his ranch was about as exciting as anything that he'd seen lately, but thirsty livestock waiting beside a broken windmill demanded that he go on. He insisted on leaving one of his canteens with them. Ariola always carried extra water in the plane, but he quickly decided it would be easier to accept it than to out-argue the fellow. Besides, Jerry and his mechanic would be at least two hours, maybe longer.

After the cowboy left, Buck got a blanket out of the back of the plane and brought Freda's pillow along with it. They spread it on the shadiest side of the plane, but even so, the stillness of the air with the New Mexico sun beating down on them was punishing heat.

It was a long two hours. The three chatted easily, mostly about the progress of the hospital construction, and passed around the cowboy's canteen as if passing around a bottle of gin. Little was said about Freda's plans—she hardly knew what they were herself, only that she would be leaving NeeDee. She didn't tell them she had already wrapped each of her wedding presents—had them ready for mailing. She would mail them just before she left. She didn't want to go through the pain of explaining to each of her friends why she couldn't—didn't want to—keep the gifts. By the time they received them and read her note, she would be far away. Where? She wasn't yet sure.

Jerry got there just about the time they finished off the canteen and started on Ariola's stash. Yes, it was a bird, all right. Not a very big one, but big enough to mess up some lines. It took nearly as long to clean up the mess as it did to get the lines replaced.

Thinking Ariola might be a bit shaken, Jerry assumed he would be flying the plane back to NeeDee. No, Ariola insisted. If Jerry said it was airworthy, he would take it back up, himself.

Then surely Buck and the young woman might want to ride back with him. No, thanks, they said, Freda a second ahead of Buck.

Buck helped Freda into the back seat and handed her the pillow before climbing into the front seat beside Ariola. The plane took off, hardly kicking up dust on the narrow road.

The three said goodbye at the NeeDee Airport. There were hugs all around, but the two men felt helpless, at a loss as to what else they could do for her. Nothing else, she told them.

Freda had driven out to the airport in her own car that morning. It was packed and ready to go. Waving to them one last time, she pulled out.

She needed only what she had in the trunk of her Chevy.

Chapter 22

Three weeks passed before anyone heard from Freda, and when they did, it was Ariola, not Buck, who got the call. They had both wondered about her, worried about her, Buck more than Ariola. Since it had been he who had brought Paul to NeeDee, Buck still felt some responsibility for the pain that had come into her life.

She was at a small lodge on the Idaho and Montana border, and would be staying a few days. She had seen the ocean, she told him and now she was seeing some mountains. They chatted inconsequentially about the beautiful scenery she was passing through, how her car was holding up, the weather she had encountered, about all the things a traveler experiences. The conversation was light, but as he listened he could hear something else in her voice.

"We've been talking about your trip," Ariola said.

"Now, let's hear about your journey."

She hadn't intended to share her feelings—she was too fragile, emotionally, not yet past the numbness. That one little question, though, was all it took.

"Ariola, you're just too much of a romanticist. I haven't been on any journey. I've just been driving so nobody would be around to hear me scream."

She laughed sadly, then continued. "You'd be surprised at how far your voice carries if you aim it at a hundred miles of empty desert."

"Not at all," he replied. "I've tried a little of that myself. Romanticist, huh? Well now, I've been called some things, but I believe that's a first."

"I'm sorry. I know you're just trying to be kind. I'm not the first person who has gone through this."

"Poor old Buck—" she added in a shaky voice.

"Never mind Buck. You're the one we're concerned about. Both of us. All of us."

"Thank you, Ariola." Her voice sounded stronger as she began, but she sighed and it broke again.

"It's just that I still miss him so much. You know, he was the first man since—college—I trusted enough to—love."

Ariola had little to say in reply, managing a sympathetic phrase or two, but felt he didn't know her well enough to continue. She seemed to catch that, too.

"You all have been so kind to me, but I want to ask one more favor. I haven't called anyone since I left."

Hesitating a moment, her minimal excuse was extended before Ariola questioned further.

"Just not ready. I know it's crazy, but I can't. They're all going to want to know something—but I don't know anything to tell them. I don't want them to think I'm dead myself, but I just can't talk to any of them yet."

"Sure, honey. What do you want me to do?"

"If you'll write a short note and put it on the board in the lounge at the hospital, I'd appreciate it so much. Tell them I'm fine, but I haven't found a place I'd like to live, but I'll call when I do."

"Of course I will, Freda," he said, then added, "But, Freda, promise you will let us know where you settle."

She'd left NeeDee, headed west with no destination in mind. While crossing the desert, she'd been drawn to the idea of seeing the ocean. A cousin had talked for years about a childhood vacation in Long Beach and Santa Monica, but common sense had led her to give Los Angles a wide berth. She'd had her first glimpse of the Pacific near San Luis Obispo. After sitting on a boulder for an hour, staring at the endless expanse of water, she felt smaller but at the same time, stronger. However, she wasn't finished with the ocean.

The next morning, she had turned north and for three

days had driven along the coast all the way to Neah Bay before turning inland again. Still, she couldn't bring herself to stop. She wondered how long it would take.

"Freda?" Ariola questioned.

"I will. I promise. You all were so good to Paul—and to me."

He knew she meant it. At the same time, he wondered if she would do it, if they would hear from her again.

Before hanging up, Freda whispered into the telephone, "I can't describe how I feel right now. Just empty, I guess. Ariola, I loved that old man."

He knew she meant that, too. He reached for a piece of paper and began writing.

Chapter 23

Buck had arrived at the Bull Barn long before Pauline or Mary Lou, even ahead of Ariola. After making a pot of coffee, he had sat down at his desk and opened the morning paper to the markets. After reading a few minutes, he was up again, pacing back and forth in front of the shelf where a chess set nestled in folds of blue velvet, then finally stood staring at the ornate figures.

Alta had given him the set years before. She had come upon the idea of their learning chess during one of her family image-improvement phases. All she knew about chess was what she saw in movies. Watching stuffy old men concentrating intently on those tiny figures convinced her chess must be a game for truly refined people.

She pictured them by the fire on cold evenings leisurely moving the pieces until a brilliant maneuver ended the game. Nick and Billy Jack's friends would notice. The message would be spread by those friends to their families, and thus throughout the community, that the Ramseys were a typical couple, relaxing together at home much of the time. The Ramseys would become noted for something other than fast horses and, in the minds of some people, fast deals.

True, the boys had friends in and out of the house all the time, but they seldom caught Buck and Alta playing chess. The two of them never became too interested in the game. When they did play, the boys nor their friends, paid much attention. Chess came in far behind those fast horses and particularly, those fast cars the deals provided.

The chess phase didn't last long so the set was soon moved to a shelf in Buck's office. It did, however, serve a purpose, in fact, a threefold purpose.

Alta enjoyed looking at it. She still held out hope that they could get back to chess—that is, spend more time together. Finally, it made a good conversation piece. Very few people, when seeing it for the first time, failed to comment on it.

Alta had a flair for gifting. While her personal needs were modest, when it was for someone else, she gave the ultimate, searching relentlessly until finding the most beautiful item—beautiful to her, anyway. Some people would have considered the set gaudy, too fancy for a serious chess player.

He took out a queen and studied it, then picked up the king lying next to her in one hand, squeezing them, ignoring the sharp pain. When he finally opened it, his palm was red and creased with the outline of the two figures. He scooped up two other pieces and set them side by side on his desk.

His eyes were still fixed on them when Ariola burst through the door.

"What are you trying to do now? Beat yourself at chess?"

Buck gave no indication he heard Ariola.

"It seems that wouldn't be too hard to do, considering you just cut yourself a two hundred thousand dollar loss turning in that stock yesterday."

He still didn't respond.

"Buck—"

The edge in Ariola's voice brought Buck's eyes up, but they remained vacant.

That look made Ariola want to hit him in the mouth. He felt his fist clinch, but he willed it to relax again.

He began again in a kinder tone, "What could you have been thinking? You didn't have to do that. How about a credit line from the bank? Or we could have gotten an extension from the contractor."

Hesitating, he then continued, "I could have put up some

money if they were that pressing—"

Buck came alive then. "I didn't want you putting up any money. I didn't want any credit lines or extensions. I did what I wanted to do and that was to use Alta's money. It's plenty good. That boy still doesn't want it so why shouldn't I throw it away?"

After Freda had gone, Nick's visits to the ranch had nearly ceased again. When he did run in, it was to hug Ramona and grab some of her cold tamales. For Buck, there was a pleasant greeting and a cursory report on the construction, but nothing more. No more leisurely suppers and card games. Buck wouldn't ask for more time with him, wouldn't hint that he noticed the change.

He matched Nick's cool countenance, then fretted about it after he had left. Sometimes he brooded silently; other times he spewed his frustrations at whoever was closest by. Ariola was usually the unfortunate recipient. Most of the time, he listened quietly, showing little emotion. Today was different.

"Buck, we've been friends, more than friends, over twenty years, and I've never seen you like this."

"Like what? Blowing in my own money?"

"You just got through saying it. Alta's money. Yours, too. But why? Is Nick going to know it? Is the contractor going to know it? No. The stockbroker is the only one who knows it. It seems there should be a question of ethics on his part for taking the sale."

"No doubt about it. Tony tried to talk me out of it. Asked me if I was drinking. Tried to get me to let him call you. I told him I could get me another stockbroker quicker than he could call you."

"Had you been drinking?"

"You know about how much drinking I do."

"Why, then?"

Ariola was patient enough that Buck finally spoke.

"Like I said, I hadn't been drinking, but I do feel hung

over today. Nick had just left, paying his usual charitable visit, smooth as honey, just as kind as he'd treat any of his patients. I swear, I'd rather have him hit me than treat me the way he does. You can't defend yourself against it. You can't fight back because there's no fighting going on."

"About that time, they called needing more money. I thought, what the hell. It's her stock, and she wanted it given away, so why not? So I did."

"It won't take you long to go through it at this rate."

"I know."

Ariola continued talking and Buck repeated *I know* at appropriate intervals. Everything he was saying made sense, but Buck already knew—and agreed with—all of it. He regretted his stupidity, but at the time, he had thought he would explode if he hadn't done it. Every time he watched Nick's little car buzz out of the driveway, confusion boiled within his chest. Why did the boy come at all if it wasn't to see his daddy? His visits seemed nothing more than an act of kindness; he was pleasant, always polite, but so remote Buck felt shunned.

Lately, the farce had become intolerable, and had ended in one fell swoop when the contractor had called. He had hung up the phone, written a check and delivered it to the bank, telling the cashier it would be good before the end of the day. It was, but Alta's stock had suffered the loss.

The sad part of it was that it hadn't made him feel any better. Now, he was feeling the fool that Ariola was pointing out. Ariola railed, offering no pity. Buck wanted none. He had felt that way long before Ariola had come in. That money could have been used in many ways that would have pleased Alta. She would have felt nothing but contempt for his absurd loss of control.

She might have raved as loud as Ariola, but not as long. She would have been quicker to understand, and would have most likely already had her arms around him, trying to soothe away his confusion and hurt.

That third piece of onyx he had been toying with when Ariola had stormed in represented one of the needs for that thrown-away money. As Buck rubbed it, he thought of the wells that were going to have to be drilled on the ranch. The summer drought was sapping the water level and three windmills had already begun sucking air. The new wells would have to go deeper, and deeper meant more money.

He put it back in place and picked up the fourth piece, a pawn. With not enough of these lowly pieces to represent all his troubles, he moved it away from the others.

"You know this loss isn't going to bring you down," he could hear Ariola saying, "but this stunt should at least serve as a wakeup call."

"I know. Stupid of me. It was just pure stupidity. But I think I've bottomed out. I won't pull anything like that again. Just to be sure, though—" he hesitated before continuing, "I need to impose on you again."

Ariola knew what he was about to be asked. He had even intended to suggest it, but he would have taken a more diplomatic tact than Buck, pointing out that Buck might need to distance himself from the construction.

Sure enough, Buck blurted, "I've got to dump the whole thing on you."

This time, *I know* came from Ariola.

It was sorted out in short order. Ariola would spend more time in NeeDee, overseeing the construction. Buck would take back most of their out-of-town dealings.

Buck moved the pawn back beside the other pieces, then gave it a gentle thump in an effort to topple them all. The blow caused a slight wobble, but all remained standing.

"When they're so close like that, they won't fall."

"Philosopher!" Buck groused.

Picking up the pieces, he carefully placed them back into their velvet box.

Chapter 24

Once Buck let go of the hospital construction, he started scrambling for something more to do than the routine business that passed through the office. He was out of town most of the time, but on planes or in his hotel room at night, or in various board meetings, he was usually mulling over ways to rebuild Alta's portfolio.

Ariola put half of it back by selling several registered bulls from the Ramsey herd. That was all right with Buck, but since so much of the livestock had belonged to Alta anyway, it was only a matter of switching assets from one place to another. Of course, Ariola realized this, but he was hoping it might cheer Buck a little. It did—some. He appreciated Ariola's concern, but at the same time, there was no letting go of his self-condemnation.

What he wanted was to wipe out the loss from the ground up—with no help from anyone. His chance for a crack at it came one night while waiting out the weather in the Chicago airport. There would be no departures for several hours, maybe all night. That was all right with him. He wasn't too interested in going anywhere.

He found a chair in the row that ringed his gate and watched people. It was a pleasure to see the new arrivals, usually greeted happily by friends or family who had come out in the rain to pick them up. The weather in Chicago was not yet a problem, it was the connections around the country causing the holdup. The hugs, and sometimes tears, exchanged by the arrivals and their greeters, warmed Buck.

Not everyone was home when they arrived in Chicago, however, and as the area filled with people finding they would be stranded there, the mood changed. People became tense and edgy. The children, most having been running about enjoying the adventure, were now clinging to their parents, waiting trustingly for them to solve the problem. This darkening ambience made Buck want to be away from it all. Seats became scarce, and when the one beside him vacated, he also gave his up. Two older ladies, though still among the fresher members of the throng, accepted them gratefully.

He first stopped at the bar, but it was jammed. That was all right—he wasn't much interested in a drink anyway. The coffee shop was just as crowded and he was about to give up on that, too, when a man motioned him over. There was one empty chair beside him, the other two having been hauled off before the stranger had been able to shag the table.

A group of youngsters, more interested in togetherness than comfort, had managed to crowd six chairs around their four-place table. Their laughter made it clear they didn't mind any delays just as long as they were together—and with an endless supply of soft drinks and potato chips in front of them.

"You'd better grab this before it's gone, too," the man called out to Buck.

"Thanks," Buck said as he sat down. "I appreciate it. Looks like we might be here for a while."

"I wouldn't be surprised. I haven't heard any flights called lately."

"Could you hear it over this crowd if they did?"

"Oh, yeah," the man replied. "You'd be amazed at how quiet it becomes the moment that inter-com crackles."

"Including that bunch over there," he continued, motioning toward the noisy group.

"Shoot," Buck said, "They're having the time of their lives. They'll be talking about this for years."

"No doubt about it. Wouldn't it be great to be that young again?"

"To tell you the truth, I don't know whether I could live through it again."

Buck laughed as he spoke, but his reply, the standard flip remark that many people gave with no thought about how they really felt, held at least a little truth as far as he was concerned.

"Me, I'd give anything for the chance," the man said.

"No," he reconsidered, "I don't really know that I need youth again. I'm just now hitting my stride."

He pulled a postcard-size pamphlet out of his shirt pocket and laid it on the table. A pair of golden horseshoes covered the front.

"In the horse racing business, huh? What do you do—trainer, owner?"

The man laughed and turned the card around. It was now obvious the *horseshoes* were two golden arches, but Buck was still puzzled.

"Neither. This is our company logo. Ever seen one of these drive-ins?"

Buck hadn't, and he really didn't care to, but this didn't stop the man's enthusiasm.

"Well, if you haven't, you will one of these days. We're going to be everywhere."

"You run one? Where are you located?" Buck asked. "I might sell you some beef."

"Oh, no. I don't have anything to do with the operations. I sell franchises."

They talked the rest of the night. Buck was certainly not interested in a franchise, but he missed his called flight the next morning. Before he boarded the afternoon plane to Albuquerque, he had left a fifty thousand dollar check for stock that Ariola would consider risky at best.

Buck had a gut feeling it would be a good investment in the long term. In any case, he felt he had taken a step in the right direction.

Chapter 25

"What do you think of this?" Buck asked as he tossed an envelope onto Ariola's desk.

"Ever heard of it?" he continued as Ariola took his time inspecting the shares.

He hadn't. Moreover, he was quick to point out that the BAR4 usually stuck to oil stock and the only beef they dealt with was on the hoof.

"Well, I just have a good feeling about this one. They've only been around a few years, but they're really expanding. The way it looks now, they'll be going public in a couple of years, maybe sooner."

"Could be a sleeper," Ariola mused as he shuffled the papers into an orderly stack and returned them to Buck.

"Yeah, they could, and anyway, I'm going to put it in Alta's file. We'll just wait and see."

Ariola's lips parted, but he turned back to his work without saying anything. He had nearly reminded Buck they were trying to distribute Alta's estate, not add to it, but he caught himself just in time, and was glad. Buck already knew this.

Buck had flopped down on the sofa across the room, and Ariola pushed back from his desk, turning his chair to face him.

"Billy Jack and Donna want us all out for supper tonight. Ramona left you a note on the kitchen table in case she missed you."

"I don't know," Buck growled. "I was thinking about taking off for Amarillo."

"Can't you wait until tomorrow? I think this might be pretty important—to them, anyway."

"Sure. I haven't called over there. Don't know that any

of those guys will be around."

Again, Ariola restrained himself. He knew why Buck was thinking of going to Amarillo. He had started talking about selling the registered herd soon after the fiasco in the law office. Ariola believed he was rushing into something he was not ready for and tried to talk him out of it. Since Buck had been gone so much for the last few weeks, and hadn't mentioned it when they were together, Ariola was hoping he was past that idea. Now it seemed he was wrong. Livestock was the only reason Buck would be talking about Amarillo.

He skirted that issue, trying hard to stick to what he had been advising Buck to do about the boys—let him make his own decision.

"Nick will be there. And Ramona was going with me if you didn't make it in. Now we can ride out together?"

He had put it in the form of a question, which Buck answered without enthusiasm.

"Sure," he said, but didn't speculate on what the occasion might be.

"Then we'll leave here about six thirty?"

"Okay," Buck agreed again with the same detachment, then wandered outside and went to the barn. He looked out across the holding pasture at the herd, elite and separate from the range cattle scattered beyond. The pride he'd felt when Alta and he had shared the task of raising those beauties was gone.

Yes, the work had been good. They had often spent hours riding, then going over the meticulous records she kept. Now all he felt was the need to be rid of them. The joy was gone.

He was about to turn back to the house, but whistled for Shotsy on impulse. He was surprised when she trotted up so readily. She hadn't been ridden for weeks, yet so docile as he threw the saddle across her back, he surmised that she might be as pleased as he about their getting back into a comfortable routine.

Heading out to the pasture, he let the reins rest slack across his hand, but Shotsy trotted along as if it had been only yesterday since they had checked the herd. She moved among the grazing animals. Most didn't look up, but kept munching at the lush grass. Buck let Shotsy take him where she would, and didn't use his rein to turn her back until he saw Ariola leave the Bull Barn.

He would have just enough time for a shower. He knew Billy Jack wouldn't mind if he showed up smelling like Shotsy, but Ramona would remind him—in such a gentle way that he could take no offense—that this was a special occasion and Donna would expect him to show up dressed accordingly. That's what Alta would have expected of him. Even with different wording, both would know that was what she meant.

He was ready and waiting when Ariola pulled under the portico, Ramona beside him. As he closed the front door, he was just about to tell Ariola he would follow them in case he decided to leave early. Instead, he slid into the back seat so they could all go to Stone Creek together—that, too, being what Alta would have expected of him.

The occasion for the special family dinner didn't remain a mystery for long. Matt met them at the front door and announced, "We're having a baby."

After the commotion had settled, Donna laughed, then said, "Well, so much for the big toast. I didn't need wine, anyway."

Chapter 26

Speaking as casually as if it were no more than a routine call, Ariola said, "I heard from Freda yesterday."

He hesitated, then added, "She said she might have seen Rica in the clinic."

Speechless at those last words, Buck whirled around. Ariola sounded calm and unruffled, but the restraint in his voice was no match for the pain in his eyes. Buck understood just how hard he was fighting for self-control.

He took a moment to consider what Ariola had said, then asked, "Might have seen her? Now what does that mean?"

"That's it. She might have treated her, or at least she thought so."

"Come on, man. What are the odds? You've looked all over the country for Rica. Besides, Freda hardly knew her. Probably just someone who looked familiar."

"No. She thinks it might have been Rica. She spoke of having lived in Santa Fe, also mentioned NeeDee." Ariola licked his lips, then continued, "But she didn't mention me."

"Mentioned NeeDee, but not you?"

"Well, she didn't exactly. They were just chatting, you know, and when Freda said she'd come there from NeeDee, Rica reacted strangely. Looked a little startled, scared was the way Freda put it."

"Ariola, that could mean anything."

Ariola didn't hear him, but said instead, "I've been thinking about it all night."

All night! He had gone through the evening before as if there'd been nothing else on his mind, as if he hadn't a care in the world while his insides must have been on fire. He had to be the coolest, no, the most caring, person Buck had ever known—wouldn't allow his own troubles to cloud the joy of the family dinner. Putting others first was a trait that Buck admired but had never mastered.

"It could be Rica—I really believe it is."

"Why, Ariola? What would she be doing there? Freda just thinks it's Rica? She didn't give her name?"

"No, she said her name was Silent Water, but Freda said she wasn't Indian. Dark haired, but not Indian."

"It was the way she acted. A nurse understands these things—how Rica was acting."

Ariola talked faster now. "I just have to go see for myself."

He then drew up, hunched over his desk, head in hands, his voice raspy, barely audible.

"She said her name was Silent Water. She's married to an Indian and she'd going to have a baby."

Laying his hand on Ariola's shoulder, Buck said, "We'll leave in fifteen minutes."

They left, instead, in about ten, a move they were both to regret. Ariola had his car gassed up and ready, his grip in the back seat. He had planned on making the trip alone until Buck had insisted on going with him.

Buck had thrown a change of clothes and not much else into a bag. Neither of them thought to pick up a jacket on the way out.

They drove to Gallup then headed North. Two days later, stepping out the door of the lodge where they had spent the night, they found the mild weather left behind in NeeDee had turned into an early cold snap. Ariola would not consider waiting until a nearby store opened. A new building that had been aged to resemble an old fashioned trading post, Ariola said it probably wasn't stocked with anything other than curios and trinkets. It looked like a tourist trap to him.

Buck was certain it must stock parkas, blankets and

anything else unprepared travelers might need, but he didn't argue. Having listened for the last two days as Ariola had run the gamut from despair to anger and back again several times, Buck knew it wouldn't be wise to insist on waiting around to buy a jacket.

He did manage to get him into the lobby for a cup of coffee. The coffee was fresh and too hot for Buck to swig down, but before they were half finished, Ariola was ready to go. Buck gave the desk clerk five dollars for the mugs and refilled them before they left.

Ariola would not be held back. He remarked as they left the parking lot that Rica might be only fifty miles away and she might be in trouble.

Or she might be perfectly healthy and happy, Buck thought, but he only nodded and sipped his coffee. He knew Ariola didn't need any rationalization—in fact, would tolerate none. Buck also knew Ariola would never give up on finding Rica and he didn't intend to let him do it alone.

"What's your plan, exactly, Ariola?"

"To be frank, I have no idea. We'll go to the clinic. Freda will be at work by the time we get there. After I talk to her, maybe I'll know something. I might even know enough to head back home."

The only noise from Buck was his sipping his coffee.

Ariola continued, "But I might have a chance of finding her."

"Man, Freda said she's married and expecting a baby."

Having said that, Buck immediately regretted it, for Ariola nearly lost control of the car at his words.

"That's it," Buck said, surprising even himself at his calmness, "stop the car. I'm taking over."

Even more surprising, Ariola immediately stopped. He got out and came around and opened Buck's door. Buck stepped out, but instead of getting inside, Ariola stomped about so long that Buck began wondering if he would get back in at all.

Buck just leaned against the fender and waited.

Finally, Ariola stopped in front of him and stuck out his hand. After they shook, Buck started to speak but his throat was so tight he only managed a hoarse *Ariola,* before Ariola cut in, "You're right—"

"No! No, not at all. What I—" Buck said.

"Oh, yes. This is crazy. I'm crazy. I don't even know what I'm doing here," Ariola replied.

"Just grasping at straws," he continued. "I could have waited until I knew more."

"You had to come," Buck insisted. "What I was trying to say is that you might be expecting too much. You have to be prepared that she might actually be—"

Ariola wouldn't let him finish. He didn't want to hear it voiced by someone else—that if the young woman Freda had seen was indeed Rica—

He went straight to the words he loathed to hear. "If she is married and pregnant, okay. I just want to find out. I want to know that she's—"

His voice broke then, and he couldn't continue because that was not at all what he wanted. He wanted to find her, but to find her waiting for him, needing him to come and take her home.

It was colder than it had been when they'd left the lodge, but neither seemed to notice. If anything, it cleared their heads a little. They got back into the car, and Buck drove on.

Freda was taken aback when the two walked into the clinic an hour later. She hadn't expected to see them so soon. She had begun having second thoughts right after calling Ariola.

Even after thinking about it for a few days, her fingers had trembled as she dialed the telephone. Now she was distraught at seeing them. What if she had been wrong?

She was at the front desk going over the day's schedule when they came in. The desk was ordinarily manned by a volunteer but since no one had shown up, Freda was trying to get her workday organized in case she had to handle it alone.

"You guys. Already? You made good time."

After some hugs and sociable inquiries, Freda took Ariola's hand and said, "All right, friend. I know you didn't come to see me."

"Now Freda, you know why I'm here, but you also know we're glad to see you."

"Sure," she said. "Come on over here and sit down. I can't show you her file, but I can tell you what I think—at least what I thought at the time. Right now, I'm asking myself if this could be possible."

"That's what Buck's been telling me and what I halfway think myself, but—I just—I just had to come."

"I understand." She looked out the window, suddenly far away.

"Freda," he said, "You're not doing too well yourself, are you?"

"Oh, heavens, yes. I'm just fine. Working long hours. Loving my work. And these people—so appreciative. Still, there's that same old story. We need a better clinic and more help. Mostly more help."

"It looks like you've found your niche."

She nodded in agreement before Ariola continued.

"So I don't suppose there's much use in asking you back to NeeDee, say, as Director of Nurses."

"Oh, Nick's been calling about that, but," she chuckled and continued, "I've been trying to get him up here instead."

"It might not be all that hard," Buck spoke up. "I think he'd like to cut loose from us—"

"Not at all," Freda intervened. "All he talks about is getting that hospital finished for his mother. He's really proud—" she stumbled a little as she spoke.

"Go ahead, Freda. I'm not some kid who just found out

someone is talking about him behind his back."

Immediately after saying it, that was exactly the way he felt—like a kid.

She was shocked by the edge in his voice, but that didn't stop her. Before continuing, however, she went over to Buck and sat down beside him.

"Now, Buck, I knew all about the blowup with your boys the day it happened. After all, that's NeeDee for you. Everyone knows everything."

"Sure, I know that," he said and managed a chuckle.

"Anyway, Nick couldn't be happier about that hospital. He really is, Buck—"

She stalled again and he knew it was time to let it go.

"I know he is, Freda. And anyway, Ariola's taken over and he won't let Nick get away, but I don't think he'll give up on getting you back to NeeDee, either."

"He might as well," she laughed again and turned back to Ariola.

"She hasn't been back in here, but I did ask around a little. She's lived here for some time now with an old woman several miles out. No one seems to know much of anything about her."

"How did she come to be here? Who is the old lady she lives with? Could we go out there and see her—the old woman, I mean?" Ariola pummeled Freda with questions.

"If she's found herself a husband, I guess she—" Buck regretted his words the moment he'd spoken. The bloody look Ariola threw him served notice.

"Hey, I'm sorry, man. You know I'm with you on this. I don't know what I—"

"I wish the hell you'd stayed home."

"Oh, no. I mean it. I'm with you, and you know it."

Ariola's face was dark, but he did manage a nod that served to sooth Freda's rising uneasiness. She had thought for a moment that the two men were going to fight, but in the next instant, her concern was for anyone who might get in their way.

"Look, you guys. I have no idea there's anything to this. In any case, though, she will most likely come back sometime this week. The doctor wasn't here that day, so she'll surely want to see him. She wouldn't make an appointment then, and that was one thing that concerned me, she seemed so uncertain."

"Rica never liked appointments," Ariola said.

Buck held his tongue this time, only saying, "What we can do is just wait around until she does come in."

"You're right," Ariola agreed. "If we try going out there, she might take off again."

"I still don't understand why she disappeared in the first place," he continued, "but when—if—" he paused, "when she comes back in, I'd like to see her."

"Sure," Freda said, then drummed on the desk. "I don't know how that will work out. How the clinic would handle it. I might have spoken out of turn when I called you—"

"Then why did you call us?" Buck cut in.

"I—" Freda began.

"She didn't call us. She called me."

Another look from Ariola shushed Buck, but not Freda. She continued cautiously.

"Buck's right," she said, her eyes darted between the two men.

"I—I'm afraid I didn't act very professionally. I just had a feeling when I saw Silent Water, but now, I'm not sure."

"We'll just wait and see, Freda. She might not want to talk to me, and if she doesn't, I can accept that. I'll know she's all right—I'll at least know something."

They didn't make any real plans—they couldn't, but Freda was relieved to see the first patient walking up the steps. No doctor had shown up, but one would sooner or later. In the meantime, she could deal with minor ailments and send them on their way. In any case, she would be busy. With that, the men knew it was time to go.

Buck suggested they find a jeep to rent in order to get a look at the rough countryside and Ariola agreed. He wanted to keep his car out of sight.

Since he had been chilly all morning, as soon as they got the jeep, Buck pulled up to a likely looking store. Ariola was glad he did, although he had paid little attention to the temperature so far.

Ariola soon found a heavy gray parka and went outside to wait in the jeep. After walking each aisle, pulling out anything likely only to find it either too large or too small, the best Buck could come up with was a cream-colored wool jacket with bright bands around the bottom. He said he felt like a Hudson Bay blanket, but he was warm. The sight of him even caused Ariola to grin for the first time in two days.

They spent the morning driving over rough terrain, mostly on mining roads and a few trails that dead-ended at fishing spots. Buck continually pointed out pretty sights, even a couple of small waterfalls, but all Ariola managed was an occasional nod. He checked his watch constantly. He was to call Freda at noon and insisted that Buck start back to the village early.

They arrived back at the lodge before noon. Ariola had wanted to go straight to the clinic, but Freda insisted that he call. If Silent Water happened to be there, she didn't want her to be surprised—she said *surprised*, but meant shocked.

Silent Water hadn't been in when Ariola called and Freda was shamed at the relief she felt. She had to work through her lunch hour and was glad she did. When Ariola had asked her that morning to meet them for lunch, she had been tentative. Everything hinged on the clinic workload, she said. Sure enough, they were loaded and she could truthfully decline.

She felt wretched. She had only wanted to help Ariola—he had been so kind to Paul. Now she feared she was about to be responsible for the most searing pain he could feel. Suppose Silent Water was indeed Rica? That was what Ariola was hoping for. But what if Rica didn't want to be found, or rescued?

Silent Water didn't show up during the afternoon, but Freda stewed about the possibility enough that when Ariola called, asking her to join them for dinner, she could again truthfully decline—her head was splitting.

"I'm afraid we've given Freda a headache," Ariola told Buck.

Buck didn't comment. He was working up to a headache himself.

Without Freda around to point out the best place, they decided to eat in the lodge dining room. They had made the right choice, she told them later. Nearly the only one, she added. Both men had trout—brought in that very day, the waitress assured them. An old Indian, she told them, made his living by fishing the streams and supplying the restaurants with fresh trout.

"We ought to try to get in some fishing ourselves," Buck suggested.

"Why?"

"Just a wild hair," Buck said and shrugged. "Might even relax you a little."

"I doubt it," Ariola answered.

"Oh, well, we don't have the stuff we'd need anyway," Buck said, mostly to himself.

Buck looked down at his new jacket, then glanced around the room and spotted three more nearly identical to his. But they probably had rubber boots back in their cabins, he thought, and rods and reels and bait boxes and—he gave up on the idea.

He tried to draw Ariola into conversation, but Ariola was intent on his trout. Buck finally did the same.

As soon as they'd finished, Ariola said he believed he would go up to his room. At the same time, Buck decided he'd try to persuade a young woman sitting alone at the bar to dance.

She agreed, but was no more talkative than Ariola had been. When a tall bear-like man cut in, Buck, too, headed up stairs. He glanced back as he rounded the corner. The bear was wearing a jacket exactly like his.

Ariola was already working on a large platter of ham and eggs by the time Buck got down to the dining room for breakfast. He usually liked a cup of coffee and a look at a newspaper before ordering, but he immediately waved the waitress over. After his experiences of the past few days, he thought it best to grab breakfast while he could.

No matter the circumstances, Ariola could do no less than eat in a highly mannered fashion while Buck didn't mind eating at top speed. They finished at the same time, and sure enough, Ariola, was ready to go.

"We've fooled around long enough," he said.

Good man. Buck was glad Ariola had at last come to his senses. They would call Freda and say goodbye, then head home.

"It's not as though we're trying to do anything criminal," Ariola added.

Exactly, Buck was thinking. Soon after they'd first talked to Freda, Buck had begun wondering why they'd chased off up here in the first place. Now Ariola was beginning to realize just how unlikely it was that this Silent Water person was Rica.

And what if she happened to be? Rica had left—disappeared—only a week before their wedding date. So what? She'd done it before—more than once. Ariola had gone through hell—Alta, too—trying to find her.

They'd never once found her. Instead, she would simply walk into her gallery as though she had never been away, remembering nothing—with Ariola asking nothing.

"We're heading to the clinic right now."

Buck nodded. Ariola's head was finally clearing.

"If Freda hasn't heard from her by now, I'm on my way to the reservation. I need to see her— talk to her. If not—"

It dawned on Buck that *fooled around long enough* did not mean the same to Ariola as to himself.

He sighed audibly, but Ariola didn't hear him.

Ariola cruised the parking lot looking for a space on the graveled area close to the front door—handy enough for watching the steady steam of people making their way in or out of the clinic while also avoiding the mud that seemed to be a village-wide problem.

It didn't take long. Ariola noticed a young man coming out the door, heading toward his car. There was an air about him, his upscale clothing, the leather briefcase he carried, even the neat gray sedan he stepped into, that set him apart from the locals. Most likely a salesman. Ariola stopped and waited for the parking place.

The moment they stepped inside, Freda left her desk and motioned them toward an office. Her face was unreadable as she passed through the crowed room, but the moment she shut the door behind them, she lost her professional composure.

"Oh, Ariola, I'm so sorry to have put you through this. I was wrong. Silent Water's husband just left. He stopped by to get her records—on his way out of town."

"What do you mean, he came by? Why didn't she? Why did she need to take her records? Why did she want them? What was the big deal about that one visit?"

"He said they were leaving and wouldn't be back."

"She just came in that one time, didn't she? Didn't even see the doctor? Where were they going?"

Again, Ariola was firing questions, the same questions over and over, faster than Freda could answer, if she could answer them at all.

"Please, Ariola. Sit down. I'll tell you everything I know."

She had asked the young man more questions than she

felt comfortable doing, but he had seemed willing, even anxious, to tell her about his wife—at least some things.

He did choose his words carefully.

Buck and Freda sat down, but Ariola paced back and forth in the small space.

"Ariola?"

"I'm sorry, Freda. Go ahead. I'm listening."

"This morning was the first time I had ever seen him, said all he needed was to pick up her medical records. The only thing in it was that one visit, of course, so I wondered myself why he wanted it."

"What was his name?" Buck asked.

Freda's face fell again.

"I didn't even ask. He just said he was Silent Water's husband."

"He didn't sign anything?"

Her lips quivered. "You know, this isn't a big city hospital we have here," she shot back. "We don't have a form for that."

"He simply asked for Silent Water Blackhawk's folder and I handed it over—but not before I asked a few more questions."

"I'm not blaming you, Freda," Ariola interrupted. "I just want to find out as much as I can about Rica. And I do think this definitely confirms that Silent Water is Rica. Otherwise, what reason would her husband have for coming in instead of she? Do you suppose she found out I was here and went to all this trouble to avoid seeing me?"

"I don't know about any of that, Ariola. I just hate that all this happened," Freda said, on the verge of tears.

"Oh, no, Freda. I at least know she's alive and well. That means everything to me. Just tell me what else you found out."

Freda felt a little better at those words, not a lot, but enough to continue.

"She came here back during the summer. Stayed out at

the reservation with Irene Blackhawk."

"Why did she go out there?" Buck asked. "Did she know this Irene?"

"She apparently just showed up and Irene took her in. Irene is a patient here. Getting on in years, but a nice old lady who would do something like that."

Freda hurried on, wanting to get her story out while she was up to it. Neither of the men interrupted her again. Ariola sat down beside Buck.

"He said he was here on sabbatical from a small college in Missouri. He and Silent Water married very soon after they met. Irene is his aunt, the only one in his family left, and she was going back to Missouri with them to take care of Silent Water and the baby—when it comes. He cut his stay short."

Freda was finished and leaned back in her chair, wilted.

"Well, at least we can go out there and talk to her," Ariola said at last.

"No," Freda answered. "Silent Water and Irene left three days ago. He stayed to pack."

Now it was Ariola who was deflated.

"I still don't understand why he made such a big deal about that one office visit."

"He only said they would never be back and he wanted nothing left behind," she repeated.

The three sat in a long silence, and it was Buck who finally made the move.

"It's time to go, Ariola. Freda has a roomful of patients waiting out there."

"Sure," Ariola said softly. He stirred and stood up, putting out his hand to Freda.

She stood up and hugged him.

"I'm sorry, Ariola," she said.

"Don't apologize again, Freda. You were only trying to help."

"I just thought, just hoping—"

"I understand. It could have been different. Don't think about it again."

"You know I will—a lot. I won't be able to forget. I was just so sure. I was thinking—maybe it was really Rica and when you saw that she was all right, it would comfort you."

"Sure you did. And I'm grateful you called me, Freda. You helped me to close a door."

"I hope so," she said and turned toward a door of her own, but a different kind of door—one a little easier to handle. Her patients were waiting.

"Freda, remember we'd sure like to have you back in NeeDee," Buck said.

"I'll remember," Freda replied, but none of the three expected it would happen.

As they went down the steps, Ariola pitched the keys to Buck.

Before they were too far out of town, Buck spoke up.

"We have some time to kill. What do you say we stop off somewhere?"

"Fine with me. Anywhere but Missouri."

Buck grinned and sped up a little. When the time came, he headed toward Reno.

Chapter 27

Buck felt good for a while. He gave Ariola a few miles, then tried to loosen him up with a little talk. The two of them had never been at a loss for conversation—until this trip. He wasn't that set on talking, he was just hoping to lift Ariola's spirits. Finally giving up, he drove on in silence.

Only then did he begin noticing the scenery, so magnificent his chest tightened at the sight of it. Twenty miles per hour was about top speed on the twisting road. It was also sprinkled with sharp curves that required braking down to ten, but he didn't mind. Around each curve lay another vista outdoing the previous sight.

Soon the ache changed courses. He thought of Alta, and how she had loved driving through country like this. She'd never cared much for stopping at the tourist attractions along the way, nor the restaurants and beer joints—in fact, she preferred stopping at a grocery store for some bologna and bread and a jug of milk. What she enjoyed most was the drive.

Ariola, still sloughed in his corner, still staring out the window, looked like pure misery to Buck. Perhaps he, too, was feeling—or remembering, some ride he had taken with the woman he loved.

Although Buck was attuned to Ariola's torment, he didn't know how to—did not want to, actually—comfort him. He was still selfish about his own grief. His was real—Alta was dead.

It suddenly seemed irrational to Buck that Ariola should be hurting so badly. Why should he be sitting there, ready to cry like a baby? If anything, he should be mad as hell that Rica had run off and married some Indian.

His anguished thoughts of Alta gradually changed to anger toward Rica.

He pulled off at the next fishing side road.

"I'm going to look around," he said as he got out. What he really needed was to cool off a little.

Ariola nodded, but stayed put. As Buck pushed his door shut, Ariola laid his head back against the seat and closed his eyes.

Sucking in the cool morning air, Buck walked to the stream. He stepped out onto a rock, stooped down to catch a double handful of water and splashed it against his face. Icy shock waves shot through him, but did little to get rid of his irritation.

He walked further down stream, then whirled around and stalked back to the car. Ariola didn't stir when Buck reached through the open window to retrieve the keys from the ignition, but he did open his eyes at the sound of the slamming trunk.

He watched as Buck set a fifth of Scotch on a fallen log, then went over to the stream to relieve himself before coming back to the log, sitting down and taking a long swig from the bottle.

Ariola had to grin as Buck shuddered and let out a swish of air as the burn of the liquor hit bottom. He wiped his mouth with the back of his hand, then gingerly placed the bottle back on the log. He kept it close to his side. It appeared that he didn't want to take a chance of spilling any of it, though several minutes passed before he took another drink—this time with more caution.

Ariola got out of the car and walked over to join him. Buck handed over the bottle without a word. He didn't even look up. Ariola took a drink, then held on to the bottle. He didn't want to spill it either.

They passed it back and forth a number of times before Ariola finally spoke.

"Pretty good Scotch. Where did you get it? I've never

known you to carry a stash of liquor."

"Last night at that bar. After you went upstairs, I thought a nice bottle at my table might entice someone to sit down, but it didn't help."

"It's smooth. They'll never know what they missed. Of course, it would go down better if we had some ice and water."

"Yeah," Buck replied. "If we just had a glass, we could at least have some water." He gestured toward the stream.

"No thanks," Ariola said and chuckled. "I saw you go in it."

Buck rolled his eyes. He had to have another swig at that one.

"Those few drops of mine are already to Colorado by now. We'd best be concerned about a grizzly upstream."

"Whatever," Ariola said. Resignation in his voice, he added, "We don't have a glass anyway."

"If we did," Buck, beginning to see the brighter side of the situation, added, "all it would do would be to weaken this stuff."

"On the other hand, it would've lasted a little longer," Ariola said, matching his logic.

"I don't think so," Buck reasoned. "Just like me eatin' chilies. The hotter they are, the faster I go after them."

"This stuff is hot enough," he added, holding the bottle at arm's length, studying it as he spoke, "that I just had to gulp it. I don't think I'd enjoy it near as much if I was just sipping."

"You don't seem to be enjoying it too much as it is," Ariola said.

"Oh, yeah, I am. Doing me a lot more good than it did last night with those women."

The subject appeared to have been so well analyzed that they both fell silent. After a while, one of them made a move. It must have been Ariola. With the whiskey almost gone, he could see no reason to spend any more time sitting on the log.

They stumbled, arm in arm, toward the car. The struggle was great—great enough to cause Ariola to wonder aloud how they had let themselves get into this mess.

After giving the remark some thought, Buck replied solemnly, "It was that son-of-a-bitch that left us his parking place."

Ariola jerked his arm away, and Buck fell down landing on his knees.

"Why'd you do that?" he questioned, puzzled.

Ariola said nothing, but kept on walking.

It dawned on Buck. Ariola tolerated no cursing other than a hell or damn once in a while, no matter who it might be or what it might be about. Even with his brain in its present state, Buck could recall many a young cowboy reduced to red-faced shame by Ariola's scathing reprimands about cursing.

As for himself, he had never felt obliged to follow Ariola's strict discipline. Even in his now uncertain condition, he wasn't about to give up although his main concerns at the moment were his throbbing knees—he happened to land on some fair-sized rocks—and his whirling head, which felt like it had been hit by a few of them. He lay down, making himself more comfortable, before calling out to Ariola.

"You know who he was. It was that Indian that came out of the clinic carrying a briefcase. And you know what was in that briefcase. And in my opinion, he was a son-of-a-bitch, a real one."

Ariola was quickly at his side again, yanking his arm, dragging him back to his knees.

"Nobody asked for your opinion," Ariola growled, before letting Buck drop back to the ground. At the same time, Ariola gave a little push that landed Buck on his back *again.*

He looked up, puzzled—but not so puzzled that he couldn't grab Ariola by the ankle, landing the man right beside himself. Ariola lay silent for a moment, winded by the fall.

The silence sent a shiver of concern through Buck. What if he had hurt him—or killed him? He rolled over, intent on checking Ariola's breathing. His face hovered above Ariola's. Although Ariola's eyes were closed, Buck could hear the soft reassuring sound of his breathing.

Just as he was about to lie back down to rest a little more, Ariola's eyes opened and he grabbed Buck's chin.

Their blazing eyes locked. Ariola, who still had a grip on Buck's chin, said, "You didn't shave this morning, did you?"

Buck would have laughed had Ariola's long fingers not been digging in so hard. Instead, he managed to get out of the side of his mouth—the fingers were holding most of it closed, "Shit no."

At those words, fighting words to Ariola, he gave a twist to the chin that turned Buck over, and landed Ariola on top. From there, they rolled back and forth, first one and then the other in command, stirring up a great cloud of dust as they went.

It might have continued much longer had a burly hand not reached down and yanked Ariola, who happened to be on top momentarily, away from the fray. He lay there, winded. He had put more into the scuffle than Buck had, and he was also a few years older.

"What's troubling you girls?" a harsh voice demanded.

"Keep your hands off my brother," Buck shouted. He was on his feet immediately, ready to light into the intruder.

"Just settle down, boy. I'm not interested in breaking up any family scuffles. I just happened to see this cloud of dirt and was afraid a grizzly had somebody down."

Still suspicious of the way the big man had handled Ariola, Buck charged on.

"What is it? You just look into every dust storm you run across?" Buck demanded.

He was feeling enough of the Scotch to embolden him beyond his ordinarily mild nature, and also enough of it that he hadn't noticed the uniform the man was wearing.

"Hell, no," the man said, with no way of knowing a few simple curse words were what had started all of this.

Buck darted a look toward Ariola, half expecting him to jump up and start something again. However, he just lay quietly where he was, thankful for a chance to rest.

"Lucky for you, I just got off duty and they don't pay me no overtime. I would have intervened if it had been a grizzly, but I'll just let you boys get back at it."

He turned to leave when he noticed the bottle.

"Come to think of it, instead of scrapping around anymore, you might better sleep it off before you get back on the road. Like I said, I'm off duty, but I ain't the only ranger around here, and they don't tolerate no drunks on the road. Don't want anybody running over no deer. Don't want nobody running off a bluff, either."

Ariola was on his feet by now. He knew how to be contrite when the situation merited contriteness and he knew this was one of those times.

"I'm sorry, Officer," he said solemnly. "We'll be resting here for quite a while."

He glanced at the nearly empty bottle, and added, "It wasn't full when we started."

Buck had had one shot out of it the night before. It did have that much missing when they'd started.

In any case, the ranger seemed satisfied.

"Be careful," he said as he left.

They walked back to the stream. Kneeling side by side, splashing water over their faces, they cupped their hands to drink. Neither minded drinking out of it this time.

Neither of the men felt like talking about the scuffle. Probably never would. Both only wanted to sleep.

Chapter 28

They walked back to the car in silence, opened the doors in zombie-like unison and crawled in, Ariola in the back and Buck in the front. Ariola handed Buck his jacket and hat, then stretched out. He lay on his stomach, feet hanging out the open door and was asleep before Buck had gotten around to making himself a pillow out of the jacket.

The wool cloth ate at his neck even worse than the dried grass had. He turned the jacket inside out, and tried again. The shiny lining provided only slight relief, but enough that he, too, was quickly sleeping.

They slept at least a couple of hours and then, were probably awakened only by the other's snoring. In any case, they both woke with a start, both hungry.

"Scratch around back there and see if you can find some crackers or something," Buck growled to Ariola.

Ariola shuffled things around a little, but knew it was a futile effort.

Anyone who would head for the mountains of the Northwest without a jacket—with fall not too far away—would be unlikely to think of picking up crackers and fruit to take along.

Each man knew he hadn't been that thoughtful, but was hoping the other had.

"Rica always brought a little basket of goodies along with us. She liked to nibble."

"Oh, yeah. Alta would've, too."

They fell silent again, each man thinking of the woman he'd lost. Soon, though, they had to return to their immediate need, food. Their griping bellies needed filling, but more than that, each hoped food might soothe his splitting head.

"Surely we'll run into something on down the road," Ariola said as he slid behind the wheel.

It didn't work out that easily, however. He backed into a shallow water wash as he was turning to leave. It must have been hunger, or perhaps headache that caused it. Ariola, ordinarily the epitome of good judgment, gunned the motor and the wheels spun, quickly burying to the hubcap.

Shocked but calm, Buck said softly, "Why don't you try backing up a little more so you can make a run at it?"

Ariola tried—again with a little too much vigor. The car shuddered and bounced out of the ruts but crashed with whiplash potential against a large boulder.

Both were stunned momentarily. Ariola spoke first, but he chose the wrong words.

"Any more advise?"

Buck gritted his teeth and said, "I wish there was something left in that bottle. I need a drink."

Ariola gave him a look and stomped on the gas again. The engine roared and the tires, whirling like stone grinding wheels, burned off rubber, sending up great billows of black smoke. The bumper was hung on the rock. Buck looked around wildly, but Ariola seemed unaware that he was there. He gripped the wheel, intent only on getting the vehicle loose—so intent Buck thought crazily he might defy the laws of physics and lift the automobile off the rock that held it captive.

It did finally break loose, careened across the shallow ravine, and stopped. The motor sputtered and died.

Ariola ground on the ignition. Nothing happened, but he kept grinding. It managed to cough to a start then immediately shut down again.

At the same time, something began seeping from under the hood. Buck jumped out and raised it, but was met by a solid cloud of steam. He wasn't burned, but addled enough to think it was smoke.

He grabbed his hat from the dashboard and was back

with a hat full of water by the time Ariola had managed to get out of the car.

There were several trips, but each splash caused more steam—*smoke*—and Buck could picture the motor bursting into flames.

He threw his hat down and they both began scraping up handfuls of dirt and throwing it on the engine.

Matters finally seemed under control—and about time, too, since the engine was full of dirt and gravel. They had just stepped back to survey the situation when the ranger pulled up.

He got out and walked over in heavy measured steps, a carved club swinging from his hand.

His eyes traveled the length of the car and back again before turning to the men, first scanning Ariola up and down, then giving Buck the once over.

"I knew I should have hauled you boys in. I was on my way into town when I saw all the smoke. Thought you'd started us a forest fire."

"Smoke!" Buck said defiantly, "It was just steam. We found that out after we'd filled the motor with dirt."

As far as Buck could tell, the ranger hadn't heard a word he'd said.

The big man glanced down at his club, slapped it against his thigh, then eyed Buck again.

"Works pretty good against bears, especially the smaller ones, them that aren't any bigger than a man."

Buck was silent. He had finally realized that nothing was sometimes very good to say. He'd read something like that once, but had never thought to put it to use until now.

The ranger then got back to business.

"It was smoke, all right. Look at these," he said, and kicked a tire.

Ariola ignored that. He spoke up cheerfully. "Glad you came back, officer. We do seem to have a little trouble."

"Yeah?"

The ranger said no more, but walked around the car, Ariola following him.

Now Ariola, taking his cue from Buck, was also silent. They walked, Ariola looking intently at the car, as if the sagging bumper might be the problem. It wasn't, but was close to it.

The ranger was the one who made the discovery.

"Looks like you boys stirred up quite a bit of sand and gravel with all your spinning."

He pointed to the tail pipe. A rock, just the right size, was jammed into it. The ranger hit the side of the pipe with his club and the rock popped out.

Surprised, yet relieved, Ariola, brought out a money clip and extended some bills toward the ranger.

"In any case, we'll need a tow truck if you'll send one out. We thought the motor was on fire, but since it now seems to be full of mud, I doubt it will run."

"Yeah. Seems to be. Whose bright idea was that?" he asked, looking pointedly toward Buck.

Buck didn't hear the jibe or see the look. He was kneeling by the stream, enjoying the rush of cold water against his stinging hands.

Ariola pretended he didn't notice it either, in fact, acted as if it had never been spoken, but he did put the bills back into his pocket. The timing didn't seem right.

"I'm afraid we were a bit overwrought at the sight of the steam. Thought at first it was smoke."

"Well, I knew right from the start that what I saw was smoke. Real smoke. Coming from your tires."

"About the tow truck officer," Ariola said as he again extended the bills.

This time the ranger waved them away with a sharp flat-handed signal that told Ariola in no uncertain terms that there would be no tow truck coming.

"You boys are coming over to the station with me for a little talk with the captain. I don't believe these forests are safe with you two running loose in them."

"Officer," Ariola began again, but a jiggle of the rangers club closed his mouth.

As they walked over to the stream, Ariola was hoping Buck would be as easily convinced as he.

He was. He was tired and hungry and his head still hurt—nearly as much as his hands.

Chapter 29

The car *was* towed, then impounded all before Ariola and Buck had a chance to talk with the captain, much less get any food.

The captain wasn't in—he was thirty miles away—but the ranger was sure the captain would want to hear the whole story before he made any disposition of the case.

Buck's head hurt, and his neck and hands—and now so did his stomach.

"What do you have to do to get something to eat around this joint?" Buck asked

That remark nearly made them subject to a hearing before the judge, also thirty miles away.

When the ranger heard the station referred to as a joint, Buck—and Ariola, too, since they were together—was informed that only inmates were fed. That sent a shock of alarm through Ariola—Buck, also, but not so much that he wouldn't have minded being locked up if it meant getting something to eat, plus a couple of aspirin.

The young clerk at the corner desk took it all in. He knew perfectly well the station didn't have any place to put inmates—he'd had to suppress a giggle when he heard Carl say that, but from the look on Carl's face he was glad he had held it in. He just kept on typing, even though it was only a letter to his girlfriend.

He also thought of suggesting that the two men walk down the road to the lodge and get something to eat while waiting for the captain, but he didn't. Carl seemed to think he had them in custody. Maybe he did. Maybe they were some kind of criminals. You'd have thought so, from the way Carl kept such a close watch on them, and the way he regularly slapped his club against his thigh.

They probably were. Carl was supposedly off duty, so it must be something. Carl prided himself in being a good judge of character, and it was obvious they were up to no good, especially the blonde-haired man.

The Mexican mostly sat looking out the window, but the other one just couldn't keep quiet. He really exploded when he saw Johnny dragging in the car.

It was a good thing the captain came in about the same time, or else Carl might have had to use his club, especially on the white man. The Mexican seemed not to care.

Carl and the white man were standing toe to toe when the captain finally arrived. It was obvious that trouble was about to erupt, but the captain didn't seem concerned. He told Carl to sit down, and he did. The Mexican put his hand on the white man's arm and it settled him, too.

Carl told the captain what had happened, then the captain turned to the Mexican. He told the same story, but it didn't seem nearly as exciting as Carl's version.

The young clerk was just finishing his letter. He wanted to get it out of the way before the captain noticed what he was doing. Nothing much going on here, he wrote. Same old, same old. Love, Jacky.

The captain turned to Jacky, telling him to write up a receipt for the towing.

"We'll put your car behind the fence for safe keeping until you can get a truck up here to haul it," the captain said to Ariola.

He glanced at his watch, and continued, "Jacky's getting off in a few minutes. I'll let him go a little early so he can drop you men off down at the lodge."

"Sure thing," Jacky said as he picked up his letter and headed for the door.

Ariola and Buck thanked the captain and were right behind Jacky.

He walked along with them as they went over to the car for their bags.

"Nice," he said.

Ariola thanked him in his usual cordial tone, but said nothing more.

The only other vehicles in the lot were an old blue Ford and a jeep over in a far corner. Buck wondered what their owners had done to land them there—but he didn't wonder aloud.

A nice hot meal was in front of them before they wanted to talk about what to do next. They could probably rent a car somewhere, or hire someone to drive them to a train or airport, or call Jerry to fly up and get them. By the time they had eaten, they had decided to call Freda. It wasn't far back to her place and they could do something from there.

Buck smiled as he listened to Ariola telling her about their plight. He again made it sound a little tamer than Buck remembered it to be.

"She's coming," Ariola said, hanging up the phone.

"Be here in less than an hour, but she didn't sound too happy."

"Maybe she is tired. Probably just got off work," Buck replied.

"No, it was more than that. She sounded, I don't know, perhaps a little sad."

"Could be the prospect of putting up with us a few more days," Buck said as he laughed.

He had never been much on analyzing another person's feelings. Usually turned out to be completely off track. Even if Freda did sound sad, he didn't want to hear it. He was tired of sadness. The best he'd felt lately was when he'd been rolling around in the grass with Ariola. His neck still itched, but he wasn't sad.

"If she's sad, we'll cheer her up," Buck said.

He walked over to the curio counter and bought a red bandana, then went to the men's room and scrubbed his neck with it. He was ready to take on Freda's sadness.

Freda wasn't sad, she was mad. She arrived at the lodge

with her car packed.

"It turns out they had a form to be filled out for patient's records after all," she said curtly when they gasped at the startling sight.

The packing had obviously been done in a hurry and sloppily, as if the packer might have been blind with rage— or tears, as she worked. Opened boxes filled with kitchen utensils rested on her bedding that had been stuffed into pillowcases. Two suitcases, one with a bit of red silk caught peeking out, the other with one broken clasp that caused a bulge in one corner as if it might pop open at any minute, took up the rest of the back seat. She had thrown several pairs of shoes and two goose down jackets onto the floor. A box of books filled the other side of the floorboard.

"It's a good thing you guys called when you did. I was on my way out the door."

Ariola took it all in and immediately knew her flippant words only veneered her real feelings.

"Well, it's the first bit of luck we've had today," was all he said. She'd talk when she was ready.

Buck didn't wait, however. "Where, for cryin' out loud, were you headed?" he blurted out.

He didn't want to mince words. He wanted to be down the road, and if Freda was going someplace, she could drop them off wherever they could rent a car or catch a plane or a train. He wasn't particular. He just wanted to get out of this place.

He had asked a question Freda couldn't answer, but after a stuttering attempt, she burst into tears. She waved away their offers of assistance. Buck even held out the wet red bandana that he'd stuffed into his hip pocket.

She cried hard. The tears lasted only a minute, but it was a long minute to the men. Stopping almost as abruptly as she'd started, she then accepted the bandana from Buck.

"I only washed my face with it," he said meekly. "But then I rinsed it out, too," he was quick to add.

He was taking no chances on upsetting her again.

She scrubbed her face to a rosy hue, then handed it back to Buck.

"Sorry about that," she said, then sniffed loudly to finalize the process.

"We'll all have to ride in the front," she said, even as the men wedged their bags among her boxes.

Buck slid behind the wheel without asking.

"Where to?" he said as Ariola helped Freda into the seat and slammed the door.

They were three good-sized people cramped into a small space, but none of them minded. All three were glad to be leaving.

This time she didn't burst into tears. She was through with crying.

"Just head for NeeDee," she said. "I'll drop you off, but I don't know what I want to do after that. I haven't made up my mind where I'll go from there."

Neither man commented.

Several miles down the road, they stopped for coffee. It was then she started talking. She circled the mug with her hands as she talked and it warmed her enough that she could tell her story without emotion.

The doctor hadn't been in—which was often the case, Freda said, a sardonic edge creeping into her voice—when Silent Water's husband had come for her file. While going over the morning's work sheet with the doctor, he became upset, not upset about the half dozen shots administered in his absence, nor the stitches she'd put in, nor the other ten patients rescheduled because of his late arrival, but about the missing record.

It seemed that records were the basis for his pay. He hadn't treated Silent Water, but records were important. Perhaps he could get someone with more experience to replicate the missing record. Henceforth, she would not touch administrative matters.

There had no doubt been other words, but Freda chose to go no further.

And so it went the same way when the three showed up back at the ranch a few days later. No one questioned Freda's arrival back in NeeDee with the two men—they were only hoping she would stay. No one asked about the disappearance of Ariola's car, nor the quick delivery of a new one. No one asked about Rica—of course, only Mary Lou and Pauline had any inkling of why Buck and Ariola had taken off in the first place. There was an aura about it all that could have brought questions, but they were never voiced. No one even noticed Buck's black eye.

Chapter 30

Freda had been holed up in Jimmy's quarters—where Paul had lived his few months at the ranch—three days before Nick had been told she was back. She had asked Buck and Ariola not to mention her presence to anyone—she needed some time to think. Ariola had obliged by parking her car in his garage, and Buck had done his part by calling Nick and Bill to let them know they were back, but busy catching up on things in the office. Ramona sent meals out. Whether it was Buck or Ariola who carried them, or one of the household helpers, no one was invited to stay and chat. All gave her the space she needed.

She took three days, but might have come around sooner had the weather been better. They arrived at the ranch late at night, dense fog having slowed them to a crawl the last few miles. The dawn was soupy and unseasonably cold. By mid-morning, heavy drizzle was falling. Buck was thankful for the moisture—the pastures were brown, not from early frost, but from the toll of New Mexico's broiling sun. Ariola appreciated the rain, yet he closed the blinds on his office windows to block out the sight. Rica might be traveling through it, and wherever she was, whomever she was with, he wanted only sunshine for her.

Paul was on Freda's mind constantly but she was also puzzling her plight. She had come to NeeDee right out college. She'd left, never expecting to return, but she was back, trying to decide whether to stay or drive on without calling anyone.

She paced the small apartment, finding an occasional reminder of Paul. The most treasured was his belt. The heavy buckle, scratched from years of wear, austere, yet still impressive, lay nestled inside the coil of worn leather.

She let out a happy cry at the sight of it.

Removed by the medics, then placed on the dresser by the cleaners who came afterward, Freda now rubbed it, the lettering coming alive beneath her touch The word, Cheyenne, arching across the top and the numbers, 1934, curving upward from the bottom rim, told everything. It wasn't as ornate or as large as the buckles worn by many of the young cowboys who had dropped by to see him, but it said enough. They glanced at the buckle, and respect, even awe, shown in their faces.

"That was the big one for me," he told her once.

"But what about me? You were to be my big one, Paul. You promised me a brand new life, but then you had to go and die on me, you bastard."

She was appalled by the name she had called him, and at the same time, chagrined at the sound of her voice with no one else to hear it. Shame won out. She began sobbing, clutching the belt in both hands, pressing the cold metal buckle against her throat.

"That's all right, honey. I'm mad at me for dying, too," she could hear him saying.

A light knock alerted her that supper had arrived, and the low growl of a familiar voice told her it was a new tray-bearer at the door.

"Shake a leg, will you? It's raining out here."

Wiping tears with the back of her hand, she opened the door for Nick.

"What are you? Some kind of Greta Garbo?"

She grinned in spite of his sarcasm, and would have hugged him if a large tray hadn't blocked her reach.

"Put it on the coffee table," she said.

"Thanks for bringing it out," she added in a dismissive tone.

"Wait a minute. Let's put it on the table. I brought me a little something, too, and I can't enjoy a steak unless I have my elbows on the table."

He headed for the kitchen without waiting for her reply.

They were half way through their steaks before much more was said. Nick, intense about everything he did, rarely did more than one thing at a time. If he was eating, he ate; if talking, he talked.

He lay down his knife and fork and looked at her.

"Okay. Where've you been and what do you mean not calling me the minute you got here?"

His brusque tone didn't phase her. They had always been blunt with each other. Their relationship centered on it.

"I don't know. I couldn't see anyone," she said softly.

She was not at all blunt. Her listless response alarmed him. He didn't know how to deal with this strange new Freda.

He patted her hand lying idly beside her plate. She, too, had stopped eating.

"Freda, I'm not just anyone. At least, I hope I'm not. I've always assumed I'm not."

"Of course you aren't, darling boy," she said, lips beginning to tremble.

He'd noticed the traces of tears on her cheeks when he'd come in and could see them resurfacing.

"Hold on now, woman. Don't cry on me. Pretend you're sponging out a gunshot wound or something."

"Don't worry about me. You'd be the shaky one in that case."

The Freda he knew was back. He gave her hand a squeeze and went to work on his steak again.

"How did you happen to be out here? I thought you and your daddy were kind of on the outs," Freda said.

"That's exactly how it happened. Buck's always—"

"Daddy!" Freda snapped.

"That's exactly what's wrong with him."

"Okay, okay," Nick conceded. "Daddy's always aching about me not coming around enough, so when he called the other day, his attitude just made me a little curious."

"Curious?" Freda said. "Admit it, you big baby."

"Okay, okay. So I wanted to see the old man. But I also wondered what was going on out here."

"And I'm glad I did," he continued. "I've missed you as much as I've missed Daddy."

Freda brought her napkin toward her face.

"Freda," he warned. He couldn't tolerate this new, soft Freda, unaware that it was his own words causing the tears.

Though Paul had complained each time she had come in late from the hospital, no one else before or since had missed her.

"Freda, I don't know why they let you stay out here. You've just been moping around here thinking about Paul."

"Well, he's mine to think about. That's all I have left."

"But you're just making it hard on yourself. You should have been out seeing people. They should have at least insisted you stay in the house—"

"Of course they insisted. But I didn't do it. Trying to take care of me like I was some long lost kinfolk! I don't even know your family very well. I don't believe I'd ever been in the same room with any of them until I met Paul."

"But I did have to accept Buck's kindness for a few days," she added, her eyes surveying the room. "I need a few days to see if I can tolerate being here since Paul—"

"We'd all just met Paul, too, but it didn't seem like it, did it?" Nick said.

"Nope. It didn't take long to feel you'd known Paul forever."

She gazed out the window, her eyes as cloudy as the relentless drizzle.

Nick didn't leave until after midnight, but when he did, he left knowing that as soon as Freda found an apartment and settled in, she would become the new Director of Nurses. With that decided, she slept well. So did he.

Chapter 31

Freda was at work on Tuesday morning. She had found a house near the park, a little brick that needed only a quick coat of paint inside. The husbands of three friends had shown up early Saturday morning. Loaded with ladders, brushes and paint, they had it finished before the four women returned from furniture shopping.

The furniture was delivered early Monday morning, and placed according to Freda's directions. Efficient from years of giving and taking orders, she had decided on the placement before it arrived, but the deliverymen could have done just as well without her.

The small house had only one living-room-wall that would accommodate the sofa and corner-windows offered the obvious choice for her overstuffed chair, ottoman and reading lamp. The same rule applied to the bedroom; it was designed with one wall wide enough for the bed while the others, broken up by doors, were meant for the chest and dresser. However, being veteran deliverymen, plus knowing from hard experience how much it meant to a woman to direct the arranging of her furniture, they waited patiently for her instructions. They placed her little chrome and yellow dining set in the tiny kitchen while she was on the telephone and she waved them out the door in less than an hour after their arrival. It was neat, but plain, and Freda wanted nothing more.

The second bedroom remained empty. As she looked around it, a daybed for guests and a desk for herself crossed her mind, but that must be left to the future. She didn't expect guests, and her restlessness allowed her to sit at no desk other than amid the hubbub of the nurse's station. She closed the door and went for a walk in the park.

Her first week as director of nurses was one of restraint. She had to restrain herself from pitching in to help with an exceptionally rough delivery. Then twice, when a light flashed red on the board, she was nearly out of her chair and on the way down the hall ahead of the charge nurse. Midweek, when a young nurse needing to stay home with a sick baby called in at the last minute, she made rounds with Dr. Kraft. Only then was she in her element. She felt alive and efficient.

Afterward, having a quick cup of coffee with the doctor, she was about to tell him she wanted to go back on the floor when he spoke up.

"Seems like old times, doesn't it, Freda?" He then added, "After Agnes left, we were in a real mess before you stepped in."

Agnes had begun as the unofficial director of nurses from the day the NeeDee Hospital had opened its doors thirty years before—unofficial, because with only six nurses, working in shifts of three, there had been no real need, nor funding, for a director of nurses. After staying with the hospital through two additions, her title became real. Bad knees had forced Agnes into retirement only weeks before, but since then, the hospital had been in the worst need of a replacement.

Freda nodded and mumbled, "Oh, yes," losing the heart to say more.

Back at her desk, she only glanced up, giving a perfunctory wave in response to the doctor's sharp knock on the corner of her desk as he left the hospital. She had plenty of work to do.

After work each day was another story. Those first two weeks, two, sometimes three, different women, mostly nurses, dropped by nearly every afternoon. Freda was glad to see them, to offer them a glass of iced tea and hash over the day, but they appeared to be more interested in the state of her house than of refreshment.

They often wandered through the house, glass in hand, chattering about pillows and afghans and her favorite colors.

"They're just in the nesting mode," Nick laughed and said when she complained to him about her friends' behavior. "They're happy in their nests and want the same for you."

She let him know she didn't appreciate his remarks. He laughed that off, too.

"Relax, Freda. They're probably just planning a little housewarming for you."

"They did something like that not so long ago," Freda retorted.

Didn't Nick, didn't they all, remember that she had returned every one of the wedding gifts before leaving town?

"This is different, Freda. They love you. We all love you. They just think buffing up your new house a little will make you feel better."

"Told you," Nick said, winking at Freda, that following Saturday afternoon when Freda returned from the beauty shop to find her back yard full of smoking grills and her house full of people.

"I knew how you felt about gifts," Nick said, feigning a look of complete innocence, "so I just brought the steak and beer, and it will all be gone by sundown."

She grinned, at the same time giving him a look that let him know she would have plenty to say later. He was positive she would, too.

There were no gifts to unwrap. Pillows had been thrown on the sofa, the afghan over the arm of her chair, a new comforter and shams on the bed, with towels already shelved in the bathroom and cookware and dishes put away in the kitchen.

Likewise, no thank you notes were necessary, or even possible. There were no names on the gifts.

"Everybody just pitched in," she heard from one after another person as she made her way around offering thanks.

"Well, I do know where the afghan came from," Freda said. "I've been noticing Jane crocheting like crazy on her breaks."

"Yeah, but you don't know who furnished the yarn, now do you?" Jane answered quickly.

She shook her head and grinned, saying, "Don't worry. I'll get even with each and every one of you sooner or later."

Chapter 32

Two days later, Ariola showed up soon after Freda got home from the hospital.

She was surprised, but not unpleasantly, to see him instead of Jane when she opened her door. She did momentarily wonder if her hair was in place. At the same time, she felt aggravated with herself at the tinge of regret that swept over her. She'd thrown on her worst looking faded jeans as soon as she'd gotten home, but if they were all right for Jane, they were certainly good enough for Ariola. Besides, he wouldn't even notice what she was wearing.

He smiled, a little apologetically, and thrust a wrapped package toward her.

"They called from the hospital and invited me over for the party, but I didn't want to interfere with you and your friends."

Freda had instinctively reached out to take it as soon as he started to hand it to her, but at his words, she felt immediately rebuffed. So much so, in fact, that her hand dropped and she almost missed the transfer. There was momentary fumbling from both of them, putting the package in peril. His hand accidentally brushed hers. It was warm and hard and smooth, so different from Paul's. Then she understood. He was Paul's friend, not hers. At that realization, she was suddenly flushed and disoriented, protesting vehemently against his bringing her a gift.

She could hear herself, but couldn't seem to be quiet, hoping at the same time he hadn't noticed her flush.

He did notice it, but took it to be part of her protest about the gift.

"Please. After everything you did for me, I want to give

you this. You might not even like it and if you don't—" he paused and shrugged.

"Did for you? I just stirred up trouble—" she declared.

"Please," he said again. At that moment, he seemed the more flustered of the two.

Both still had their hands on the package, but neither let go of it, perhaps each expecting the other might let it crash to the porch.

One of them had to break the impasse, and Freda did it with a grin and a few words. Looking down at their hands, both scrambling, then clutching, she smiled and said, "I hope it's not glass."

He returned her smile, saying please for the third time, but presenting it as a question.

She shook her head negatively, but while doing so said, "Come in, Ariola. We'll talk."

She released her hold on the package and he brought it safely inside.

Once there, before the ritual could begin again, Freda took it and said, "Let me put it over here."

Leaning it against the hearth, she turned back to Ariola and continued, "We'll talk while we're having something to drink. I have iced tea already made, or I can fix us a pot of coffee."

"Sit down," she said, on her way to the kitchen before he could answer, she called over her shoulder, "Which will it be?"

He had only intended to bring the gift and leave, but answered that tea would be fine, and followed her into the kitchen instead of sitting.

"How about trying out your new table?" he asked.

"Sure. I have some chocolate cake left from the party." She gave him a questioning glance.

"You bet," he said and sat down.

She soon joined him with the iced tea and cake.

As they began eating, Ariola slicing into it boldly, Freda

gingerly picking at hers, she worried aloud, "Coffee would have probably been better. I had pretty much forgotten about this cake."

"No, no. This is great," Ariola insisted.

They chatted pleasantly, never mentioning the package. Freda, however, couldn't get it out of her mind. She felt an unexplainable reluctance to accept it, but was at a loss as to how to refuse. She worked on the cake as long as she could reasonably do so. Ariola finished his quickly but passed on seconds. He got up and helped himself to another glass of tea while she was still nibbling.

When she finally pushed it aside, unfinished, she made a hollow remark about how her friends must be trying to sabotage her diet.

"No such thing," Ariola protested. "You're not on a diet. You surely don't need to be, anyway."

Freda blushed again. She could have bit her tongue. Talk about diets, at least his remark about her not needing to be on one, sounded too personal to her liking. Why had she said such a silly thing? She wasn't on a diet. If anything, it was loss of appetite and lots of mountain hiking that had slimmed her down.

Her flush had not gone unnoticed by Ariola this time. Why had he made such an insinuation about her body? She did have a nice figure, but it wasn't up to him to comment on it. She must think him a clod.

A few seconds passed, but it seemed eons to the people sitting across the table from each other. Freda finally jumped up.

"Let's go back in there and get this gift thing settled."

He rose immediately and headed for the sink with his glass and saucer.

"Just leave everything. I'll take care of them later," she said, as she brought hers over.

She spoke curtly, trying to shore up her shattered poise.

Paying no attention, he carefully placed the dishes in the

sink and ran water over them, but however calm he appeared, he hadn't missed her sharp tone.

She smiled as she handed him a dishtowel. He took it and gratefully returned her smile as he dried his hands, folded it neatly and placed it on the counter.

As an afterthought, he looked at the dishes, then back at the cloth and said, "I should have washed those."

"No," she snapped, "I have the whole evening to wash two glasses and two saucers."

They both laughed, each at last feeling close to a tie with their volleying.

"Let's just get out of here," she said as he followed her into the living room.

"Now," she said the moment they sat down, "I don't want a gift from you. I didn't expect a gift from you. I didn't even want all this," she said, gesturing around the room, "but apparently the girls thought differently."

"I can understand your feelings," he said. "But I can also understand why those people wanted to do this."

"I just feel foolish," she continued, not trying to analyze his statement. "I didn't want it, but of course, I can't tell them that. I don't know how to make them realize how I feel without hurting their feelings."

"You can't. But I'll tell you what. *I* won't force a gift on you. It's," he glanced at the package and continued, "just something I think you'd like. I'll give you a little time, then we'll see about it. Okay?"

It seemed there was no pleasing her. Now feeling asinine about the commotion she'd made, she handed him the package.

"Okay," she said, then added, "No hard feelings?"

"Not at all," he answered.

As he left, he smiled, asking, "I'll see you soon?"

"I hope so," she said, not quite sure she meant it.

The next morning she was at work early, engrossed in scheduling before Jane flew in, a little late as usual.

"Sorry I missed coffee yesterday," she said, giggling as she hurried by.

"Me, too," Freda answered without looking up.

Thirty minutes later, she came back up the hall and stopped in front of Freda's desk.

"Okay. You know I didn't forget about coffee. I just didn't stop. Now, dish."

Freda shrugged, then said, in what she hoped was a nonchalant tone, "He just came by for a minute."

Freda had spent a few sleepless hours wondering why he had shown up at her door with a gift and why she had been so adamant in her refusal of it. She hadn't figured it out, but didn't mention that to Jane. She simply offered what she hoped Jane would take as a plausible explanation,

"You know, he was a great friend to Paul."

"Of course," Jane said. She started back down the hall, then turned and added with a grin, "Should I try it again this afternoon?"

"Of course," Freda mocked as she returned her grin.

Jane didn't make it that afternoon, however, because she again drove on by after seeing that same black car parked in front of Freda's house. Freda was surprised when her bell rang. Jane usually just called out knock, knock as she came through the front door.

"Not a gift, not a gift," Ariola spoke up as soon as Freda answered it.

He carried a teakwood-framed painting. Freda realized from its size that it had been in the package she had refused the day before.

"No way," she said, rolling her eyes in exasperation, yet unable to contain a smile.

"It's not a gift," he repeated. "Just give me a few minutes."

She pushed open the screen door in reply and he set the picture back on the hearth. Freda brought two mugs of coffee out of the kitchen without asking.

She wasn't as shaken by his unexpected appearance as she had been the day before. In fact, she was pleased to see him.

He took a couple of sips before setting the mug aside.

"That was my favorite of all her paintings," he said.

It was large, nearly three feet tall, and almost that wide. Showing a hazy overcast and two ethereal figures shrouded in fog walking arm in arm through a wilderness, it was a picture warranting study, and they both did that, intently, silently.

He finally spoke again.

"I took the rest of them to a gallery in Taos. As they sell, they'll take their commission, then give the rest to charity."

"It's lovely, Ariola, but I—"

"I would appreciate your hanging it for awhile, Freda. It's not a gift," he repeated.

"I just don't want it at my place, at least for now. It's still my favorite, but there's just something about it that reminds me of how Rica was so much of the time—"

"Maybe it's all in the way you look at it, Ariola. I don't know about you, but the way I see it, it's not troubling, simply two people emerging from the mists."

His eyes popped. "You know, you might be right, Freda, but I'd still like you to keep it for a while."

"Sure," she said. "I need something on the mantel."

Ariola laughed when she added, "It's a good thing I didn't accept it as a gift. I might not have wanted to give it back when you change your mind."

"Don't worry about it," he replied, "Just enjoy."

Ariola propped it there and placed a large polished stone in front of the frame for security. Freda pushed the rock over until it was slightly off-center and they stood back to study it.

"Perfect," she said.

Ariola nodded his agreement.

After finishing their coffee, Ariola carried some boxes of books in from her empty spare room. She had left them with her former landlord who now insisted on returning them. As he helped her fill the small bookcase to one side of the fireplace, he commented that a person's library could tell quite a story about them.

"Well, I don't know about that. All these biographies belonged to my daddy. I did read some of them as a kid, but I'm a sucker for every mystery that rolls off the press."

"I can see that. You have a nice collection here."

"What do you read?" she asked.

"Oh, mostly poetry, I guess. Something I can pick up for a few minutes. Truthfully, though, anything in the pocket in front of me on a plane. I'm on the road so much, I do most of my reading in the air."

"Looks like you're set for the winter," Ariola added as they finished filling the case.

"Looks like," she chimed in, but the prospect of so many cold evenings of reading alone seemed suddenly dull.

Chapter 33

"Well, it's a good thing you're alone. If his car had been out front today, I was just going home and start planning the announcement party," Jane remarked as she zipped through the front door and across the room.

Freda couldn't come up with the hot retort she knew Jane expected, so she went to the kitchen and came back with two mugs of coffee. Jane was already nestled on the sofa with her feet tucked under her, studying the painting.

Freda handed her a cup and sat down across the room.

"Well?" Jane asked, wondering why Freda hadn't mentioned the painting at the hospital.

Deep dimples on each cheek twitched in anticipation. Jane threw her whole self into whatever excitement could be managed from her rather mundane existence, but now she felt on the verge of witnessing something exciting—in her own forthright expression, something *big*.

"What?" Freda asked.

"What, yourself," Jane shot back.

Freda had held in her grin as long as possible, but once it broke free, her only hope was that her indifferent tone would belie the giddy feeling Jane's first words had brought out.

She knew Jane was waiting for an explanation—no, she was waiting for Freda to *dish,* a pet expression of Jane's.

"He gave that to you! That's why he was here, wasn't it?" she questioned.

"No, he tried, but I refused it," Freda answered.

"Then what's it doing here? Why wouldn't you take it? It's beautiful. It was done by Rica, wasn't it?" Jane was relentless.

"Is that the reason you didn't want it, because of Rica?"

"But at least, you got him to come back the second day by refusing it," she ranted on, never slowing for answers.

Freda wasn't holding out. She simply didn't know how to answer any of this. Even if she did, there had been no chance to do so.

She didn't want to talk about it. There was the guilt she felt at having called Ariola about Rica, and the remorse for her poor judgment in handing over the young woman's medical records to a stranger, albeit she still believed he was simply a protective husband. Then again, she probably shouldn't have made the call at all. Her chest still tightened at the memory of the resulting confrontation that sent her cramming her belongings into her car even before Ariola had asked for a ride home.

Freda knew what Jane was thinking, or at least what she was hoping. With one husband already out of the picture and a boyfriend on shaky ground, Jane often wondered aloud why Freda never seemed concerned about the lack of men in her life.

She had been adept at fending off her efforts at match making in the past, but now Jane was back in full form. It seemed that Paul hadn't counted with Jane.

Jane could picture the beginnings of a fanciful encounter for her friend, and she was eager to help Freda cultivate it. In fact, she was set on it blossoming, but Freda was equally determined that it not.

Here was a man, a tall, handsome man, not to mention, a tall, handsome, rich man and not just *any* tall, handsome, rich man, but Gabriel Ariola, simply—in Jane's eyes—the most eligible man in NeeDee. It was *the* Gabriel Ariola's car she had seen parked in front of her friend's house two afternoons in a row. Jane was full of curiosity—and, moreover, hope for her friend.

Jane, of course, knew nothing of the impulsive call that had sent Ariola and Buck hurrying across three states to find Rica, but returning with Freda instead, nor why Freda was back in NeeDee. However, Freda, never having been one to talk about herself, didn't feel that she was deceiving Jane. She was simply not ready to talk about the situation.

"Jane, it's nothing. He's clearing out Rica's art, taking it all to Taos. Apparently, he wanted to keep at least one, but not at his house, so he thought of me."

She laughed and added, "Knew I didn't have anything on my walls."

Just as quickly, Freda's stern mood was back as she asked, "By the way, what on earth possessed you all to invite him here in the first place?"

For Jane's part, she declared herself innocent, pulling her sweater tightly around her shoulders and said with an indignant air, "Well, I certainly know I didn't."

Freda doubted that. Jane was in on most everything. If she hadn't asked Ariola herself, she more than likely knew who did—in fact, made sure that the invitation had been extended.

"Oh, yeah. Like he's been coming to our parties for years," Freda said.

Jane was about to put on an apologetic face, but quickly decided against it. No need to waste that. Judging from Freda's flip remark, she was confident that not only was her friend going to forgive her, she would bet anything Freda was glad Ariola had been invited.

"I can kind of understand you guys showing up with all this," Freda said, gesturing around the room, "because we're buds, you know, but Ariola? He's hardly one of the crowd."

Partially forgiven anyway, Jane thought.

Freda's voice softened. "In fact, I doubt if he knew my name before Paul."

Her tone always changed when she spoke of Paul, but there was no need staying sad forever, so Jane plugged on.

"Well, he knows it now. Otherwise, he wouldn't have been here two days in a row."

Freda wilted. The look on her face sent Jane scrambling for words to buoy her friend and bring their coffee talk back to its normal chatter, but before she could find the words, Freda began to talk. She told Jane about every encounter she'd had with Ariola. She rambled, not even trying to keep it in any sequence, simply telling things as they came to mind. Her voice lilted when she spoke of his graciousness toward Paul and herself, and broke ever so slightly when she told of the call she'd made to him about Rica. She ended with their trip to scatter Paul's ashes, noting how he'd tried singing a little. Freda was sure it was meant to mask the silence coming from the back seat.

"You know, he has a darn good voice," Freda said, then laughed.

Jane knew the story was finished, but still wasn't satisfied.

Sensing this, Freda added, "Now listen, Jane. I just can't take this anymore. We're"—with a sense of generosity, she alluded to *we're* instead of *you're*, "acting like teenagers pining for the quarterback who's going steady with the cheerleader."

"Not me," Jane chimed in. "I *was* the cheerleader."

"Well, I wasn't," Freda snapped. "Just forget all this silly stuff about Ariola. I doubt that I'll come within two miles of him again."

"But suppose you do," Jane posed.

Would Jane's goading be so cavalier if Freda were a widow? One day. She had been one day short.

"Jane—you're starting to aggravate me."

Jane could see that indeed she was, so decided it was time to give it up—for the present. She still didn't know how Freda felt about Ariola.

Chapter 34

"I need you, Gabriel."

Ariola drew in a sharp breath at the sound of Rica's ragged whisper, and asked immediately, "Where are you, my precious girl? I'll be right there."

Ariola listen intently to her shaky-voiced directions. He landed in Springfield, Missouri a few hours later, then rang her doorbell an hour after that.

Her face, gaunt yet indescribably beautiful to him, lit up when she opened her door.

He gathered her to him without considering that he was holding another man's wife, only that she had called and he was there. She didn't attempt to stop him, but instead slid her arms around his waist as he kissed her forehead.

Inexpressible relief at seeing her, touching her, blocking out reality, he was hardly aware of how large she was in her pregnancy.

"It's so good to see you, Gabriel," she finally whispered into his shoulder.

With that, he released her and she took his hand, leading him to a sofa. For a moment, he considered taking a chair across the way so he could drink in her face, but holding her hand won out.

She then attempted to explain away the months he had searched for her.

"When I left Santa Fe, all I wanted was to disappear—from the face of the earth, I guess, but I was just too much of a coward."

Ariola protested occasionally, but she wanted to talk and he wanted to hear.

"I don't know how I ended up on the reservation. Perhaps a kindly truck driver took me there. And I don't know why Aunt Irene took me in, but she did."

"You shouldn't have needed someone else to take care of you. I should have been the one. All I've wanted was to take care of you, to keep you safe. We were planning our wedding. We were—"

"I know, darling. I can't explain what I did. I just had to get away. Your world is just too big for me."

"I could have changed all that."

"No," she protested. "I know you believe you could have, and there's no doubt you would have tried. But things wouldn't have changed enough."

He didn't interrupt again—just listened, relieved that she was safe, but bitter that she had run away from him, yet turned to a stranger. As painful as it was, he needed to know how she had come to this point.

"I had been with Aunt Irene a few weeks when Warren came back home."

Ariola winced at hearing his name for the first time.

"He was disappointed with his life on the outside, as he called it, and intended to stay right there—never again leave that wonderful place he'd grown up. He was going to teach in the reservation school."

"But now you're living on a college campus."

She chose not to hear him.

"Oh, Gabe, you can't imagine how beautiful it was, how serene—how safe I felt."

Ariola laid his head back against the top of the sofa. *Rica, oh, Rica, why couldn't I make you feel safe?*"

"His old family home was there, empty, waiting for him, waiting for me, he said. After only two weeks, he began insisting we marry. Two days later, we did. Then the baby was soon on the way. A month later, the college was calling, asking him to come back."

She hesitated, then said with finality, "Now we're here."

Why? She should have been his wife. This should have been his baby she was carrying.

"I didn't think I could bear it, leaving the reservation. But Aunt Irene came with us. She gave up her home there in that beautiful place, among her friends, to take care of the baby and me. And I need her. He's gone so much. I do need her. He's a good man, Gabe, and he does love me."

"Do you love him?"

"I—I—must. The baby."

Must? Did *must* mean an obligation to love her husband, that she *should* love him? Or was she actually puzzled about her feelings, only presuming that she *must* love him? He made it easy for her.

"Yes, you do. You do love him, and you should. There will be other babies. And you will be strong and able to take care of them and love them—and him."

"Oh, Gabriel."

"Yes, you will, you must. I insist."

"Gabe, you still don't understand. I'll always love you. I don't know why I kept running away from you, but I just couldn't stay. I would promise myself that everything was all right, then an uncontrollable urge would come over me—an urge to run, to disappear."

"Let's don't try to explain away five years, my dear. We can't. Let's just remember the good times. And there were good times."

"Yes. So many."

"You know, I might have come upon the crux of the matter. You were afraid of me."

"No. No. How could I have been? You are the most loving, the kindest, the—you're perfect. If there was any fear, it was of your lifestyle."

"Oh, Rica. I grew up in the most desolate place on earth. I could have taken you back there. I could have taken you to your wonderful place you say you intended to spend the rest of your days. I could have—"

"Don't you see? I didn't go there looking for anything. It just happened, somehow. Everything was so beautiful."

"I felt so safe, she continued, "and once I got there I knew I never wanted to leave."

"There had to be more, but we can't change anything now. In any case, I don't believe you want to."

"Oh, Gabe, I—"

"Rica, you have a husband and a baby on the way and you love them both."

"Yes," she said softly. "Yes, I do."

"And you also have a friend right here. Be happy, Rica. I want you to be happy. Again, I insist on it."

"Now, my darling, tell me why you called. What can I do to help you?"

"My dad has died, Gabe."

"I'm so sorry, Rica."

She nodded, and he took her hand again.

"Will you be able to attend the service?"

"It was a few weeks ago. I only found out yesterday. They knocked on my door—his lawyers, of course."

"So he had known where you were? How did he take the news of your marriage—and the baby?"

Her eyes clouded as she told him, "I didn't talk to him, but I guess he knew how to find me. His lawyers did, anyway. I suppose they contacted Palo's family."

So at least Palo had known where she had been all along. Why Palo? Why not me?

Rica read his reaction.

"I just had to let Palo know I was all right, Gabe. His mother always said he went crazy worrying about me. After all the problems they have with him anyway, I couldn't put them through more because of me."

"He certainly was always protective of you. I even came to appreciate that."

Ariola thought of the young Indian, blind, yet ready to fight anyone whom he thought might harm Rica. It was usually his own hostility that caused the disturbance, but Rica could calm him with a word or a touch. Even without sight, Palo had made it his life's work to *watch over* Rica.

"I guess Daddy did too. He never liked Palo when he was alive, yet, would you believe? He made provisions for him in the trust. I guess he knew what Palo means to me."

"Oh, yes. There's a trust. He provided well for me," she continued, her voice flat.

"He always did. I guess he didn't know what to do with me, except that," she added, then squaring her shoulders, turned to the reason she had called Ariola.

Her father had left his entire estate to her, his only heir, as it should be, but Ariola was astounded as she told him why she had called. She wanted him to serve as the trust officer. Then he was truly stunned as she asked him to be her baby's godfather. It was what Warren wanted, too.

As they talked, he concluded it was something he could do, somehow muster the strength to handle, and be glad to do for Rica.

On the way back to NeeDee, something else was on his mind. How was he to convince Freda to be the baby's godmother?

Chapter 35

Jane squealed, dashed to the kitchen, emptied her cup in the sink, grabbed her jacket and headed for the door all before Freda was hardly aware of it.

"Gotta go. See you at work tomorrow."

"What on earth?"

"You'll see in a second. Tell me all about it first thing in the morning—that is, if you make it."

She opened Freda's front door just as the first knock sounded.

"Oh, hi, Ariola. I was just leaving."

Slipping past him, she dashed toward her car.

Ariola glanced at her, then turned to Freda, a question on his face.

Freda answered with a shrug.

"I hope I wasn't interrupting something."

When Freda didn't reply, he hesitated, then asked if he could come in.

"Of course. Come in. That little display kind of threw my brain off track."

"Seriously, I could come back later. I should have called first. I just got back into town and came straight here without thinking."

"No, no. Come in," she said, not realizing she was blocking his way.

"Well?"

Her cheeks colored slightly as she stepped aside and directed him toward the sofa.

"We were just having coffee. I'll bring you a mug, but I can't promise I won't spill it on the way."

"I could use some caffeine, but I'll get it myself."

She followed him into the kitchen, where he poured two

mugs, setting them on her table.

"Okay?" he asked as he pulled out a chair for her.

She nodded in agreement, yet felt a slight jab at her sensibilities. Shouldn't she be more in command here? At the same moment, it felt good having a man pouring her coffee, pulling out her chair, little niceties that she had missed since Paul's death.

"Freda, I'm sorry, just showing up like this. You probably have plans, but could we talk a few minutes?"

"Sure we can. I don't have any plans. And any that might have come up just ran out the front door."

"That Jane. She's quite a gal, isn't she?"

"To say the least."

"Why was she in such a hurry?"

"Who knows? When she saw your car pull up, she just split. To be blunt, she probably thought oh, hallelujah, Freda has a gentleman caller."

"Well, that's not so farfetched. But I'm afraid I'm here to burden you even more than I already have."

"Please don't say that. You haven't burdened me at all."

"Yes, I have. For one thing, I cost you your job at that clinic."

"You didn't, for pity's sake. I just didn't use common sense up there. Anyway, I'm glad to be back here—should never have left."

"A lot of people around here are certainly glad you're back, too."

"Let's just get off this—please. You said you wanted to talk about something."

"Yes, I do, Freda." He paused, then continued. "I've just gotten back from seeing Rica."

"Well, that's good to hear. How were you able to find her?"

"I didn't. She called me."

"She called you? So things are better between the two of you. Oh, Ariola. I'm truly happy for you. Is she all right?"

"I believe she is, Freda. Better than she's been in a long time. She was frank about her past behavior. Now, she's married with a baby on the way, healthy, happy."

Freda was amazed that this man, after searching for months, was complacently telling her that Rica was happy, as if her happiness had been his only concern. What about himself? She was hesitant to ask, but she did.

"So what's next? What are your plans?"

When he had finished his story, she said, this time without wavering, "Well, it looks as though you've been relegated to caretaker."

"That's all I've been for a long time, Freda."

"What does her husband think about this?"

"Surprisingly, he's all for it. He realizes they both need help. That tells me he's confident enough of her feelings for him that he's willing to allow me to do this."

"Did you talk to him?"

"No, he was in class. And frankly, I wasn't quite ready for a meeting."

"But," he hurried on, "if my being in the picture could cause any trouble for Rica, I'll not be doing it."

"Ariola, I just think you're setting yourself up for more heartbreak."

"No, I believe I'm freeing myself. I haven't searched for her at all since Montana. Now she's called me—and then only because of the trust. We talked for a long time and I came away believing she loves her husband. She still needs me, but as a friend and father-figure."

"And you can live with that?"

"I'm certain of it. Her husband's aunt lives with them, and adores her. And Rica loves her so much. She's the mother Rica never had."

"Let's see. Husband, baby, mother, at least mother-figure, and you—the father-figure—it seems she's in a utopian world. Do you think it will last?"

"I pray it will. It's her only hope, Freda."

"That was kind of snippy of me. I'm sorry."

"Point taken. And forgiven."

Their mugs were empty but she didn't offer to refill them. Their talk was over.

"Well, you've had quite a day," she said. "I honestly do hope everything works out the way you've planned."

Ariola got up and refilled the mugs without asking.

"Thank you, Freda. There's something else."

His tone made her leery. Did she want to hear this?

"Rica has asked if you will be the baby's godmother."

A silence hung between them. Ariola took a sip of his coffee while Freda left hers untouched and stared at him in disbelief.

"What?" she finally said. "I hardly know her. I don't really know her at all."

"You were kind to her at the clinic. She's actually lived her whole life without friends. I suppose Montana was a new beginning for her, and you were a part of it. And you're a friend of mine. Would you consider it, Freda?"

So this was the reason he came by. For a moment, she had been as silly as Jane.

He sipped his coffee, waiting for her reply.

Why me*? Here was this young woman, as frightened as a fawn, coming into that clinic to find out if she was pregnant. Silent Water! Hiding her real name. Then her young Indian husband taking her records and disappearing. Now she was asking Freda to be her baby's godmother?*

"I'm at a loss, actually. I don't know her husband's name, except Blackhawk," she confessed.

"Warren Wilson," Ariola replied.

"Warren Wilson. Has a substantial ring to it," Freda said.

"He grew up on the reservation using that name, Blackhawk—his aunt raised him—then went off to college. Now he's teaching at a little college in Missouri."

"Surely she has someone."

Ariola shook his head, and said, "No one."

"But surely," she repeated, "there's cousins, his aunt, some of his friends? Someone—"

"No one she wants more than you," he pleaded.

"She wants to have someone from her side. It seems that everything so far has come from his."

She began to understand Rica's feelings.

"Why not? I've never been a godmother. And I do love babies. All babies are lovable. Tell her I said yes, I'd be honored."

"She'll call you, but asked if I would approach you first."

"Ariola, you are a good man. And she's a lucky young woman to have you."

"As you said, I'm just her caretaker. And that's all I intend to be," he resolved.

She believed him.

"Rica's been alone all her life. Oh, her father adored her, but the most he could do for her was to see that she grew up in luxury. She was raised by housekeepers and nannies, but now she'll be surrounded by family. I talked to Warren's aunt before I left. The aunt is like a mother to her, and tells me all his relatives dote on her."

"Well, that's good, Ariola," Freda said, feeling the need to comfort him.

"Actually," he continued, "Warren is the best thing that could have happened to her."

"Being a part of his family—they'll be spending summers back on the reservation—and now with a family of her own—"

He stopped talking momentarily, causing her to jump in.

"Ariola, are you sure you're up to this?"

"Absolutely," he declared, his old demeanor back. "My only role will be as trustee, and I'll be out of that when they're ready to take over."

"You'll always be the godfather," she reminded him.

"And you, the godmother," he said and smiled.

Again, she was certain their evening was over and again she was mistaken.

"Thank you, Freda. Now, this was certainly a load lifted. Makes me feel like celebrating. Let's go somewhere and have dinner."

"I have things on hand. Why don't I just fix something here?"

"No offense. I'm sure you're an excellent cook, but I'd like to go out. In fact, I just feel like taking you dancing."

They did have a nice dinner out, but didn't find a club for dancing open on a weeknight. That suited Freda just fine. She wasn't sure how she would have fared dancing with Ariola. She hadn't been dancing for years—never danced with Paul. He had been on crutches until their last few days together.

Besides, as she told Jane the next afternoon—Jane demanded every detail—she did not feel comfortable going out with Ariola. Suppose his only interest in her was as a godmother?

"Suppose it isn't." Jane replied with a sly wink.

After continuous badgering from Jane about whether or not he had called, Freda had finally forbade Jane, with threat of banishment from their daily coffee ritual, to mention it again. That didn't hush Jane completely, nor did it keep Freda from thinking about it.

Ariola said it would be a few days before he talked with Rica again. Legal matters had to be dealt with, and he did not intend to talk with her any more than necessary. He would communicate with Rica only through her attorneys. He didn't want to disturb the delicate balance of her world.

He didn't say so, but Freda surmised it had to do with Warren Wilson, and how his feelings might change if his beautiful wife found it necessary to talk with Ariola often.

When she did think about it, fearing at times that the

situation might culminate in a real crisis, she was torn between concern for Rica and sympathy for Ariola.

There was no more Rica *and* Ariola, he had assured Freda more than once.

Perhaps it was pity she felt for Ariola. No, he had been hurt so badly, but he was strong.

Then her thoughts would turn back to Rica. She must have severe emotional problems to flee from a man such as Ariola.

Another concern was her involvement in the whole matter. She became more anxious each time she thought of how her conversation with Rica might go. She never doubted they would be able to talk pleasantly and become casual friends, but being a godmother was a personal matter based on deep friendship and trust. How could that be established over the telephone? She would take her cue from Ariola.

Those thoughts sometimes brought on whole clusters of feelings, with flashes of anger and disgust crowding out the more pleasant ones.

She was thankful her job was demanding, thankful that she often had to work late, leaving time for little else, yet too often her mind was in turmoil by the end of the day.

One afternoon, she actually closed her front door and pulled her blinds against Jane's anticipated visit, only to run and open them, calling out to a dejected Jane. After another warning about the subject of Ariola, they enjoyed their coffee.

Each truce lasted a day or two, but Jane invariably threw out that door opener, *had he called*? Freda began paying little attention to the speculations and theories that Jane came up with, responding with only a shrug.

Jane had a tendency to take everything Freda said as gospel and that prompted Freda to keep her lips sealed.

When she was alone at night, her emotions swirled. At times, she would dwell on how light and comfortable she had felt while having dinner with Ariola. Rica had not been mentioned again, yet there'd been plenty to talk about and they had—at least, she'd had—a delightful evening.

Sometimes though, she was consumed with outlandish thoughts. What if Ariola had taken the role of trust officer just to stay involved so he might have a chance of winning Rica back? What if Rica disappeared again, this time leaving a husband and baby? Would she be expected to help raise the baby? How could Warren Wilson be thinking of turning over his wife's fortune to her former lover?

When her thoughts did settle, she would take a more realistic approach. Ariola would get the paperwork done, then call, saying that as much as Rica had been set on the idea at first, she now had someone else, a family member, to act as godmother.

Freda would then be free of any involvement. Ariola would again become one of the people she nodded to when they happened to meet at an intersection, nothing more.

She would go back to the role of chubby friend who didn't have much of a social life, and didn't want one, but was usually available to baby-sit, always happy to do it so a young couple could have an evening out.

There was also pain from another source. How had she become a part —if she were a part—of Ariola's life in the first place? Paul. Ariola was Paul's friend, not hers. If not for Paul, those pleasant evenings at the Ramsey home would never have taken place. That trip to sprinkle his ashes—not for her, but for Paul. Anything she'd had to do with Ariola had been due to Paul.

She would end up wishing that time could be turned back to the days before she had met Paul. Life was so simple then.

That thought usually vanished quickly. Although she'd had Paul only a few months, those memories rekindled the searing pain of losing him. At the same time, she knew it had all been worth it.

Chapter 36

"Mr. Ramsey?" A vaguely familiar voice floated across an aisle lined with red wagons. Who would he know in a Denver toy store?

Milling shoppers paid him no attention. He scanned the crowd trying to match the voice with a person. Then their eyes met. Ah, yes. The eyes. He remembered the eyes.

A tentative smile flickered across her lips as her fingers fluttered in a hesitant wave.

"Well, I'll be. Valentine Swenson."

They made their way toward each other through the crowd.

"Mr. Ramsey. I wasn't sure it was you at first."

Meeting midway, he clasped her outstretched hand.

"You haven't changed that much. It's just that I hardly saw you without your hat back then," she continued, then laughed. He remembered that laugh from the times she had been at the ranch with Joe, but the last time he had seen her, there had been no laughter.

"Valentine," he said again.

"Well now, what brings you to Denver?" She asked, then glanced around, answering her own question.

She would have no way of knowing about the seemingly endless string of board meetings, business luncheons, conferences, dealings that had once been challenging and exciting, but had now turned so dull, so oppressive, they had become a weight he wanted to shake off.

The young woman would have no reason to care either. He explained concisely, "A board meeting, but I slipped out after lunch. I don't intend to go back to NeeDee without a load of these wagons. My very first Christmas with grandkids."

"Grandkids, huh."

"Yep. Three boys. Bill married a girl last year with three kids. They're expecting another this summer."

"Wonderful," she said, then looked down at her hand. He released it.

"Hey, there's a coffee corner over by the front door. If you have a little while, I'd like to hear about everyone."

"What's it been? Eleven, twelve years?" he asked as they made their way across the crowded store.

"Nearly thirteen," she said. Walking on in silence, they took their coffee to a corner table and sat down.

"Grandchildren. I'll bet Mrs. Ramsey is having a great time with them."

Buck studied his coffee cup before answering.

"We lost Alta this past summer, Valentine."

"Oh, no." Her eyes misted. "Oh, no," she repeated.

Biting his lip, Buck finally looked up. "Cancer," he said.

She waited for him to say more, but he could not.

"I just can't talk about it today, Valentine. Sometimes I can, but not today. So close to Christmas, I guess."

"No, don't. I'm just so sorry," she said, and patted his hand.

She feared she had caused him more pain as she told him, "Oh, Mr. Ramsey, you'll be receiving a Christmas card from me—to the both of you. I've been working in London for the past year. Just got back a few weeks ago, and—smart aleck-like, I mailed my cards before I left England. I'm so sorry."

"It'll be all right. I knew you and Alta always exchanged cards. I know I'll get some others from people who haven't heard."

"But still, I should have been more in touch. I should have known."

"Enough of that, Valentine. Just tell me about your life. What are you doing in here? Shopping for your children?"

"No children. I'm shopping for my secretary's boys."

Her face brightened. "They've sort of adopted me."

"That's good. Kids really liven things up, don't they?"

"Oh, yes. I usually just go skiing over the holidays."

"No 'home for the holidays' stuff for you, huh?" he asked.

"I lost my parents in a car accident a few years ago."

"Of course. Alta told me. I'm sorry. I'm afraid I've been the one out of touch."

"Please," she demurred.

"All right. Then tell me about London. What are you doing over there?"

"Was there. I'm back in Denver, hopefully for a long time. I was doing some editing for our London house. Did some seminars. I also have another book coming out in the spring."

"Well, I'm impressed," he said, pleased at the turn in their conversation. "What's the name of your new book?"

"Can't tell you," she said with a lively smile. "They insist on a press release being issued across the country. An agent thing. Anticipation, you know. Trying to boost sales."

"Sounds like it's just good business. I'll be looking for it. Wait until I tell Matt I talked to a real live author today."

"Matt?"

"The youngest. David and Jeff are the other two."

She glanced at her watch. "I must get back. I'm afraid I've missed a couple of appointments already."

They rose and he took her hand as they said their farewells. As he watched her walk away, another morose thought crept over him. Joe. If things had been different, she, too, could have been the mother of his grandchildren.

He had a rough trip home. His mind raced from one extreme to the other.

What a cruel hand life sometimes dealt. One moment he might pleasantly recall the young girl Joe had brought home to meet the family and the next, his mood had plunged to dark depths as he thought of the sophisticated young woman he had left at the toy store and the life with her that Joe had missed out on.

Valentine looked well adjusted. She had apparently gotten over losing Joe. Alta had mourned him until the day she died.

The next second, he felt silly. He was thinking as if Joe had just died. Why shouldn't she be adjusted? It had been thirteen years.

Valentine was a beautiful young woman. She said she had no children, but that did not rule out a husband.

Joe had mentioned her in every letter he had written to them. And why not? It had only been his class ring, but it meant a lot back then—when a boy went off to war.

She had been living in England. He wondered if she had ever visited Joe's old base as Alta had done. Why should she? Maybe it would have only brought back heartache.

He wished he hadn't seen her. She had been part of the dim past—he seldom thought of her, hardly remembered her—yet seeing her today had stirred so many regrets. It turned losing Joe back into a fresh wound. If only Joe had lived. He could have been hauling six wagons instead of three—or even dolls and tea sets.

By this time of year, Alta would have had a Christmas tree up and the house decorated. She even put wreaths on each side of the gate.

He could imagine the fuss she would have been making over the three little boys, the Stuart-Pitts boys, thanks to the speedy work of the law office and the judge. Billy Jack had been in a hurry for the adoption process to take place, anxious to get all his chicks in one nest. Old Bill—father of three, another on the way.

Buck was happy to have those three wagons in the back seat. Maybe the boys weren't the right age for red wagons. Too old, too young? It didn't matter. Nick had been too young when he got his, but it worked out fine. Jimmy pulled him all over the place in it.

That little gold locket he had given Alta—still in her jewelry box the last time he had looked. And the saddle—it had taken them six months to finally put a horse under it, but Joe had used it from then on. Wouldn't consider getting another one. Joe. He would be thirty five now—probably still using that old saddle.

It was really something, running into Joe's girlfriend. Only one he'd ever had. Alta would have been so tickled to see her again.

Oh, Alta. If he could make it through this first Christmas without her, maybe things would get better. Right now, though, he was going to see that this was the best Christmas for Bill and his family. If only Alta could have had this one Christmas with them. No telling what she would have cooked up.

The closer he got to home, the more his mind churned. Those red wagons he'd been so pleased with suddenly seemed inadequate. No, she had liked that red wagon he'd gotten for Nick. It was still out by her garden patch. There probably wouldn't be a garden this coming spring.

He pulled up to the portico and stopped, then sat in the car, gazing at the darkened house, before finally pulling in by the front door. He didn't want to go in. He always dreaded the nights, but he had to spend nights somewhere. Somewhere else might be better tonight.

When he opened the front door, Matt was standing there. He could hear the stereo in the library. Christmas carols. Donna, Billy Jack and the other two boys were waiting. They had decorated a tree. Its twinkling lights glowed in the dusk.

Chapter 37

Ariola paced back and forth across his office. Buck Ramsey, on the other hand, in a complete reversal of the two men's personalities, sat quietly on a sofa, waiting for Ariola to cool down and be reasonable. That is to say, to bend to Buck's will.

They couldn't agree on plans for Christmas.

"You've never missed a Ramsey Christmas for the past twenty years."

"I've never known you to be so concerned about Christmas in the last twenty years," Ariola retorted.

"That's just it. I guess I depended on Alta to take care of everything. She always did, and it always turned out just the way I wanted it."

Ariola nodded his agreement. "It did, didn't it? The way we all wanted it."

"This one would have been so great for Alta. Those three little boys—I just want everything to be the way she would have done it, things back the way they would have been—if she were here."

"It's never going to be the same, Buck. They're a new family. Let them do things their way. You can certainly be a doting grandpa, but just show up about mid-morning Christmas Day —unless you're invited earlier."

As for himself, he couldn't bear the thought of being at a Ramsey Christmas without Alta—or without Rica, yet he was uncomfortable expressing those feelings about either of them. He didn't feel entitled. He had loved Alta like a sister for all those years, but he felt Buck and the boys had more of a need to mourn her than he. The same for Rica—he had declared to himself and to the world only a few weeks before, that he no longer had any claim on her other than as her trust officer.

He must now act accordingly. He must be the strong one, defer to everyone else's needs.

Alta had usually had a large gathering in for eggnog and a dessert buffet on the Sunday afternoon before Christmas, then hosted a smaller group on Christmas Eve, and finally a family dinner at noon Christmas day. Ariola nixed every bit of that, pointing out that Donna and Billy Jack might want to take over some of those festivities and start some family traditions of their own.

It wasn't clear which of the two had the thought, or who finally spoke the words, but they did come out.

"I can't believe we've come to this. Two old nickel nuts arguing over how to celebrate Christmas."

They laughed at the irony of it. Neither had gotten the holiday spirit, yet here they were, trying to come up with the perfect plan to hide their fragile feelings. After sparring a while longer, they compromised. They'd have the family and a few friends in for dinner the week before Christmas. Their own *doings* would be out of the way.

As it turned out, the dinner was a perfect solution to a problem that hadn't been a problem to anyone except the two men. It had been close enough to Christmas to serve as their contribution to the holidays, but low key enough that their lack of high spirit didn't put a damper on the evening. It was like so many other Ramsey dinners except for the heartrending absence of Alta and Rica.

Freda was there. Ariola had called, asking about her plans for Christmas. She had already volunteered to work both Christmas Eve and Christmas Day so the people with families could take off, she told Ariola. She cheerfully told Jane the same thing. She knew in her heart, however, it had more than likely been a matter of self-defense. If Ariola happened to call, she would have a ready excuse to decline his invitation. If not, working would serve the same purpose—she couldn't have gone anyway.

When he asked her to the dinner, she had no excuse. She hadn't volunteered for anything that particular evening.

Nick also came out. His presence was, in itself, enough to make Buck happy, but a private moment they'd had made the evening absolutely perfect.

Returning from his room with an armful of books to take back to his apartment, he came over to Buck and whispered that he had seen the wagons stored in his closet. Nick then looked Buck in the eye and told him his own red wagon had been the best Christmas gift he'd ever received.

As the evening wound down, noticing Ariola helping Freda with her coat as they were about to leave, Donna commented to Buck, "They seem so comfortable together. How long have they been dating?"

"I don't know," Buck replied, "but if you asked either one of them, I'll bet they'd be quick to tell you they aren't."

Chapter 38

"Well, what's it going to be, Buck? Are you coming with us to the Brown? You can't beat a steak like that, not even out of the BAR4 herd."

Most of them knew the Brown's beef might very well have been Ramsey cattle, but that was not the point. They were just trying to gently lift their friend's spirit. Buck was undecided, but after a few more soft, yet badgering, remarks, he waved them away.

He was thinking about grabbing a sandwich next door, or skipping lunch all together, but didn't say as much. Some of them would be after him again.

He walked out into the brisk January sunshine, breathed deeply, already feeling better, yet knew he had rather be most any other place than where he was right now.

Continuing on, picking his way through the crowd, people passed him in all directions. Paying little attention to any of it, he gazed up and down the street, looking at nothing in particular. When he saw the quaint three story brick building that housed Valentine Swenson's publisher, he impulsively cut across toward it.

Jaywalking was not a wise thing to do on a busy noontime thoroughfare, but he felt reckless enough to try it, and at the same time, so listless he could have gotten hit by a car without caring one way or another. However, he made it. Maybe that was a good omen, and ending up where he did, an even better one.

He went inside, stopped at a pay phone and deposited the toll, before realizing he didn't know her number. He fished out his wallet and fanned through several business cards until he found the one Valentine had given him before Christmas.

Miss Swenson was not in. Could she give Miss Swenson his name? No, he'd try again later, but doubted he would.

He turned back to the entrance. Being outside was better than eating, anyway.

Nearly to the revolving door, he heard her call out, "Mr. Ramsey. Funny running into you here. Did you know you're in my building?"

"Hello, Valentine. Yes, I did. I just called upstairs to ask you to lunch."

"In town for another board meeting?"

"Right down the street.I didn't think about your working so close by until I happened to see your building. I had about decided to skip lunch and just walk instead. But, how about it?"

"You know, I was, too. I had some errands. But, sure, that sounds great. There is a little diner right here in the lobby. Pretty good, if you know what to pick."

"Fine. Just lead the way."

They found a table by a window. At her suggestion, he had the chef salad and she had a fruit plate.

"So how did those red wagons go over?" she asked after they had ordered.

"Just great," Buck answered. "In fact, the whole holiday was great. I was kind of worried, you know, Alta being—"

"I understand. The first Christmas after my parents died, I didn't make any plans, just kind of let it happen."

"That's exactly what I did, but only after some pretty straight talk from my partner—you remember Ariola?"

She acknowledged that she did.

"Well, I was set on having everything just the way Alta would have. Ariola convinced me to accept the fact that things—" he said, his voice faltering.

He straightened up when her eyes clouded with concern.

"He told me to let them start their own traditions, be the doting grandpa, but show up after they'd had their family Christmas, unless I was invited earlier."

"So that's what you did?"

"Yeah, and after thinking about it, it turned out exactly the way she would have wanted it. Donna and Bill had us out to their house for Christmas dinner, then New Years, we went up to Willowbranch."

"Willowbranch?"

"It's a cabin we built back in the hills. Alta named it Willowbranch."

"Willowbranch. What a pretty name."

"Not any more," he said in a cut-off tone, then added, "Here I've been going on about myself and didn't even find out about yours. What did you do?"

She hesitated, then said, "Oh, it was all right. I saw a few people."

He waited to hear more, but she closed the subject with, "It was great."

Their lunch came just in time. Christmas was forgotten.

They chatted as they ate. Buck found himself slowing to her leisurely pace. This was so refreshing—the food was better than he had tasted in a long time.

He knew that if he had not skipped out on the board luncheon, he would be wolfing down his food along with the others because of time, and try joining in their lively banter. One thing he could do in a crowd was cover himself with meaningless words. With Valentine, he didn't find that necessary.

He watched her as they ate. She had a dainty way about her, but so self-assured her style was beyond that. Elegant would seem a more accurate assessment. Elegant. Yes, elegant, but at the same time, so relaxed.

She had a polished look, too. Her hair in that same sleek French roll, the crisp, red suit, just the right cut and weight to be the harbinger of spring, nails in the same bright hue as the suit, short, but beautifully manicured, all adding up to that one simple, yet indiscernible word, elegant. What he returned to, however, was her poise.

There was no pretense, no special *company* manners meant to impress a new friend—new in the sense that he had not talked to her other than those few minutes in the toy store last month, for thirteen years.

He didn't actually remember much about the times she had been at the ranch, but Alta had happily talked about Joe's girl for days afterward.

Valentine remembered Buck, congenial, but usually just waving to the group on his way out, glad they were having fun.

Even though she knew Buck was only ten years older than Joe, to her nineteen-year-old way of thinking, he was her boyfriend's stepfather and therefore an old, old man.

They had not spoken at Joe's funeral except for one cordial hello. For a time, she felt a twinge of resentment that he had hardly acknowledged her presence. Later, she realized she had not been snubbed. He had talked very little to anyone that day.

Alta had explained that in the flurry of notes exchanged during those first months of grieving.

Moreover, even though Joe always called him Buck, she knew, as far as Joe had been concerned, Buck was his dad. In Valentine's mind, he had remained so. She was having lunch with Joe's dad.

Buck had reconnected with a friend at a time when he really needed a friend.

Chapter 39

As the hospital neared completion, the next phase had to be addressed—operating funds.

Buck came to the meeting a little late, but he came well prepared. Walking in with a thick folder in his hand, he laid it on the table in front of Ariola.

"Everything we'll need is in there," he said, and sat down beside his partner.

Ariola already knew what was in it. It was the Ramsey Registered Cattle file. Buck had been working hard to recover the huge loss on Alta's stock and was making considerable headway. He had also added more stock looking at long term growth. The portfolio was in good shape, but what Buck had just placed before Ariola would put it over the top.

The proceeds would be earmarked for the hospital operations fund, although there could have been other means to handle that.

There were many reasons for the sale of the herd, some holding more importance to Buck than others, but all were intertwined in his mind to the extent that he couldn't sort them out.

The prospect of taking over such an intricate business was a major drawback to Billy Jack's accepting his inheritance. He didn't want to be desk bound. Buck could also see years ahead when buyers would still look on the herd as Buck and Alta Ramsey's stock, making it hard for Bill to establish himself—understandable since it would be the same location, same brand, many of the same people around.

Buck also took the house into consideration. He had worked hard on convincing them to accept it.

He had gained a powerful tool with the announcement of the new baby. Why should a family of six be at Stone Creek while he lived alone in a huge house? The baby had won out. Sure enough, they would be moving into it soon.

So many activities connected to the Ramsey herd had taken place in that house. Would Bill and Donna feel comfortable continuing that or perhaps feel obligated but at the same time, resentful?

After thinking about it for months, Buck had decided to get rid of the herd. Clinching his decision was, without Alta, he just didn't have the heart to keep it.

Buck couldn't tolerate the thought of one last auction. He wanted the sale to amount to nothing more than a business transaction with papers signed and hands shaken so he had contacted three large operations that might be interested in it.

Mary Lou and Pauline had already begun the task of calculating a fair price for the whole herd. Ariola would take care of the transaction and he would be out of town, or at least not in sight. With that, another part of the BAR4 would be gone.

Chapter 40

Buck pulled into Valentine's driveway, turned off the engine, then sat there feeling rather foolish, so foolish, in fact, that he was hesitant to even ring the doorbell.

He had come to Denver to look at some land but hadn't so much as driven out that way. Instead, he had stopped at a service station on the edge of town to ask directions. He had never been on her street—she'd never invited him.

So, now what? The place looked deserted. He glanced again at the address. He was at the right spot, but she must be out of town for the weekend. He certainly *was* interested in the land, so he would have been in Denver anyway, but in addition to that, Joe's album lay on the seat beside him. He did want to show it to her and give her some of the pictures. He had been thinking about bringing it since she had told him one day at lunch that she had no pictures of Joe.

Her mother, with love and the best of intentions, wanted to help her daughter get on with her life following Joe's death. Valentine, strained and remote long past the time her mother thought she should be, had finally relented to her mother's unusual solution. She put the snapshots, souvenirs and his class ring, into a box and handed it to her mother. Valentine would not be getting rid of them, only putting them away until she was emotionally strong enough to enjoy the good memories, her mother had assured her.

When Valentine returned to her classroom, the small cedar handkerchief box was left behind. She had wound the little cylinder inside and listened as it plunked out its sad, tinny melody one last time, never to see it again. After the death of her parents, it had disappeared in the sorting and moving.

The new owners of the farm had cleaned the attic where Valentine suspected her mother had stored it, safe from her sad eyes when she came home on visits. She had told Buck she would never again keep anything that had to be put in the attic.

When she told him the story, she spoke with little emotion, simply explaining to Buck why she had no pictures of Joe. The years had dulled the pain and she accepted it as a cruel twist of fate. Hearing it for the first time, Buck felt a deep sense of loss for Valentine. Her mother's reasoning might have been quite logical, but he still wanted to give Valentine some pictures of Joe.

He now sat in an empty driveway. Oh, well, he could drive out to the land, then call Valentine if it wasn't too late.

He started the engine and was about to back out of the driveway, when she came around the corner of the garage. He had not seen her approach, but heard her call out. He was getting out of the car before she got there, but she couldn't resist saying it anyway.

"Since you're so close, why don't you get out and stay awhile."

His face flushed, but he only hoped she hadn't noticed.

"I don't know why I didn't ring your bell. It looked like you weren't home. I had some business up this way, so I decided to bring those pictures by."

"I thought I heard a car out here and I'm glad it was you. I need you."

He didn't like his twinge of delight at those words. This was, after all, Joe's girl he was talking to.

He recovered quickly, and asked in a bland, hopefully indifferent, voice, "What's going on?"

"I'm putting up shelves in my garage and need you to hold the hammer," she said, displaying that same radiant smile, this time coupled with a mischievous glint that found him hard pressed to turn his eyes away from her lips.

He was glad this lapse had gone unnoticed by her and said agreeably, "Sure. I believe I'm up to that."

"And I see you're in your work clothes," she said, eyeing his jeans. "Come on."

He followed her to the side door of the double, oversized garage. Valentine's little red MG, dwarfed by the huge space, was parked close to the far wall. It occupied only about a third of the floor. In the center, a number of cardboard boxes, obviously sealed and labeled by professional movers, stood in a neat row. Four boxes were labeled china while another three were marked crystal. The last was marked silver serving pieces.

"Mother's dishes," she stated decisively, then hesitating before continuing, "I don't see how three people could have used so many dishes, but we did. She was always cooking for a crowd and enjoyed setting a pretty table.

She used most of this every Sunday. If I have people in, it's usually barbecue out back."

"They look well-packed," Buck observed.

"I guess they are. They've survived several moves. Always took up badly needed space in the apartments I've lived in. And you know what a premium closet space is in an apartment."

Buck nodded, although he actually had no idea about closets and apartments.

"So," she continued, "when I got my own place, I decided to put up some shelves out here. I hate to get rid of all her beautiful things, even though I'll probably never use them."

"Well, it looks like you have plenty of room. Have you lived here long?"

"Only a few months, actually. This is my first house. I bought it right after I got back from London."

She surveyed the pile of boards lying in wait, then continued, "I'll show you around when we finish."

"Good," he said. "I'd like that."

She had completed the frame earlier, nailing two by fours to the wall and floor. As they worked, she explained that she had drawn a diagram of the shelf she envisioned, and ordered all the material delivered, precut.

"Looks like you're a pretty good engineer," he said.

"Pretty good?" she admonished, smiling to take the sting out of her words.

"Real good," he corrected himself. "You remind me of Alta. She could do anything that needed to be done."

"Well, being an only child, Daddy taught me to do lots of things. When he needed some help, I was his boy. I spent a lot more time on the tractor and in the barn than helping Mother."

"You would have fit right in at the ranch," he said wistfully.

"Thanks," she said.

After that, they worked in silence except for occasional directions from her. The shelf was finished in about thirty minutes. Buck stacked the boxes on it and stood back to look at their handy work.

"You could have a dance in here now," he said with genuine satisfaction.

"Lets go dancing, ourselves," she replied gaily. "Such good carpenters deserve it."

"Yes, we do," he agreed, delighted at the prospect, then glancing down at his denims, he continued, "but this is all I have with me."

"Come on," she chided. "I know a joint where you'll be the best dressed guy in the room."

"Well, all right. Why not?"

"Let me she show you my house first. Then I'll give you a glass of tea while I change. After that, we'll be ready to roll."

They sat at her kitchen table, a heavy round oak on pedestal stand—one of the handful of pieces she had kept from her childhood home.

She took only a few sips of tea, then excused herself. He watched moisture condense on his glass while looking around her kitchen. It was light and roomy and homey. Lots of white tile and metal. Mesh bags of garlic, onions and red chilies hung from a wrought iron rack. Another rack held brightly polished copper pans and kettles. A green, slightly tarnished, metal baker's rack was filled to brimming with brightly colored pottery. Despite its wide mixture of themes, it was a pretty room. Perhaps that was the charm of it. The room simply served as a backdrop for its owner's lifestyle. She apparently believed in being surrounded by things she loved and enjoyed.

More than the few minutes she had promised passed before she returned, but he didn't mind. When she did appear, she looked completely fresh in a soft peach colored skirt and blouse. Her tiered skirt, nearly ankle length, rustled slightly as she walked. The blouse, its drawstring neck fastened with a pretty bow, matched the skirt perfectly. She wore a heavy silver belt and flat tan sandals.

He nodded his approval, saying, "It was worth the wait."

"Thanks," she said, and smiled that smile.

Glancing around her kitchen, he said, "I thought you didn't cook."

"I don't. I just want to have it in case I change my mind. Besides, I love to smell it. Don't you just love the smell?"

He had to agree he did.

"Ready?" he asked, anxious to show her the land. After all, that was the main reason he had come to Denver.

They were well out of town before it occurred to either they had missed lunch. They had worked on the shelves past noon. Then after a tour of her back yard and a quick view of the living room before ending up at the kitchen table, another hour had passed. There were also those well spent minutes she used to change and freshen up. It was near mid-afternoon, so they decided to drive on and have an early dinner.

The land, about two hundred acres of rolling hills and lush meadows dotted with small groves of pine and aspen, was crisscrossed with well-kept gravel roads. A small stream ran close to a large clearing suitable for a house. While driving over the land, Buck thought about the first time he had taken Alta to Willowbranch. Things had been so different then. He and Alta were approaching their happiest years that morning. Today, he was simply looking for a place to lick his wounds.

The young woman beside him was sincerely interested in seeing the land because it was, after all, a beautiful property.

She would enjoy having Buck so close to Denver. She had begun to genuinely like him. He would be a pleasant lunch companion, and after tonight, a sometimes dancing partner.

He had yet to tell her why he was looking for a new place. He didn't know her well enough. Perhaps it might come out later by bits and pieces, perhaps not. He might never reach the point that he wanted to talk to her about it. At the moment, he just wanted to show her Joe's album.

Chapter 41

Buck drove across the clearing and stopped as close as possible to the stream. The moment he parked, Valentine was out of the car and down the gentle embankment. He saved himself from calling out *be careful*, or *watch out,* or some other senseless warning that adults instinctively give children, knowing all the while they will go unheeded. He smiled instead, reminded of Alta. She would have cautioned the boys to watch out for snakes. He'd heard her warn them countless times, although during all those years, he doubted they had come across more than fifteen or twenty, and most of those only bull snakes, usually long and fierce looking, but harmless. That was simply Alta's way of telling her sons that she cared for them, that she wanted them to be safe.

He didn't know why he was compelled to look after Valentine. She was certainly no child, but she had been Joe's girl. Perhaps that was the reason he felt so protective of her, why he wanted to race after her, make sure she came to no harm.

He was alarmed at his feelings, and knew she would be, too, so he trailed behind her down to the stream where he remarked casually, "Do you suppose there might be any trout in there?"

"Could be. If we don't have any soon, they'll begin stocking upstream. You'll have all you can eat before you know it." She was obviously a more experienced fisherman than he.

"Sounds like you've done some fishing."

"Quite a bit," she said. "Daddy's girl, you know."

"I used to do a little when the boys were younger. Haven't for a few years, though."

"Well, are you in luck! Today I taught you to build a shelf. Soon I'll have you fishing like a pro."

He liked the sound of that. Her chatter, along with that smile, prompted him to come back with uncharacteristic repartee of his own.

"And don't forget about tonight. It's been a lot of years since I've been dancing. Probably step all over your toes. And you in those sandals."

"I might not be of much help there," she said. "It's been a long time since I've done any dancing myself."

"That's not all bad. Neither of us will have any need to be embarrassed," he reasoned.

"Right. We can relearn our moves together," she said.

He liked the sound of that, too.

She abruptly turned her attention back to the stream.

"Look at those pebbles," she said. "They're beautiful. I've never seen quite so many black ones together. Could I have a few of your pebbles?"

"They aren't mine yet, but I don't think Mr. Fleming would mind. Anyway, we won't mention it to him."

He reached down into the stream and came up with a double handful.

"Thanks. Oh, but now you've gotten yourself wet."

"No problem. I dry fast. But we'll spread these out on this rock for a little while."

Laying them down, he dried with his handkerchief.

"Lets give them a minute and go on back to the car. Remember, I brought along that album."

"Sure," she said.

As they walked back up the incline, that same fleeting confusion crossed his mind. One moment he was with a beautiful woman talking about fishing, going dancing, with a hint of a developing friendship. Then he was walking beside a girl, intent on showing her pictures of his dead stepson. She would have been his daughter-in-law, if life had gone the way it had been intended.

That solemn reminder quickly dispelled the confusion. It was the girl who walked beside him now. The woman had been left at the stream, admiring the glossy pebbles that he had gathered for her.

He helped her into the car and started to close the door, but she suggested it be left open to catch the breeze.

He got the album out of the back seat, handing it to her before sliding in behind the wheel.

"It's not at all what I thought it would be," she said, studying the brown leather binding.

She had envisioned a faded old book, worn and brittle from years of use.

"Oh, it's new. It's one of the last things she did. Last year. She fixed up one for Nick and Bill, too. I guess this one was for me. I found it in her desk."

His voice trailed, and sensing that he was not ready to begin looking at the book, she remained silent, waiting for him to continue.

"Our bunch was always on the run. We had boxes stuffed with pictures, but never enough time to sort them out. Seems as though you only realize a little too late that there are things a lot more important than all that running."

"We all live with some regrets," she offered.

"I have more than my share," he said. He was loaded with them. For a moment—but only for a moment—he felt the urge to say more.

He slid closer and opened the book that lay on her lap.

She laughed with delight when she saw the first page. The only picture on it was the black and white photo of all of them ringed around a drilling rig.

"Alta always said that was when our life began."

There they were, all six of them. No, seven. Ariola was in there, too. The four boys were covered with mud. Buck, Alta and Ariola were grinning from ear to ear. So were the boys, but they dared not open their mouths too wide. They had already found the gritty sand to be sharp to the teeth.

Sam Whitlock had taken the one shot, but that was enough. Many copies had been made through the years. A large print hung in Buck's office, and Alta had put one on the first page of each of her son's picture albums. Buck's album contained the small original, its edges tattered, the only picture on the first page.

That picture, meant to bring laughter, delight at seeing such a scrappy, but joyful bunch, should have caused the very reaction that it evoked from Valentine.

For Buck, at least for today, the sight of it brought on a feeling completely opposite to what Alta had intended. As he looked at it, a wave of remorse, so deep he couldn't bear having her turn the page, swept over him. He wanted that day back. He longed for yesterday.

Yes, this was when their life began, Alta had said. Her simple truism had been correct, but now it was all gone. It had ended where it had begun, with Alta.

He had to get himself together. It had been his idea to bring the album to show her. She would have little patience with a blubbering old man. Besides, he felt pretty foolish. He was supposed to enjoy showing her the album.

Valentine's laughter finally penetrated Buck's gloom. He listened as it grew softer, finally turning into sporadic giggles. That lighthearted sound brought him back to this sunny afternoon where they sat, looking at his life.

"This is just precious," she said. "Look at that Nick. How old was he? About two?"

"A little over three," Buck mumbled.

After one final gaze, she did turn the page, and he was able to watch as she lingered over each picture.

There were few baby pictures, only one studio picture of Joe. The rest, snapshots, all four boys at various stages, some individual shots of each child, and a couple of the four sitting on the porch with their grandparents. There was one of Alta, about age twelve with her blonde hair in braids, none of Jack and her together. None of Jack, period.

"They just didn't take many pictures back then," Buck remarked.

"Maybe the breeze is a little too much after all," she said, and reached over to pull the door closed.

She turned those next few pages. When she arrived at the section of the book where Buck was in the pictures he began talking more as he pointed out the various events that had been captured with Alta's little box camera.

Among the first was one of Alta and Joe side by side, both in jeans and long sleeved shirts, both with blonde hair that curled around their ears.

"Oh, my gosh. They looked like twins, didn't they?"

"When I first met them, it was hard to tell them apart," he said and laughed softly.

"She was thirty and he was fourteen."

"Gosh, just sixteen years old with a baby," she said.

"Yeah, kind of young to start a family. She quit high school to marry Jack. But she did all right. She was little, but tough as nails."

"Well, she was a beautiful lady," Valentine said.

Buck nodded.

They continued looking, the pictures dredging up scraps of pleasant memories.

When they came to the section that contained Joe's NeeDee High School days, Buck said, "There's some of you in there."

"Not many. We moved right after my sophomore year."

"You're in there. Alta found a picture of you in Joe's box. You were a cheerleader, right?"

"I can't believe it. Let me see that," she barked.

When they found the page, Valentine looked closely, frowning a little, but giggling at the same time.

The picture of Alta pinning on Joe's wings came soon after. Valentine looked at it for a long moment, but did not comment. He searched for a change of expression on her face but noticed little.

The last page contained an enlarged snapshot of Joe standing beside the Alta Vista. She looked at it, her eyes tearing slightly, but still said nothing. She closed the book and looked out the window, turning her face away.

He waited for a time before speaking. "I brought it so you could take some of the pictures."

When she faced him, her eyes were clear.

"No."

"No?" Buck questioned. "Really. I don't mind. And I know Alta would have loved for you to have them."

"No," she said again firmly, rubbing the book that still lay on her lap. "This is for you and your family. Alta made it for you. It should stay with you, intact. Besides," she added softly, "I don't want any of them."

Buck was stunned at those words. *How could she not want them?*

His silence prompted her to go on.

"Look," she said, "That was all so long ago. Joe was a wonderful young man. I wore his high school ring and promised to wait for him. We would probably have married. I say probably because, looking back, I can understand how war changes people. Both the ones who serve and the ones waiting at home."

It was now he who looked out the window.

"You know, I realized several years ago, and I'm sorry to say, only after quite a lot of bitterness toward her, that my mother was right all along. Mom having convinced me to store those pictures was the best way for me to get on with my life. I was twenty one years old, and would you believe, to this day, some of my relatives still think the reason I never married was because of losing Joe."

Buck remained silent, still looking out the window. Her voice softened as she continued.

"I hope you can understand why I don't want any of those pictures. It's not that I never think of Joe. I do. I just don't want to think of him standing beside that B-24.

When I see a little red airplane? That's when I think of him. And when I think of him that way, I smile. You can't imagine how sophisticated I felt when he would fly down to Eastern to see me. And all those other girls hoping their boyfriends could borrow a car to take them to the drive-in." She laughed as her voice trailed off.

That brought Buck's head around and a smile to his pained face.

Her next remark brought a deep, spontaneous chuckle out of him.

"You must realize, Mr. Ramsey," she said wryly, "you are not looking at a war widow, you are looking at an old maid."

"But a pretty one, for sure," he said, returning her grin as he took the book from her and laid it in the back seat.

"We'd better go pick up your pebbles. It's getting pretty late and remember, we haven't eaten yet."

"How can I forget?" she said in mock anguish, patting her stomach. She reached for the door handle.

"Just a second, Valentine. I think I might have a box in the trunk."

Her hand withdrew as if she had changed her mind about getting out.

"And that's another thing. This Valentine stuff has to stop. My mother named me that, over protests from my dad."

"Born on Valentine's Day?"

"Goodness, no. My birthday's in August. It was after some actress, I think."

"It's a nice name," he said.

"If you're an actress, I guess it is," she replied tartly.

"Anyway, all my friends call me Val. Grandmother is the only one left who calls me Valentine."

"I still say it's a nice name. A pretty name."

"Oh, go ahead then."

"No," he said, a bit surprised at her sudden petulance.

"Val it is, if you'll stop this Mr. Ramsey this, Mr. Ramsey that. Makes me feel old."

"Okay. If we're going dancing tonight, we should be on a first name basis. Right?"

"Agreed, Val." He stuck out his hand, and she took it in a firm handshake.

"Buck," she said, then added, "Seems as though we've cleared the air of lots of things."

She never again called him Mr. Ramsey, that is, except under very special circumstances. In years to come, if he heard Val calling him Mr. Ramsey, it could only mean one of two things. He was in for a lot of trouble, or in for a lot of fun.

That said, they gathered their pebbles and drove back to Denver for a nice dinner. Later that evening, they went dancing. They found they danced very well together.

Chapter 42

Buck had been home from Denver about ten minutes when Donna came through the back door with some news. Lorene Eagle would be arriving in a few minutes and hopefully be spending a few days at the house.

He was astounded to hear that Lorene was in NeeDee in the first place, and surprised to find that Donna had insisted she come to dinner, but he was more than a little perturbed when she added she was hoping Buck would invite her to stay at the house.

"Have you ever considered that there's two real good motels in NeeDee, and a couple more that aren't so bad?"

"We can't ask a lady like Lorene to stay in a motel, especially with her injured leg. You're gone most of the time anyway. Besides, she won't be here very long."

A lady like Lorene was a phrase Donna grabbed loosely. She actually didn't know what kind of a lady Lorene was—in fact, she knew nothing about her, having been with her only those few hours in Las Vegas for the wedding. But she did know how grateful they all had been for Lorene's expertise.

"Then have you considered what happened the last time we had a houseguest with a broken leg? We kept him around long enough for him to die."

"She only has a bad sprain. And as I said, she won't be here long."

"And how long is that?"

"I don't know exactly. Only long enough to be able to handle her car, I guess. Nick said a week or so."

"So Nick's in on this, too."

"No one is in on anything. This isn't some sort of scheme, Buck."

"I just happened to be at the service station when she fell. She'd stopped to use the pay phone—to call you, as a matter of fact. I recognized her from Las Vegas."

She regretted mentioning Las Vegas when Buck's jaws balled into tight knots, but she had to make her point. He wasn't taking the news well—an unexpected houseguest not of his choosing, certainly not a beautiful blonde one that he hardly knew—so she hurried on.

"Well, naturally, I took her to Nick's office."

"You?"

"Not exactly." She looked down at her huge body.

"I couldn't do much. Ray helped her into her car and drove. I just followed along in mine."

"He was the only one working, and had to close the station to do it."

"I'll bet he was plenty glad to shut down—to get her out of his driveway and to the hospital."

"It wasn't that way at all. No one was blaming him. He was just being kind."

She frowned, adding, "A lot kinder than you're acting."

He grinned at her. She could push him further than any of the rest of them and she knew it.

"So how about it?" Donna questioned as she returned his smile.

Before he could reply, the question had been answered. Nick pulled under the portico with Lorene Eagle in the seat beside him.

Buck and Donna went down the steps in time to help Lorene inside. The men supporting her at the elbow, she hopped clumsily up the steps. Donna carried her crutches, which she'd not yet managed to master.

"Nothing like making a grand entrance, I always say," Lorene said dryly after having been seated in a soft chair and handed a tall glass of iced tea.

"You can handle an entrance with the best of them," Ariola said as he came in.

"You were magnificent in Vegas."

No one else commented, so he added, "and taking care of all the rest of it so professionally."

Everyone else, even Buck, seemed bent on pushing the Vegas wedding out of their memories. The staging of that wedding had been the most appalling task Ariola had undertaken. He, too, tried to push it out of his mind, but seeing Lorene here today brought it all vividly back—yet he was genuinely glad to see her. He gave her all the credit for pulling it together as well as it had been.

He had come in the back door just as Nick had driven up, needing only a few minutes with him to go over some construction details, but when he saw Lorene there in the library, he sat down for a long visit.

"Nick seems to think you'll be off that foot for a while. How is Las Vegas going to get along without you?" Ariola continued.

"It seems Vegas is going to be getting along without me just fine," she said, then added quickly, "but that's another story. Right now, I'd better be thinking about getting a ride back to town with Nick and find me a place to stay."

She clearly didn't intend to say more about Vegas.

Buck knew what Donna expected of him.

"No way," he said.

His voice cracking like a kid fumbling for the correct words, he stopped to clear his throat, then continued.

"We're planning on you staying right here."

"That's nice of you, Buck, but I wouldn't dream of it."

"Sure you would," Nick joined in. He looked at Buck and said, "We can put her in Paul's quarters, what with these stairs and everything."

"Oh, no. I don't think she would care for that," Donna intervened.

Buck momentarily wondered when he'd gotten to the point that his children had started making decisions for him, then he chimed in.

"This makes into a bed," he said, patting the sofa on which he was sitting. "Never been used as far as I know," he added.

They all looked toward Lorene.

She shrugged her acceptance, then said, "But I have to warn you, Buck. I make a terrible houseguest. Sleep late. Drink tons of coffee and use dozens of towels."

"No problem," Buck said.

"I have to be in Chicago by tomorrow night, but we have plenty of coffee and plenty of towels. Anything else you need, Ariola will be right here."

Chapter 43

Freda was never quite sure how or why it happened, but her world made a complete turnaround in a matter of days.

On Monday, she arrived at the hospital to find that Jane had eloped with the boyfriend she had declared only days before that she never wanted to see again. He had landed a good job in Houston. In the burst of excitement created by that feat, they not only reconciled, he proposed. Jane hesitated a few moments—long enough to consider the hundreds of miles between NeeDee and Houston, and to think about the months that might pass before he could return to NeeDee for a wedding—before saying yes. She then called her mother in Tucumcari, and that nice lady performed an even greater feat. By the time Jane and her fellow got there, she had a preacher, flowers and a cake, plus several friends, waiting at her house.

Jane told Freda all this when she called on Tuesday night. Freda had been in Santa Fe for a rare weekend of shopping, and had missed it all. She had to smile at the thought of the bustle that must have gone on.

By Wednesday, Freda was missing her friend's drop-in, after-work visits. She even missed her incessant chatter about Ariola. While Freda had constantly insisted that Jane not mention him, she now felt the absence of that chitchat.

Two days later, Freda received the call that Ariola had told her to expect. Rica offered a self-effacing apology in the first minutes of that conversation, which Freda had quickly brushed aside as unnecessary.

With each additional call, the two became more relaxed. Freda talked about her challenging new job at the hospital while Rica spoke of having been invited to join the faculty wives club and the whirlwind duties of keeping a house going and a husband happy, plus preparing for the baby.

There was the layette to be planned and names to be considered. Warren was certain he would have a son, and Rica would settle for nothing less than Warren Wilson, Jr.

Freda never told Ariola of Rica's vibrant demeanor, in fact, seldom mentioned her at all. While he was concerned with the care and protection of a bewildered girl, Freda was talking almost daily with a young woman basking in the excitement of a fulfilling life and dazzled by the love and attention of a handsome, dashing new husband.

After some of those calls, having had dinner with Ariola the same evening, Freda awoke in the night. She loathed that wakefulness. The lack of sleep didn't bother her—she had long been able to steel herself against the grueling hours of nursing—it was an ache, a sense of sadness that overwhelmed her. She felt something happening that ought not to happen. Her feelings for Ariola were changing.

She'd had only two relationships, both ending badly. The first, her senior year in college, while she was positive he was the love of her life, he was drowning in frustration. With graduation in sight, he had dropped out of school and disappeared.

Now, with Paul still a searing pain in her heart, how could she feel anything for Ariola other than what their relationship was meant to be? Rica was the only reason they saw each other.

Friendship was all Ariola wanted from her. After one of those dinners, they decided to try dancing again. As they danced, she looked up at him and smiled. When their eyes met, she felt his arm tighten slightly around her waist.

He's thinking about Rica. She looked away quickly to hide her trembling lips.

He must control himself. She's thinking about Paul.

Both soon decided they'd had enough dancing, and made an early evening of it.

She slept a few hours before that wakefulness returned.

Chapter 44

Buck was on his way back to Denver well before his upcoming board meeting. In fact, less than a week since he'd been there, he was again racing up the highway, this time, with part of his family and some of his friends in tow. Lorene was at the wheel.

Val had mentioned to him that she was having a signing the coming weekend and would be delighted to have them all there.

Nearly everyone had been reluctant at first. Ariola's schedule was already overextended. Nick was busy at the hospital. Billy Jack didn't want Donna riding so many hours. Jeff and David, even with a side trip to the Denver Zoo, couldn't give up their weekend of horseback riding. Only Matthew stood firm. He was anxious to meet the lady who had written his most recent favorite book.

He had never yet managed to see a real mouse, but he was curious to see if a real mouse's tail was as long, its ears and eyes as big, its coat as glossy, as that mouse in his new book. Could it really talk, and was its smile so bright it sparkled? He wanted to meet that lady.

Matt prevailed in the end. Most of them were on their way to Denver. Jeff and David were agreeable when it was worked out for them to fly up with Nick and Ariola.

Nick had been totally indifferent when Buck had first mentioned the trip. He still felt a bit of disdain at most anything from Buck, but this time Buck persisted strongly enough, or perhaps long enough, that Nick agreed to go. The deciding factor that finally caught Nick's attention was curiosity. Why Buck's interest in a book signing? He hadn't seen Buck this persistent about anything since their confrontation in the attorney's office.

Just a nice gesture since Val and Joe had been so close, Buck told him. It would mean a lot to her for them to be there since she had no family of her own.

Ariola gladly changed his schedule. He was anxious to go, feeling this outing would be exactly what Alta would want for her family. Perhaps this could be the beginning of healing. The last thing they had done together as a family, besides Christmas, of course, had been to bury Alta.

It was probably Donna who had finally convinced them all to go. She seemed to be taking Alta's place as the family peacemaker. There was no denying they needed it badly.

It was Billy Jack and Donna who didn't go after all. Donna had to admit at the last minute that she wasn't up to the trip.

Ariola called Freda and explained the situation. He hated to impose on her weekend, but would she please accompany them to Denver? Donna wasn't able to go, and she would feel more comfortable about the children having Freda with them. Lorene Eagle would be going, but she had plans to fly out of Denver back to Las Vegas. He would also be delighted to have her along.

Of course you would.

"Tell Donna I'll be happy to do it," she said. "See you in the morning."

"Freda, I'm glad you're going," Ariola said again, but the phone clicked off before he finished.

They saw Ariola, Nick, Jeff and David off at the airport and were about to leave, themselves, when a problem arose. In spite of being the most enthusiastic of the group, at the last minute Matt became reluctant to leave his parents for a whole weekend. Buck was anxious for him to go. After all, it was a signing for Matt's favorite book, and none of them would be going if not for the children. Matt would not consider going at all unless he was in Papaw's lap in the back seat.

Lorene volunteered to drive.

She had been thinking about trading off her Ford, and would like to see how a larger car handled on the road.

Freda noted what a problem solver Lorene was, and how simple the solution had been. She, on the other hand, had not thought about driving. *She could see she wasn't needed on this trip.*

Nevertheless, Freda found herself enjoying Lorene's chatter as the miles zipped by. Soon after they left, Matt had his papaw involved in story telling. Not too long after that, Buck's soft drone, and Matt's even quieter comments, had silenced. Freda glanced back, and nodded to Lorene. They were both asleep.

As the two women continued talking, Freda's spirits lifted. She was now determined to enjoy the trip.

The first order of the day was a late lunch with Val. They were to meet her at a restaurant near the bookstore. Ariola had gotten a car at the airport, and he, Nick and the boys were waiting with Val on benches in the foyer when the others arrived.

Nick had spotted Val right away, but she was a little uncertain of him. He soothed her embarrassment by noting that he had changed more in thirteen years than she.

Val and Ariola were glad to see each other again. After Ariola introduced the boys, they were soon busy with coloring books she had brought along in case there was a wait, while the adults enjoyed renewing old friendships.

Val and Nick were soon engrossed in conversation. Ariola sat back, listening. Nick was at his most charming, yet cutting enough to draw Val's ire. Ariola soon realized that she had the verve to hold her own and then some, with Nick

Nick was impressed to be in the company of a writer, but after a pleasant discussion of the latest New York best sellers, he asked why she had chosen something as mindless as children's books when she could have gone into serious literature.

Ariola was aghast at such a remark, but noting Val's poised countenance, he relaxed and again retreated to his listening.

She began explaining part of the process of writing for children, something Nick apparently knew little about.

The first step, at least for her, was to come up with a prototype of the main character.

"You don't do your own illustrations?" Nick asked.

"No way. My publishers couldn't get a single copy off the shelf if they depended on my illustrating," she replied with a smile, then continued, "but I lay the story out and have my character's personality figured out enough to get it across to the illustrator with a sketch pad."

"You mean to tell me you can sketch a character's personality?"

"Sure," Val answered. "I try, anyway, and have a pretty good grip on it most of the time. People's personality shines through, Nick—and reflects their looks. All that red hair, that twinkle in your eye? Even as a kid, you were such a cut-up."

Ariola intervened, "Do I hear a pun there? Cut-up? Surgeon?"

Nick guffawed and the little boys giggled, even though they had no idea about what a pun might be.

After that, Nick and Val continued talking more seriously, with Val going into the targeted age level, their attention span at that level, the psychological affect of the story line, and other details to be considered.

Nick nodded in what could have been taken as understanding and appreciation, but when a hint of a patronizing smile appeared, she continued. She had taken her first degree in early childhood development, but had gone deeper into children's literature in graduate school.

By then, he was truly impressed, but she couldn't resist adding, "Nick, don't worry. I won't be switching to surgery any time soon."

"Whoa, whoa," Nick said, throwing up his hands in submission. "I left myself wide open for that one."

"And you got it, too, you little twerp," Lorene chimed in. They had all arrived, all laughing.

Everyone was introduced, then seated quickly. Buck had made sure a table would be waiting. Ariola pulled out a chair for Freda and ordered a booster seat for Matt, who had requested to sit by her.

"Well," Nick spoke up, "since we're choosing, I dibs on sitting by Val."

Buck was pleased to see them getting along so well.

Nick had won a place beside Val, but he failed at monopolizing her conversation. Val included everyone.

While they were working on their salads, she asked Freda about her involvement with the family.

"Buck and Ariola took me in when the man I was about to marry died."

Ariola interceded, "That sad beginning turned into much more. We're very close now."

"Good friends," Freda added.

In hopes of lightening the conversation, Val turned to Lorene, asking if she had lived in NeeDee long.

"No, I've been in Vegas the past several years, but we do go way back. I left NeeDee two days after they arrived there."

"How did you happen to reconnect?" Val inquired.

Lorene realized, from the silence of all the adults, that Val was unaware of the Vegas wedding she had arranged.

She continued in her guileless way, "They took me in, too, for a few days—with a sprained ankle—but, I imagine they're relieved that I'm on my way back to Vegas."

Lorene had made another save.

They were about to finish eating when Val excused herself to get to the store.

Buck looked at his watch and said he believed he'd have time to take them out to see what they thought of the land.

Buck had talked to Ariola about it, but Nick was taken by surprise.

"More land?" he questioned. "What are you up to now, Buck? Gonna buy Denver?"

"Just a couple of hundred acres. Bill and Donna are about ready to move into the house, so I figure I'd better be looking at something."

"Are *you* moving?" Jeff asked, alarmed at that thought.

"No, no. Don't worry. There's not even a house on it."

The little boys sighed with relief.

"Don't know what I'll do. Might even move into the bunkhouse," he said.

A simultaneous cheer went up from the three. That had not crossed his mind before this moment, but it seemed to have served him well.

"You can't do that, Buck. They'd be spoiled rotten," Lorene objected.

"Not these fellows. They're too big for that."

"Can't you come with us, Val?" Nick asked.

"I wish I could, but I have to get over to the store and set up," she replied, then turned to Buck.

"Is it the same land you showed me a few weeks ago, Buck?"

He nodded.

"It's a beautiful place," she said to Nick. "You'll all love it," she added.

Lorene started to comment, but just smiled instead.

Val stood up. Buck was half out of his chair but Nick was up quicker and said, "I'll walk you to the door."

"I'll see you all at the signing," she said to the group as they left.

The book signing began at four o'clock. A slow moving line of children waited patiently—as patiently as could be managed at that age, each clutching a book A number of mothers and teachers stood close by, Freda among them.

Matt stood between his two brothers. He was one of the

youngest in line, but one of the most interested. He was enthralled with the book, and after having met Val, even more taken by its author. Watching this, Buck beamed. The boy must be advanced for his age, he thought.

Ariola, Nick and Lorene chatted quietly, but Buck was hardly aware of them. He scanned the line until his eyes rested on Val's table, then on Val, herself, where they remained most of the time. He liked the way she handled each signing.

As a child handed Val a book, she asked for his or her name. Turning the book in her hands, she studied it as if that child might have picked the most special book from the stack on the counter. She then inscribed it with the small owner's name and the words *enjoy this book. May it be the beginning of a lifetime of reading.*

For many of the children, it was.

The signing over, Val had to leave immediately on an unexpected business trip. One of her associates had become ill, and she had to take his place. She apologized for having invited them up, only to leave.

Lorene was undecided about which one was more disappointed, Buck, Nick or Matt.

After dinner, Freda took the boys up to the suite they were sharing. She supposed the rest of them also made an early evening of it, but was tired enough that she didn't give it thought. After a few hours of sleep, that wakefulness was back. She got up and sat by the window, looking at the scattered lights of Denver.

With Lorene on the plane to Vegas, Ariola and Nick already half way back to NeeDee, the three little boys, content and tired after the promised visit to the zoo, asleep in the back seat, Freda and Buck spent most of the ride home in comfortable silence.

Chapter 45

Freda called Jane Monday night. They usually talked during the weekend, but after she'd unpacked and read the paper Sunday night, it was too late, and besides, she was feeling a little too gloomy to talk to anyone.

Jane was feeling just the opposite. She had meant to call Freda, but had been dragged around every waking hour looking for a house. They'd moved into a furnished studio apartment and would have to buy furniture, too, but must decide on a house before looking at anything. Her new husband was wonderful, had the best job imaginable, wouldn't let her consider finding a job until they were in their own home, and then, only if she could find something strictly nine to five. He had to have her with him every night. She couldn't imagine how she could have said all those bad things about him during the time they had been broken up.

This news, all spouted in less than three minutes, served a good purpose though. It brought Freda out of her doldrums.

After Jane finished, she asked about Freda's weekend.

"I went to Denver—to a book signing."

Jane gasped. That sounded like a bombshell to her.

"With Ariola?"

"No—well, yes, I guess you could say that, but also with Buck and his three grandkids, and Nick and a lady named Lorene that you don't know."

"But did Ariola ask you?"

"No. Yes. Oh, for heaven's sake, Jane. He did ask me, but to take care of the kids. Donna is too far along to travel."

"But he did ask you. You're the one he depends on."

"No, I'm the one Donna depends on. She'd probably like to hire me as a nanny if I were willing."

Freda's edgy tone let Jane know she'd hit a nerve.

"Well, she *is* a nurse. And apparently, she didn't want this Lorene person to take care of them. So she got Ariola to ask you. See? Even *she* knows you two are close."

"Get off it, Jane. I did go. I took care of the kids. I had a pleasant time. That's it."

"What about this Lorene? Why was she along? Buck's new girlfriend?"

"Jane," Freda said in a threatening tone.

"Well, I just wondered. I've never heard of her, and I've just been gone a few weeks."

"I hate talking like this. I'll say it once, and I don't want it mentioned again. Is that clear?"

"Sure," Jane said meekly.

"I'd never met her until a few days ago. She knew Buck and his family years ago, before either one of us moved here. Now she lives in Las Vegas."

"So she's back here visiting—going to Denver with Buck, and you tell me she'd not his girlfriend?"

Freda was silent.

Jane, never one to tolerate silence, continued, "There's nothing wrong that I can see with his having a girlfriend. Is she pretty?"

"Yes, and very nice—a lot of fun to be around, but she's already back in Vegas. And no, she's not his girlfriend."

"I'll bet she wishes she were."

"Jane, I'm going to finish this thing, and be done with it. Understood?"

"All right," Jane agreed.

"You remember that fiasco last year about Buck and Alta having never married?"

Freda didn't wait for a reply—Jane and everyone in NeeDee and far beyond knew it—but continued, "Well, Lorene was the one who organized the wedding."

"Wow," Jane said softly, and was truly through asking more questions. She thought too much of Alta's memory to mention it again.

"I don't know why I can't keep my trap shut, Freda. I'm sorry, really sorry."

"Forgiven and forgotten," Freda replied.

"So, what about you?" Why don't you come to see me? Help me house hunt."

"Can't. I'm too busy. The hospital will soon be opening, and we have three doctors and several nurses and some more staff coming in. Besides, I'm sure that husband of yours doesn't need any help."

"Well, yeah, but we could at least just sit around the pool," Jane rationalized, before rushing on to a better topic.

"New doctors, huh? I hope you'll catch you one," Jane said giddily.

In the previous few seconds, Jane had gone from contrite to conciliatory to giddy, and of the three, Freda preferred giddy, but not enough to let go and join in her friend's fun.

"Jane," she replied in a huffy tone, "I won't be trying to catch one. If anyone is interested in me, they can try to do the catching."

Jane knew she had pressed to the limit, but still kept the hope that Freda might be calling later with a change of heart.

After they hung up, Freda poured herself some more coffee, but let it sit until it was cold before finally picking up the phone again.

"Rica," she said lightly enough to offset the heaviness in her chest, "I've been away over the weekend, and thought I might have missed your call."

"Oh, no," Rica replied, "but I'm so glad you called. I've been away myself, and planned on calling you tomorrow. I've just been dying to tell you everything."

"Well, it certainly sounds like good news," Freda said.

"Oh, it is. Warren just decided out of the blue Friday afternoon that we'd fly up and visit some of his family. Aunt Renie went with us, of course, and Warren had gotten someone to open her house and air it out so we could stay there. You can't believe the number of cousins I met, Freda. He has such a big family," she gushed.

"Now they're all my family, too," she added softly.

"I'm so happy for you, Rica," Freda said. She, at once, was reconsidering what she had intended to say. Why put a pall on Rica's exuberance when her own words could wait until another time?

Before she'd had a chance to decide, Rica had something better to share.

"There's more, Freda. I'm seeing a therapist."

Freda drew in a sharp breath. "That *is* wonderful news," she said, and meant it with all her heart.

"It was because of you. Our talks are such a blessing. Gabriel tried for so long, but I wouldn't hear of it. But Warren told me I must. He says he depends on me to take care of him. Imagine that, me taking care of anyone," she said lightly, then continued.

"He says I must be strong for him, and for our baby, Freda, and I will. I promise. And I promised him."

"I believe you will, Rica, but I can't take much of the credit. I believe it must go to Warren, and, to yourself," Freda said, then added, "And there's Ariola, too."

"I know. He's so wonderful. I think I would have been dead long ago without him. But, it's different talking to you. Anyway, I hardly talk to him anymore, and when I do, it's about the trust."

"Don't you see?" Rica continued, "I can't go on like this with Warren, or Aunt Renie—that's Irene, Warren's aunt. I call her Aunt Renie now, just like Warren does. But you're the one I really talk to—just to talk about them."

"Rica, that brings up something else I've been meaning to suggest."

"We do talk on the phone often, and I do enjoy it, but since you now have so many people closer to you than I, have you considered asking someone else to be the baby's godmother?"

"Never," Rica protested.

"When I say *closer*, I mean distance *and* relationship. Your aunt sounds like a delightful person. I know she would be so pleased if you select her."

"She would be," Rica admitted. "But what about two? Can't there be two?"

"I don't see why not, but even if you have two, from what you've said about your weekend, there's no doubt others who would love to be chosen."

"You're right, Freda. You're always right. But this doesn't mean we won't be talking. You'll always be my friend."

"Of course, we'll be friends, Rica, and we'll be talking, but probably not as often. You're going to be so busy with your family and the friends you've made and the many more you'll be making, you won't have time. You'll see."

"But you'll always be the best," Rica said.

"Thank you, Rica."

Freda was about to hang up when Rica added, "Freda, take care of Gabriel. He needs you as much as I do."

She only nodded into the phone. She couldn't trust her voice to reply. She didn't call Ariola to tell him what she'd just done. She couldn't trust her voice there, either. It didn't matter, anyway. He'd find out, she supposed. Then at least she wouldn't be having dinner with him anymore, having to keep herself from touching his face, or wanting to take his hand when they walked.

Freda didn't hear from Ariola for two days. She went to work each morning and came home each evening and that was it. She couldn't get rid of the leaden weight she carried, but she did her job at the hospital and did it well. She would not allow her feelings to interfere with her duty.

When she *did* see him again, he was waiting in his car in front of her house as she returned from a walk. For a moment she nearly turned back, but he got out of his car and came to meet her.

They walked in silence to her steps, where he said, "Lets go inside, Freda. I have something to tell you."

He knows, she thought.

Once inside, he declined coffee. Of all times to refuse coffee. She'd offered it only out of habit, but having a warm cup in her hands could serve a good purpose. If words failed her, she could sip it to buy time, or at least the warmth of it might buoy her spirits.

"Later," he said, "I've been waiting to tell you this for a long time. Let's sit down."

"I've been with Warren and Judge Angouli's attorneys for the past two days. I've been talking to Warren about this for several weeks and we finally finished it up—transferring the trust to him, and to Rica, of course."

"Oh, really? Was Rica upset?"

"No, she wasn't there. But she's agreeable. More than agreeable, she's pleased."

"But why? Rica depends on you so much."

"Not any more. She doesn't need me. She needs to be free of anything connected to me, and I of her. She's going to be fine, and if she's not, I'm not the one who can help her. It's her husband and his family."

"I believe she will be," Freda said, then hesitated and continued. "There's something I need to tell you, Ariola."

He looked alarmed, but she hurried on. "I told Rica Monday night that I couldn't be the baby's godmother."

He sucked in his breath. She wasn't sure whether from anger or relief, but soon found out.

"I let go of that, too, and was about to ask you to do the same," he said.

"I'm glad you don't mind. I've been talking to her a lot, and I thought that would be best for all of you."

"All of *us*," he cut in. "I didn't want to say anything until they were completely out of the picture. I didn't want any unanswered questions hanging over us."

"This is between only the two of us now. No one else. Only us."

She apparently still didn't comprehend what he was saying, since she continued, "It's just as well that I asked her to get someone else since you won't be there. I wouldn't have wanted to be there without you."

"And I don't intend to be anywhere without you, ever again," he said, and had her in his arms, kissing her before she could say more. It soon became clear to him that she did understand what he was saying, because her arms were up and around his neck. Then she was touching his face as she had so longed to do.

Chapter 46

"You still here?"

That was the standard greeting Buck offered Lorene each time he came through his front door.

She usually countered with a silent ritual consisting of a scorching stare, followed by sticking out her tongue, then ending with a rakish grin.

Today, however, she spoke up immediately after the exchange. "Where else could you get a beautiful, talented decorating supervisor for a measly lunch of tamales and beer each day?"

"Lets don't forget that steak each evening."

"That's only when you're here, which isn't often, by the way. Otherwise, Freda and Ariola take me out to dinner."

She had arrived two weeks earlier, only this time she was minus the crutches and had already checked into a motel in NeeDee before showing up at his door. She now spent her days in Buck's house to oversee the painting that Donna and Bill were having done before they moved in.

"I did need to pick up my car," she had asserted when she arrived, "and more important than that, Donna asked me to come back. Better that I inhale these fumes than she. We don't want you having a dizzy grandchild, now do we, Buck?"

"Absolutely not. Better a dizzy blonde than a dizzy grandchild, I always say."

"Absolutely," she reaffirmed.

Besides, he appreciated her company. She stayed on for an hour or two each evening after everyone else had gone, and they enjoyed a glass of wine and lots of easy talk. He could reminisce about some of the rascally memories of his youth or talk about Alta without reservation.

One evening, after listening to a tale that left him visibly down, she intervened.

"You know, Buck, I don't usually talk about myself much, but I have a couple of stories of my own."

He made a sweeping gesture, offering her the floor, then leaned back in his chair.

"Well, as you might assume, it hasn't been all work and no play for me since I left NeeDee."

"I always hoped so," he said.

"I met some real good people, and some not so good, but the top-notch one was my first husband, D.B."

Soon after arriving in California, Lorene had met this old man through a girl she worked with. He was a nice old fellow, about fifty years older than Lorene.

"This gal assured us all that D.B. was her boyfriend, so hands off. Well, that was all right with me. He was older than my grandfather."

D.B.needed someone to drive him around. His *girlfriend* started asking Lorene to do it when she had an actual date, and Lorene didn't mind that either. She liked to drive and he was always so appreciative.

Pretty soon, the *girlfriend* was no where to be found. She'd run off with one of those other boyfriends, but Lorene had just kept on driving him around.

"He even sent me to Business College," she told Buck.

"I'm sure that's one reason I was able to get out of an apron and into an office."

"Anyway, D.B. had one hang up. He wouldn't leave his house to go out to dinner without this big old diamond stickpin he owned. He'd lay it down any place convenient, then I'd spend whatever time it took to find it. I guess that was the only vain bone in his body."

She kept driving him until he'd gotten so sick he had to have around-the-clock care. He convinced her to marry him in order to take charge of the nurses, saying it just wouldn't look proper if they weren't married.

Well, poor old D.B. had died thirteen months later and left her thirteen million dollars. No sooner was the funeral over than a couple of long lost nephews had shown up.

Rather than fight them in court, she'd said what the hell. She didn't marry him for his money. The only thing she'd gotten out of it was the diamond stickpin.

She showed Buck her huge ring, the twinkling center stone about the size of a plump black-eyed pea.

"I'll bet you never thought it was real, did you, Buck."

"Never doubted it," Buck replied.

He got up to pour more wine before continuing, "Didn't you say something about a *couple* of stories?"

"Yes, I did," she said, "and this is the best of the two."

Sipping her wine, she continued.

"Soon after D.B. died, this dancin' boy comes on the scene. I thought, for sure, I had found true love. And he was the best looking thing I had ever seen. Nearly as good looking as you, Buck," she said with a grin.

The grimace she got from Buck was not the reaction hoped for, but she, at least, knew he was listening.

"I found out I was in the family way about the same time he found out that I didn't have the thirteen million, and he was gone the next week. That best thing I was talking about was Darcy. I named her after D.B."

"So you have a daughter?" Buck said, amazed. He had never even suspected. She had never mentioned a child.

"She's in boarding school in California."

"Why California? I thought you'd been in Vegas for years."

"Oh, yeah, but I sent her away to boarding school when she was twelve. It's not the best arrangement, but we manage to spend a lot of time together. I just didn't want her growing up in Vegas. Afraid she might want to become a show girl."

"She could have been," she continued, "has the looks for it. Tall and just as good-looking as her daddy."

"Tall and good looking, huh?"

"Don't worry, I won't be bringing her to NeeDee. You'd just be trying to get her interested in Nick."

"So?"

"Too young. She'll be starting U.C.L.A. in the fall. Nick won't get near her until she has that degree."

"Sounds like a plan."

"Oh," she said, looking at her watch, "I'd better get back to town. Those painters will be out here in the morning before I am."

She was up and headed for the door.

"Lorene, Lorene, let me follow you to town. Doesn't seem right to send you off in the dark by yourself."

"I've been around the world by myself, Buck, and it isn't all bad," she said as she went down the steps. At the bottom, she turned to him again.

"In fact, being alone is good for me, but that doesn't mean it's good for everybody."

Buck watched her go. The painting would soon be finished and she'd be gone. He was afraid he was going miss her.

She was a little late the next morning, but it didn't matter. He had taken the day off just so he could spend the afternoon with her. The painters said they had only some touching up to do.

He had to be in Denver the day after tomorrow and Chicago the following day. She'd probably be gone by the time he got back. Buck knew he hadn't been the best host, but he did appreciate Lorene.

Buck now sat idly watching Lorene paint her toenails. He was fascinated by the intensity of her concentration. No smears tolerated. She wore sandals most of the time, and demanded as much perfection in the appearance of her toes as with every other part of her grooming.

He didn't remember ever seeing Alta paint her toenails, although in her later years, she did get a manicure once a week in town. Most of the time she had quickly ruined the pale peach color she preferred by working around the barn or in the office—she hated to wear gloves nearly as much as she hated hats. Ruining her hair didn't matter though. She shampooed it every morning in the shower—always a shower. She was irresistible right after a shower. If he was lucky enough to happen in at the right time, he usually joined her. She was irresistible then, too.

Buck did not see the paradox in thinking about his dead wife as he watched a beautiful blonde paint her toenails on his couch. He hardly remembered how Lorene had gotten here, although he did enjoy her company.

She was easy to talk to, even easier for him if he was the listener—as he was most of the time. He realized he should have been more alert when he thought he heard her say something about Val.

"What?" He tried to perk up a little, at the same time feeling his face automatically take on an unreadable shield.

"That young woman in Denver, Buck,"she said, flashing a delighted grin as she realized she had hit a nerve.

"I was hoping to have an affair with you myself before someone else came on the scene. Looks like I waited a little too long to make my move—again."

He sputtered a weak denial, then added, "I'm afraid I wouldn't be too good at affairs, Lorene—wouldn't know how."

"Did you know I was never unfaithful to Alta?" His eyes lowered, and when he again looked toward her, the pensive expression in them caused her to hurt for him.

"Lorene, you just don't know how much I loved that woman." He wasn't asking for pity or for praise. He was simply remembering.

"I know," she said, "The short time I knew Alta, I could tell she was a wonderful person, and I could tell she loved you dearly—and you, her."

"But that's all gone, Buck," she continued softly.

She returned to goading, realizing that was the best way to keep Buck from sinking back into his moodiness. Lorene started in again on Val.

"Every time you come back from Denver, you look like a teenager in love. No, not like a teenager. I've been there, too. Did you know I was just seventeen when I stalked off down that road, Buck, and I could tell even then that I didn't have a chance against Alta."

"Oh, for crying out loud, Lorene. You just saw Alta for about five minutes that day."

"But you looked like a family, Buck. You were just so natural together— you were a family, all right."

"Just seventeen, huh? I never knew." he said mildly.

In truth, he had never even thought about her age, had never though about her at all except on rare occasions when he and Alta had curled up before the fire at Willowbranch and talked about the old days.

Now she was suddenly back in his life, yet seemed like an enduring old friend. He too, wanted to lighten the mood.

"You looked a little older. Now I know you would have been too young to go to California with me."

"I really missed you. Nearly all the way to Bakersfield," she said merrily.

"I thought you were heading to LA."

"Was, but this trucker I met in Albuquerque was headed to Bakersfield." No further explanation was forthcoming, and he didn't ask.

"Now, about this affair, Buck. I know you wouldn't be protesting so much if it weren't for that girl in Denver."

"Forget about that girl in Denver, as you call her. Her name is Val and we're good friends. End of report."

His face and voice again changed as he continued.

"She was Joe's girl, Lorene. We could never be more than friends."

"Baloney. It hurts me to say this, but Joe is gone, too. You have to let go, Buck. Just cherish the memories."

He was suddenly irritated with her, tired of do-gooders advice.

"You want to have an affair?" he growled. "Come on. What I don't know about it, you can teach me."

She knew she had gone too far and began in her own light way, to rectify things.

"Nah, you know a person has to be careful about an affair—especially with a good friend. When it's over, and they usually are, it can ruin the friendship."

"I know that's the way it was with my first affair."

He knew she was just trying to tease her way out, so he leaned back on the sofa and listened—at least made a pretense of it.

"I was thirty years old and had had two husbands by then, so I really should have known better. I really didn't know he was married at the start, and by the time I found out, I didn't care. Oh, I cared all right. I wanted him to be free to be with me. I mean I didn't care in the sense that I wasn't about to give him up. But I did."

"It turns out his father-in-law was the head of one of the big studios. You'd recognize the name if I said it."

Buck doubted it, but didn't comment.

"He was a little B-grade actor wanting to move up, and to stay alive, probably. Anyway, after it ended, I didn't want to be in the same town with him, afraid of running into him sometime. So Darcy and me, we just headed for Las Vegas."

She added, "And I don't want to ruin our friendship, Buck."

Buck didn't understand the point of her story. Didn't care. He just knew their friendship was in good shape and he knew that neither of them wanted to have an affair.

His head ached. He laid it in her lap without much thought and she massaged it with that same nonchalance. It ached, and he just wanted to lie there and think about Alta—and Val.

Chapter 47

"If we were getting a rain like this at the ranch, all of us would likely be out running around stark naked in it, hollering for more. A little storm doesn't bother me."

"Well, I hate them," Val said.

"Honey, my whole life's been a storm."

She caught the inference he was making, but chose to ignore it.

"I'm not afraid of anything you've done, Buck. I'm not going to say I understand some of it, but I'm not going to try to analyze it either."

Truthfully, she had been appalled at the story that spilled out of him, trying several times to interrupt—to stop him—but he was bent on telling it all. It was something she didn't want to hear, for hearing him talk of his life with Alta was to remember Joe. She wanted her memories of Joe to remain as she had arranged them, abstract and perfect, didn't want to think of how he might have dealt with the story she had heard. What pain Joe would have felt at finding out the two people he loved so deeply had lived a lie, their perfect marriage—no matter how they'd loved each other, how faithful they'd been, was only a sham.

At the same time, she feared Buck's story tonight might be closing that safe barrier between them, as if by knowing these things, she could accept him as he was—or not.

She was also troubled by her determination to defend Buck against himself, against his own scathing words, wanting to protect him from his self-inflicted pain. Yet she could not put any of these thoughts into words, and didn't try.

She only said, "And we're still friends, aren't we?" The moment she asked, she regretted the words.

Suppose he had told her all this as a reason to end their friendship. No more lunches, no more dancing, no more afternoon drives through the mountains? How could she not be with him? How could she go on?

And we're still friends, aren't we? That soft voice, those words, words Buck knew he did not deserve, yet couldn't get enough of, left him mute. He could only look toward her, waiting.

She came over and sat beside him.

"You know, Buck, you're the best friend I have."

"In fact, she continued, "I don't know of another person I could consider to be as close a friend as you. Oh, I have dozens of acquaintances. I have people over quite often. But I must entertain them, you know. Make sure people are compatible—good conversation, just the right wine. But you and I—we can just hang out, and that's all we need. We're comfortable."

She paused, and he broke in. "Maybe I'm just old and dull," he said.

Being with her, just having her seated beside him, lifted his spirits like nothing else.

"Oh, you know what I mean," she shot back, elbowing him.

They were still friends. Yes, only friends, and that was apparently the way she wanted it. So did he, most of the time.

At other times, he would look at her, watching as she worked in her kitchen, running inside out of the rain, laughing, as she had tonight when the storm first struck, or delighting in a beautiful sunset, and he would want to reach out for her. But before he did, common sense took hold. He was an old man, newly widowed. She was young and beautiful, Joe's sweetheart. She would have been his daughter-in-law if Joe had come back.

She spoke at the same time he was having these unsettling thoughts.

"Decision time," she said. "The storm is getting worse and I don't want my friend to drown. And more than that, like I said, I hate storms. It's already after one o'clock and I think we're in for this all night."

"I've turned my extra bedroom into my workroom," she continued, "but there's a bath off it, plenty of towels and shampoo. And I have a nice down pillow and a blanket for the sofa."

"You'll be fine," she added breezily.

He was still torn with indecision. He wasn't afraid of a storm. His own precarious feelings were his concern. She was afraid of storms; he was afraid of himself.

Looking out the window at his rental car, hardly visible through the sheets of rain he agreed to stay. He could handle himself.

"If you get too scared, just cover your head," she said as she tossed a blanket and pillow on the sofa and grinned at him.

"Remember, you're the one who hates storms," Buck answered.

He usually read for a while before he could sleep, he told her. He could look over some reports from the meeting. Fortunately, when he had arrived at her house earlier, he had reached for his briefcase out of habit. Opening it as she turned at the hallway, he smiled and said goodnight.

When she disappeared, Buck turned his attention to the slick cover of the prospectus in his hand. Flipping through the pages, it soon seemed so dull, he put it away and picked up the newspaper that lay in a messy pile on the floor beside the sofa. After scanning the markets, he dropped one section at a time slowly back to the floor.

Buck spent another hour looking out the window and listening to the pounding storm. He'd seen worse than this. He could make it to the airport, or at least to his hotel. He picked up a pen and paper to leave Val a note. No, she was afraid of storms. Stupid thought—she'd made it through dozens of storms alone. Stupid all right, she'd think he was crazy getting out in this for no good reason. If he couldn't sleep, at least he'd stay dry, and she wouldn't think he was crazy.

He then picked up a thin volume from the table beside him. Its cover was adorned with a pair of velour kittens staring at each other through large green eyes. Her latest book—this, he could read.

After finishing it, he reached for an electric razor from his briefcase and headed for the shower. He had never seen her workroom and glanced around with interest. A wall of shelves brimming with books made it look more like a tiny study than a workroom. Although she wrote only children's books, there was row after row of thick volumes of leather bound classics along with novels and reference books. Tools of her trade, he surmised. Her oak desk was neat, with only a stack of manila folders beside the electric typewriter, a matching file cabinet nearby.

A plump brown leather chair and ottoman stood in front of the shelves. He could picture her curled up there, reading, perhaps plotting another charming tale for young children. That thought made him feel like an intruder in her private world so he didn't linger.

The shower was refreshing. Now he could sleep. Wrapping his damp towel around his waist, he shaved quickly.

A row of pretty lotion bottles lined her vanity. They spoke of a woman's world—no sign of maleness here. He was pleased, but quickly felt a twinge of guilt. Why should he care? She had a life. There were certainly friends, girlfriends—men wanting to take her out.

Yet, all too often, he thought of her as the girl who had promised to wait for Joe. He knew—she had said so more than once—that her being single had nothing to do with Joe's death, but he couldn't get over that.

Nevertheless, every time he was in Denver, he called and she was free, at least she arranged to be free. At times, she mentioned canceling or rescheduling an appointment, but always sounded glad to hear from him.

He never called her otherwise. At times, he would pick up the phone, then lay it down, believing he was reading too much into her friendliness.

Being in Denver anyway, made everything plausible, so he somehow found more and more reasons to return to Denver, calling her as soon as he arrived, casually asking if she could join him for dinner *since he was in town*. She was so easy to talk to, so lovely to look at. They were friends.

Picking up the bottle with the most bland-sounding name, he patted his face lightly with it. He preferred no scent, but needed something to offset the drying effect of the soap and hot shower.

Putting the lotion back in its place, he reached for his clothes. A clap of thunder, so loud it sent him reeling—and he a man not easily startled—rocked the bathroom.

At that same moment, Val screamed and he dashed toward the sound of her voice. They met in the hall. She, who had never offered more than a cool soft hand, was now in his arms.

"I hate storms," she gasped, and he could feel her heart pounding against him.

Their eyes locked for a startled moment, then his mouth was on hers. A tremor, perhaps only a remnant of her fear of the storm—perhaps not, traveled through her. He could feel it as he drew her closer. As her hands began a tentative upward movement along his arms, he knew it wasn't the storm she was afraid of. Then her arms were up and around his neck, and he knew she wasn't frightened at all. Still, she trembled.

"Val," he whispered, neither demanding nor asking. He wanted the sound of her name on his lips. It was the only word spoken.

There was no reasoning. He was beyond that. In a few reckless moments, all resolve had left him. Even if she had pulled away, he still could not have stopped, but she did not protest. Her needs matched his. The look on her face confirmed that. There was no turning back.

The tempestuous weather that had driven her into his arms and him to her bed continued lashing the city but silenced itself to them. They were no longer aware of anything other than the storm that raged inside them both—a storm of their own making.

Just before daylight, she struggled to rouse herself from a sleep so deep that she could not open her eyes, yet she could sense an urgent need to do so. She could feel his fingers brush back a strand of her hair. He was about to leave, but she could not awaken herself to stop him.

She was asleep in his arms, but sleep had eluded him. She seemed so helpless now, how could this have happened? As he started to remove his arms, she stirred and whispered no. Was she only protesting his intrusion of her sleep, or could she want him, too? If she awoke in his arms, he could never let her go; but he must.

Guilt, mixed with desire, but overpowered by love consumed him. He now knew that his love for her hadn't exploded in that moment in the hall. He had loved her for months.

But what about her? How could she want him? He'd ruined any chance he had with her. Oh, Val.

So many times, he had nearly taken her hand as they walked, had wanted to hold her closer when they danced. Touch her hair, to kiss her. He'd done none of that, always managing to keep his feelings at bay. Now this night, this sweet, reckless, stormy night, had changed it all. He wanted their perfect world back, wanted the chance to earn her love.

But she had said she loved him. He had heard her. Those words rang in his ears.

He then repeated his own words, whispered over and over during these past few hours.

"Oh, Val. Val. I love you—I love you—I love you."

That moan flooded her subliminal consciousness, filling her with warmth. Oh, yes. Her darling would not leave. In the safe haven of his arms, she gave in once more to a deep, dreamless sleep.

The storm, having lasted the night, ended as abruptly as it had begun. She awoke to a morning so peaceful and silent, she hardly remembered the turbulence, but the sweetness of the night flooded her. She reached out to touch his face even before opening her eyes.

"Oh, no." Her hand fell dully onto the empty space.

"Buck, no." She had heard him. He'd said he loved her over and over and sometime close to dawn, as she had struggled against that black vacuum of sleep, she had heard him again. How could he be gone?

She lay there until she had enough strength to get to the shower. The water flooded over her, but did little to wash away her anguish.

Out of the shower, still drained of energy, she wrapped herself in a heavy robe and headed back to her bed. She needed to rest. She threw her own pillow to the floor, then crashed back onto the one where he had slept. Turning and burying her face in it, inhaling deeply, she searched for even a scent of him.

She jumped at the sound of the doorbell and ran to it. He was back.

Oh, my darling. What would she say to him?

Her face fell as she opened the door to a smiling deliveryman. He handed her a large white florist box. She managed to mumble thanks, just a minute—but he assured her that had been taken care of.

She took the box, unsure that she could accept what was inside, but after closing her door, fumbled over it with trembling fingers.

The note—the note would tell it all. She read it—my dearest, please forgive me.

Her face contorted as she threw two dozen white roses across the room, but instantly, sobbing, she scrambled to salvage the shattered blossoms.

Back in her bed, she lay her hand close to the phone, willing it to ring. Finally, after an hour, she dialed his hotel. Sorry, Mr. Ramsey had checked out an hour ago.

Chapter 48

Val finally picked up her phone on the tenth ring. She had opened her eyes on the first, her fingers poised above it for the next two, then waited out the next seven with her hands cupping her mouth and nose, breathing hard, hoping to control her voice when she talked to him. After all that, she only managed a whisper.

Julie was startled at the pitiful sound.

"Val?" she questioned.

So it wasn't him. Why should she have thought it would be?

Val swallowed hard and cleared her throat before a faint yes came out.

"Val?" Julie asked again. She knew perfectly well it was her boss, but she had never heard her sound quite like this.

"What's wrong? Was it the storm? Oh, I'm sorry. I had a hard time with it, too—well, mostly it was the boys. They were so scared they both cried, and you know how tough they usually are. I was late to work myself, but it's so unlike you, I thought I'd better check, especially after last night."

Val was thankful for her secretary's non-stop talking. It gave her more time.

"Listen to me," Julie continued. "I've just been rattling, not giving you a chance to say a word. You don't sound very well, Val. Is something wrong? Besides the storm, I mean?"

"No. No, it's just that I'm still in bed."

"Oh, I'm sorry I woke you."

Val forgave herself for the lie. It was only a partial lie. After all, she was in bed. She had not implied that she had been sleeping. She only allowed Julie to assume that.

"Don't worry about it," Val said, beginning to sound more like herself.

"I appreciate your calling. Some storm, wasn't it?"

"Oh, it really was, but the streets are already clear," Julie said, waiting for a decision from Val.

Would she be coming in?

"I don't believe I'll get out." She began with a strong voice, and then faltered. "I don't really feel too well."

"Val, what's wrong? Can I bring you something?"

"No, please," Val protested. She wanted desperately to head off seeing Julie, afraid Julie would be able to read the shame on her face, in her voice.

"Whatever you need. I'll be over in ten minutes."

"No!" Val's voice was firmer than Julie had ever heard.

"I don't need anything. I don't want to see anyone. Not you—not anyone. I don't need anything. Don't come over. The door will be locked."

Julie was silent on the other end of the line.

"Oh, Julie," the harsh voice had turned to pleading. "I'm sorry. I just don't need anything, other than to be alone. I'm all right, I promise. I'll be in tomorrow. Cancel my appointments. Reschedule them. I'll be in tomorrow."

"All right," Julie said, resigned. She hesitated, then added. "But, Val, if there's anything I can do—"

"I know, Julie," Val said, regaining some composure. "I'll call. Don't worry. I'll be in tomorrow."

"Okay," Julie reluctantly agreed.

"Julie," Val said softly, "Thanks."

Why couldn't that have been Buck calling? Thinking of him brought on more hurting, but it turned to anger, then to shame. The hurting stemmed from his having left, and the anger, from his sending two dozen roses as if roses were all she needed, all she deserved. The shame came from deep within herself. Even with all that, she couldn't control the longing.

She lay there much of the morning as those emotions

filled her head. Around noon, she dragged herself out of bed, not to eat lunch, but to pick up a yellow pad and make a list of how to get on with her life.

The next morning, she was in her office early. Several of the items had been checked off before Julie arrived.

Julie was stunned when she read the list, but after a hug with only a trace of tears, Julie went to work.

Val had already taken care of the item topping the list. She had entered the office of the company president and turned in her resignation effective immediately following the upcoming conference in Hawaii. She would be staying in Hawaii indefinitely.

He was shocked, of course, but with years of work and friendship behind them, he accepted it without question. Her expression, cold, yet sad, plus the erect, military-like square of her shoulders also cautioned him. She hadn't asked for a leave of absence, or for the several weeks of vacation she'd accumulated. It was her resignation she laid on his desk, and he'd accepted it.

"I do need one favor, Henry. Please wait until after the conference to begin the replacement process. I just can't talk to anyone about this, so I'd appreciate it if—"

"Of course, Val, but if you need to talk—"

"I can't. I'm sorry, I can't. Please," she said again, and turned toward the door.

Perhaps Val would confide in him later.

She then called a realtor friend and asked her to find a furnished cottage ready for occupancy by the end of the conference. It was to be minimally furnished. She was taking the clothes needed for the conference. After that, she needed nothing, and wanted even less.

The thing she gave her most careful attention was her briefcase. Her fellow writers would receive an unflawed presentation, no matter what.

Before clicking the case shut, she added her packet of personal papers. Who knew? She might need her passport.

The rest was on Julie's list. She was to take care of finding a gardener to look after the yard, give away her houseplants, and a dozen other things. Last on the list was to have the utilities disconnected the day after Val left.

That had been her final task when closing her parents' home. As she had written that on Julie's list, she thought of the similarity. That had been after their deaths. Now Julie would be doing that for her. She felt as if she had died, too.

That night she called her grandmother to tell her of her plans. Grandma was upset. Valentine had taken so much pride in her career, she couldn't believe her granddaughter was giving it up so suddenly. More puzzling was Val's plans to be gone so long. The old woman had managed one trip to London while Val had been there, but told her that she didn't feel up to Hawaii. Val resolved that by changing her departure from Denver to Albuquerque. She would fly to Albuquerque, rent a car and drive over to see Grandma.

She had been with her grandmother only about thirty minutes when Grandma, wise beyond her considerable years, spoke up.

"It's a man, isn't it, Valentine?"

Val denied it, but Grandma was determined. She knew what was best for her granddaughter.

"Call him, honey. At least tell him goodbye."

"I'm not sure where he is," Val protested.

"If you know him well enough to be this upset, you can find out where he is," Grandma answered.

She did call him. Grandma had a discreet need to go out to the back porch and sit awhile to catch the sunset.

Buck remained silent as she spoke briskly of her plans.

"Just calling to say goodbye," she soon said.

Then it was his turn to talk, but he didn't have his speech planned. He immediately began pleading that he must see her, to try to explain things, make her understand the craziness that had made him run out, a chance to tell her how he really felt.

He didn't need to say all that. Just hearing his voice was enough. There was no way she could stop herself from agreeing to see him on her way back to Albuquerque.

Doubt set in after she hung up. She didn't expect to understand why he'd left while she was sleeping, hadn't called, hadn't anything—

It wasn't much out of the way, she reasoned in the next instant.

Val was in a quandary most of the evening, but her last thought before dozing off for her best night's sleep in a week, was she'd be seeing him tomorrow.

Chapter 49

Lorene watched as Buck drove up but she did not move to meet him at the door. She knew why he was back early and she knew what she must tell him.

"Well, hello there, pretty lady," he said as he came into the library.

She had to smile in spite of the way she was feeling. He was like that. He caused people to smile.

"I didn't see Val's car. I figured she would be here by now," he said with overdone casualness.

"Oh?"

"Yeah, she called me last night in Chicago, got the number from Pauline, I guess, and I asked her to stop by. She's been visiting her grandmother in Portales. On her way to Hawaii to do a writer's conference."

"Quite a side trip, isn't it? Portales to Hawaii? She must have really needed to see you."

"She's planning on being gone a long time." He was beginning to weaken.

"Then I guess it's you who needs to see her." Before he could say more, she continued, "You're home a day early, aren't you?"

"Yeah, well, I am," he admitted. "I just thought since she was going to be this close it would be good to have her stop."

"Some stop. How many miles out of the way? Fifty, seventy five?" Lorene questioned.

"She's never seen the place, the house, anyway. We built it after Joe died. And she's never been back, of course."

"But she called you? You've never invited her out here before?"

"I've never really thought she'd be interested."

Lorene was silent.

"She's planning on staying there after the conference. Said she needed some time away from her job."

Lorene's silence continued.

"Okay. I begged her to come," he admitted.

Buck didn't tell Lorene how he had felt at the sound of her voice last night. He didn't mention that he thought his heart was about to explode when she said she would be staying in Hawaii.

Knowing that she was only as far away as Denver had kept him hopeful. Maybe, somehow, as time passed, she'd allow him to make amends, she'd forgive him enough that they could at least be friends. He would not admit to himself that they could never again be only friends. He just knew he had to see her, touch her. He had to somehow make her love him as much as he loved her.

"Lorene," he continued, "There's some things you don't know. I didn't think she was ever going to want to see me again—until she called last night, but that was just to say goodbye. Now, when she gets here, we can at least try to get some things straightened out."

"She's already been here and gone. She's on her way to Albuquerque—to the airport."

His face went ashen.

"Buck, sit down here."

It was time to quit her cat and mouse game. She patted the space beside herself on the sofa.

"We need to talk. We have about ten minutes."

He sat down like a child waiting for a well-deserved reprimand.

"Buck, I just don't know why you can't understand. Whatever happened, she didn't come to see the house—and she most certainly didn't come to say goodbye. She came to see you."

"Oh, no. She—" he protested.

Lorene interrupted him. "The only face that looked longer than yours does right now was hers when she saw me. You didn't tell her I would be here, did you, Buck?"

"I didn't think it mattered. In fact, I thought she'd be more comfortable."

"Didn't matter! Comfortable! Buck, she's crazy about you and it's obvious how you feel about her."

"I've called Jerry," she said. "He'll be ready to take off by the time you get out there. You can be waiting for her at the airport."

She laughed and continued. "But don't waste any time. She was driving pretty fast when she left."

He was upstairs and back in a few minutes with a bag.

"Go," she said.

She would tell Ramona and Ariola where he had gone on her way out.

"Lorene," he protested.

She repeated her admonition, went to the door, opened it, then making a sweeping gesture, ordered him out.

He turned and hugged her.

"By the way, Buck," she said. "Take her to Hawaii to marry her. I know a few people there. I'll call and make some arrangements."

"Lorene," he said again. He hesitated and continued,

"Thanks, Lorene. You have to come back."

"I'll be back next year, Buck," she promised and added with a wry grin, "I want to be here for the christening of your first child."

Chapter 50

Buck sent Jerry on his way as soon as he let him out at the airport. He would not be flying back to NeeDee, no matter what. If he had somehow missed her, if she refused to talk to him when she got there, whatever happened, he wouldn't be going back to NeeDee.

Buck wouldn't give up. If Val didn't want anything to do with him, he'd simply convince her she did. He would not let her go.

According to Lorene's timing, he had thirty minutes. He found a pay phone in sight of the main entrance and used most of that time making calls.

First he called a BAR4 attorney to put into place all the necessary arrangements for a Hawaiian wedding.

He then called Pauline to let her know he would be gone—he did not mention where—and that he would be in touch soon.

Next, he called Val's office to find out where she would be staying, then to Honolulu to reserve a suite at the same hotel.

All this done, he sat down to figure out the hard part. What would he say to her? How would she feel about him?

As it turned out, he didn't get anything figured out, no preparation, no pleading. The moment she walked through the door, she was in his arms. He looked into her eyes and simply whispered marry me, Val. Will you marry me?

She simply said yes.

Chapter 51

A five-day engagement was short by most standards, but seemed extremely long to Buck and Val. Buck determined that while it would be the briefest of engagements, it would be nothing short of perfect, the proper courtship Val should have had from the beginning. When they'd checked into the hotel, Buck insisted Val take the suite he had reserved while waiting at the airport as she blazed in from NeeDee, and he moved into her room on a different floor.

The conference began early the next morning. Sessions filled the mornings with afternoons open in order for attendees to take in the islands. Val gave her all to the sessions, serenely knowing that Buck would be waiting.

The first afternoon, she and Buck picked out an engagement ring and two matching gold bands. As he slipped the diamond on her finger, he proposed again, and she accepted just as quickly as she had in Albuquerque.

On Tuesday, they drove to the airport to pick up Julie. Buck had called Val's secretary to ask her to come to Hawaii as a surprise for Val. He had spoken to Henry Ames instead. Mr. Ames had been so concerned at Val's abrupt departure that he had decided to surprise Val himself, and send Julie to join her. When he found out Julie would be serving as Val's bridal attendant instead of comforting a distraught friend, he admitted he was very pleased for Val's sake, but did not hesitate to give Buck a severe tongue lashing. Buck convinced Mr.Ames that he appreciated those words. He deserved them, he said, and knew that Mr. Ames only spoke from fatherly concern. The conversation ended cordially.

"Take care of our girl," he said.

"I will, Mr. Ames, for the rest of my life."

Wednesday, Buck stayed at the hotel to catch up on telephone calls while Val and Julie took off together. He knew they would come back with a wedding dress, but pretended unawareness. Sure enough, they returned near sunset, both loaded with sacks and shoeboxes and a long dress bag, all quickly spirited up to her suite.

Thursday, Buck was back at the airport, this time to pick up Ariola. He was to serve as Buck's best man. Buck quickly spotted Ariola, who was taller than most of the crowd. It took him longer to notice the man beside him. His heart lurched and he was glad Val wasn't with him to witness what an old softie she was about to marry.

He shook Ariola's hand and hugged Nick.

"Thanks for coming, you guys."

"Hey," Nick said. "I wasn't about to miss standing up for my old man. I'd like to be your best man, Dad."

Buck couldn't trust his voice—he just hugged Nick again. Only Ariola saw his misty eyes.

"And I'd like the honor of walking Val down the aisle," Ariola said.

"Thanks—both of you. Oh, boy, I'm gonna' lose it"

"Just hold on. You'll be doing it for me as soon as I find someone as great as Val."

"Thanks, son. I'd be honored."

He turned to Ariola. "Where's Freda?"

"Couldn't make it." Ariola was beaming. "She just finished training her replacement and now she's doing all those things ladies have to do. We're leaving as soon as I get back."

On Saturday morning, in a tiny chapel so close to the ocean the surf sounded in rhythm to a quartet of flutists, Ariola accompanied Val, in flowing chiffon, down the aisle to Buck.

On Monday, Buck and Val received a telegram from Billy Jack, Donna, Jeff, David and Matt congratulating Buck and welcoming Val into the family.

On Tuesday, they received another telegram with the news that Victoria Roxanne Pitts had arrived. Nick had gotten home in time to make the delivery.

The day after Ariola arrived back in NeeDee, Freda and he drove to Phoenix where they were married by Father Michael. They took a leisurely week-long drive to Mexico. Ariola wanted to introduce his wife to his Aunt Delores, and also show Freda his homeland.

When they arrived, they found Dona Delores had a huge wedding and reception arranged for them. In a private moment, Ariola said to Freda, "Why not? Dona Delores has her heart set on this. Besides, the more times we're married, the harder it will be if you ever decide to get rid of me."

"In that case," Freda replied, "we'll stop on the way home and have a third one."

After a week in the honeymoon suite, Buck and Val moved into her leased cottage, far away from the bustle of the city. A home, even that tiny cottage, was more to their liking. They were ready to begin their real life together.

The weeks passed and their days became routine, just the way they wanted them. He taught her to ride. She taught him to cook. For a few hours each day they went into separate rooms, he to make business calls, she to write. There was still time to explore the islands.

They soon found a special restaurant, along with a special waiter. As he watched them day by day, he deliberated about their station in life, as he did about many of his patrons. At first, of course, he assumed they were honeymooners, but still, they seemed different from the younger, carefree couples there for a few days, determined to make the most of every moment.

This couple was more intent on each other, unaware of the island paradise they were in. He watched them murmur softly, oblivious to any other people in the restaurant, and wondered how conversation could be so absorbing.

He never learned their story. They were evidently so private, they weren't about to share it. He finally concluded they must be a longtime married couple, extraordinarily in love.

The waiter began reserving his special table for them, although they never requested it. It was secluded, with the best view of the ocean, and all the privacy they could want.

Val noticed this, but thought Buck had arranged it.

"Not me," he said, "but I sure like it. Our waiter must have noticed that I can't keep my eyes off you."

"Not to mention your hands," she chided with a grin.

"Guilty as charged," he admitted. "But I'll tell you what. I know I have to straighten up, or I'll just get the rep of a lecherous old man."

"I didn't say I objected to your eyes or your hands."

"Thanks for that, my darlin', but I'm the first to admit I have a problem."

"But," he quickly continued, "I've come up with a solution. Wherever we are, whatever we're doing, anytime I call you honey, you'll know what I'm thinking."

Val watched as the late afternoon sun cast its glow on his brown legs. She did not understand how she could think a pair of forty five year-old hairy legs were beautiful, but she did. She rubbed his ankle with her toes. He reached out and took her hand and placed it, his hand still covering hers, on her stomach where it rested protectively.

From beneath a newspaper covering his face, a gravelly voice whispered, "It's nice and dark and cool under here. Come on over here, Miz Ramsey, honey."

Some time later, two airliners, one departing Mexico and the other, Hawaii, headed toward New Mexico. Among the large manifest of each plane was a couple, trying for a nonchalant air, yet unable to hide their obvious delight in each other, returning to NeeDee, then to wherever the future might take them.